The Babylon Deception

Ray Pace

For those who try to put out the fires.

My books are also available on Kobo and Apple Books.

The Babylon Deception
By Ray Pace

"By a knight of ghosts and shadows,
I summoned am to tourney,
Ten leagues beyond the wide world's end,
Methinks it is no journey."
Tom O'Bedlam, a pre-Shakespearean verse

August 1948

*"It's all a game, Saturday. You should never let anybody make the rules
for you. You lay down your cards. You take a chance."*
*He poured a shot of Bushmill's and slid it across the table to where
Saturday sat.*
*"Might as well have one. Don't know what else you're going to do.
Sorry, I don't have vodka, Subbota—that's your name in Russki, no?
Mickey Saturday. What's it really? Mikhail Subbota?"*
Saturday shrugged and sipped his whiskey.
*"Close, but as you say over here, no cigar. Can you at least help me get
out of the country? Mexico? Canada?"*
*"I can't even get you to Sausalito. I thought you had one of those
diplomatic passports. What happened? Looks like the shit hit the fan
when your boys blockaded Berlin. No more consulate in SF. Got caught
with your pants down."*
*"That happens a lot around here," she said as she joined the two men on
the large balcony. "The girls are going to miss you, Mickey."*
*She lit her cigarette with a gold lighter and sat at the table between the
two men.*
*"I could stay," Saturday said. "I've been plenty generous in the past.
That should count for something. I have some money."*
*"Let's say that maybe we broke even." She took a deep drag from her
cigarette and blew smoke toward Saturday.*
*"Truth is, money won't cut it. We can't afford to let you stay. Hoover's
boys are always looking at us, and we don't need the kind of heat you're
bringing."*
Saturday sipped the whiskey and gestured for a refill.
*"Give him one for the road," she said. "You should have been quicker
on the uptake bringing those gold bars to us. You could have waltzed
your way up to Uncle Joe with our heavy package. We spent a lot of*

1

sweat getting it from Los Alamos. I guess we'll just have to hang onto it, for now."
Saturday downed the shot of Bushmill's and turned toward the woman. "I guess it's time to leave," he said.
He turned to lean on the railing that overlooked the canyon with its fading colors of sunset.
"One last look," he said. "Beautiful."
"Yes, Honey," she said. "It's time for you to go."

August 2018

Chapter One

Nick:

The day starts innocently enough.

Except in Vegas, the day always comes with baggage attached from yesterday or a series of leftover grudges and debts from decades back. As they say, go figure.

I stand with my travel bag in front of my house as Jimmy Cox pulls up in his larger- than-Fresno Cadillac El Dorado. The sun is coming up on a day forecast to hit 112 on the Fahrenheit scale in Sin City. You could bet with the books that it will hit 113, but you'd have to give one and a half degrees to get the twelve-to-one odds.

Technically, Jimmy and I are the two people in charge of running the Galloping Dominos Casino. We're answerable only to the two owners, Jacky and Muriel. They prefer to spend most of their time in the relative comfort of 1040 Lakeshore Drive, Chicago. Their day features 78 degrees with a five-knot breeze off Lake Michigan.

Being smart enough to know our limitations, we've hired managers who understand the business school approach to running a large casino in Las Vegas. Jimmy and I, on the other hand, like the old-school approach to getting things done.

Our journey is a mixed bag. We're heading west to California, where we'll do our best to work off a list. A significant part of the list was supplied by Muriel.

Jimmy and I have a few items of our own we'll try to take care of as we go.

"I talked to that guy with the billiard tables last night," Jimmy says as I get into the car. "He can do the classic ones with the leather pockets. If we go for twenty of them for the casino, he'll deliver numbers 21 and 22 to you and me, off-invoice. We'll take a good look at his tables when we get to San Francisco. I just hope we can get around all the forest fires. Half the goddamn state is on fire."

"Yeah, and a lot of that smoke is coming over here," I say.

"We never had it like this before," Jimmy says. "Who would think that you'd go into a casino to get some fresh air. The cigarette smoke smells better than what's drifting over the state line from Yosemite."

I thought about how Dawn and I had recently installed air purifiers in our house. We were worried about the effect of all the smoke on our four-year-old daughter Molly.

"Nick, you and I have hung out in a lot of smoke-filled joints," my beautiful blonde wife said. "Let's at least do the best we can for our beautiful daughter."

We both had doubts about Vegas and its effect on our daughter when we moved from Chicago. Would it be good enough for Molly? The kid was smart, probably gifted. We wanted the best for her. So far, it's okay. The private schools are good, and there are exciting arts and music. Not Chicago Art Institute or Chicago Philharmonic, but the good stuff is around if you look.

Jimmy curses a few magic phrases designed to clear early morning traffic on 1-15. Finally, we're moving along at seventy, heading for the exciting town of Barstow.

"I call it Bar Stool," Jimmy says. "First stop is Teddy Bender's Bar and Grill, a first-class dump run by one of Muriel's cousins. Teddy will be getting a dozen Galloping Dominoes shirts, a bunch of posters and bumper stickers, and two boxes of cigars."

"You left out our good wishes."

I'll smile and tell him that Muriel loves him," Jimmy says.

"I thought that waitress, Cheryl Ann, was the one who loved him."

"She did give him the clap," Jimmy says.

"And good old generous Teddy passed :t onto his wonderful wife, Sally," I say.

"Sally was nice enough to make traveling plans for Cheryl Ann," Jimmy says. "I think she was pointing a .38 at Cheryl Ann at the time."

We were delivering promotional materials for Galloping Dominos. In reality, we were providing a care package designed to keep Muriel's relatives afloat. The posters, shirts, and bumper stickers all advertised the Galloping Dominos Casino. They were a half-hearted effort to get some of Teddy Bender's customers to come to visit us in Vegas.

"You know, if most of Bender's customers came to Vegas, they'd probably be coming to sign up for welfare," Jimmy says. "I don't know why we bother."

"You don't know?"

"Yeah, okay, smart ass," he says. "Muriel. If she's happy, then Jacky's happy. I don't know if the Cubans would be happy. We're handing out their finest Havanas to people who'd rather smoke dog shit."

"It's the thought behind the cigars," I say.

"You mean the thought beneath the cigars," Jimmy says.

I nod.

Each cigar box has a small tray of Havanas. Under the Havanas are neatly bundled stacks of hundred-dollar bills. Each box holds twenty Gs.

"I'm just glad it comes out of Chicago and not off our end," Jimmy says. "If I was working to support Muriel's relatives, I'd just walk away, Jose."

"I love it when you speak French," I say.

"Merda, my friend." Jimmy laughs. "It's all turning out to be merda."

It's the perfect Jimmy Cox told-you-so line. If you heard it as the Italian word for shit, you were probably right. Unless things got heavy, then Jimmy would come back with his, "I told you as we drove here it was going to be murder."

Jimmy:

I have a lot of doubts today. Lately, that's been me. I know I'm getting older, and maybe that has something to do with it. Mid-fifties. I'm still young, but I've heard most of the bullshit before. What we used to take for granted is now a series of question marks. Cassandra, my wonderful wife, tells me we should think about getting electric vehicles. At first, I'm shocked.

"Get rid of my Caddy, my magnificent beast?" I half-laugh. I half-laugh because I know she's right. She doesn't have to say it, but she does anyway.

"Jimmy, what kind of a world are we leaving little Molly? She's the closest thing we have to a daughter. You know we'd be the ones to step in if, heaven forbid, anything happened to Dawn and Nick."

She knows how to get me. In my sadness at the thought of losing our close friends, I'm also happy that she's called the question. These forest fires, the over-heated desert towns like Vegas and Phoenix, and the phonies who stand and claim things are better than they are - I'm fed up with all of them. A major power outage and half of Vegas would fry.

I start to think we should go electric.

I could drive a Tesla.

Cassandra would love to drive a Tesla.

I think about it and put it away for now.

We drive into Barstool.

"Maybe we could get some coffee before we have to deal with Muriel's relatives?" Nick asks.

We pull into a donut shop across the street from Teddy Bender's Bar and Grill.

"We'll get a table by the window," I say. "One with the scenic view of the junkyard next to Teddy's."

"I expect nothing less from you," Nick says.

"Damn right," I say. "You're paying."

Chapter Two

Nick:

The donut shop is damn near empty. Jimmy grabs a booth by the window, and we sit down. As promised, we have a clear view of the auto-junkyard and Teddy Bender's Bar and Grill across the road.

A guy wearing a white apron tucked under his armpits approaches the table. He looks like the thrift shop version of Morgan Freeman.

"What can I get for you, gents?"

"Coffee and a bear claw for me," Jimmy says.

"Sounds good," I say. "Make it two."

"Two coffees, two bear claws. Is that your El Dorado out there?"

"It is," Jimmy says.

"Nice set of wheels. She burns some 'tane, I bet."

"That she does," Jimmy says.

"Two coffees, two bear claws." He leaves to get our order.

Patsy Cline's "I Fall to Pieces" plays on the radio. As it finishes playing, a DJ named Rex Train comes on and intro's a Jason Aldean song."

"Shit, Aldean's the guy that was on stage when it all started to go down," Jimmy says.

"Yeah, not that I want to go there," I say.

"We were damn lucky," Jimmy says. "Cassandra had VIP passes. We would have been right next to the stage."

Her bronchitis saved us.

If there's such a thing as fate, it was working for us that day. Would we want to take Molly to the Route 91 Harvest festival with Uncle Jimmy and Aunt Cassandra? We could meet some of the performers and enjoy a crowd of people crazy about music.

We were ready to go that day when Jimmy called to say that they were staying home in the air-conditioned house to help Cassandra's breathing. If we wanted, we could take the passes and go without them.

"Nick," I remember my dear wife saying, "Why don't we take some food over to their house and let me do some cooking for all of us. Molly gets a bigger kick out of her aunt and uncle than she will out of some loud sounds coming from some huge speakers."

It turned out we did hear loud sounds coming out of huge speakers. We were sitting in Jimmy's home theater watching a Harry Potter movie when the Mandalay Bay shooter opened fire on the Route 91 Harvest festival crowd. Fifty-eight dead and hundreds wounded. Was it fate that we weren't there? Or just dumb luck? We wondered. Cassandra had called a dozen people to offer them the passes. Everyone was busy somewhere else or didn't answer their phones.

Our waiter is back at our patched-up red Naugahyde booth with our coffee and bear claws. I notice he has "Mike" written on his apron in Magic Marker.

"Mike," I take a chance on his name, "How come it's so quiet in here? Business slow?"

"Been that way lately," he says. "We get the morning rush– the coffee-to-go crowd with a dozen for the office, but after that, not much. Not much at all lately. I've had to let a waitress go. They can talk all they want about the economy getting better, but I ain't seen much of it."

"And the joint across the street?" Jimmy asks. "What's the story there?" Teddy Bender's Bar and Grill looks faded and dirty. Part of the overhang above the front door is in shambles. The parking lot is empty except for a beat-up Buick and a couple of motorcycles.

"Lots of trouble," Mike says. "Used to be a nice place to have a drink, meet some ladies. Now he's got the wrong crowd, and he ain't making any money. He comes over and tells me his troubles. I think he's getting ready to toss in the towel."

"Figures," Jimmy says.

"You know him?"

"Sort of, kind of."

"You guys from Vegas? I see you got Nevada plates."

"Yeah, his cousin wanted us to check in on him. She's worried about him."

"She should be," Mike says. "He tells me he's two months behind on the rent. That's not a remarkable thing around Barstow. He's also got the cops over there every time you turn around."

As if on cue, a police car pulls up across the road. A cop gets out, writes down the motorcycles' license numbers, and gets back in the squad car. "He's checking for stolen bikes," Mike says. "That crew that hangs out there gets busted on that a lot. Somehow, they all manage to walk. I get the drift from Teddy that the cops are getting a taste."

"Nice town you got here," Jimmy says.

"Yeah, reminds me of Al Busayyah," Mike says. "Everything there was up for grabs. I was there in '91 when we fought the Iraqis. A lot a good that did."

Jimmy:

The guy in the donut shop seems to know what Teddy Bender is involved in. He's behind on the rent, his place is a dump, and it's also a hangout for vehicular theft. This doesn't look like a place to attract visitors to the Galloping Dominos unless we're running a "Free Tickets to the Super Bowl Party" where cops round up felons with outstanding warrants.

I tell Nick and Mike to hang out while I go to the car to get Mike a Galloping Dominos golf shirt. My main reason is to get somewhere where I can talk to Chicago in private. I dial Muriel's cell phone and hope she isn't at some Lincoln Park high society meeting. I could have cut to the chase and called Jacky, but he has such low regard for some of Muriel's cousins that he'd probably tell us to shoot Teddy Bender. As satisfying as this might feel, it would also start World War III between Muriel and Jacky. It was better if she made the decision.

Luck is smiling at me. Muriel is at her club getting a spa treatment. I think about how she loves the luxury of being married to Jacky. She can have anything she wants and can block out anything she doesn't like. Several years back, Teddy Bender and his wife Sally thought they could do a surprise visit to Muriel and Jacky. They never got past the doorman at 1040 Lakeshore Drive.

At Muriel's instruction, Eddie Scarponi picked up the Benders and took them to a Day's Inn near O'Hare. She and Jacky met them once for a meal at a nearby Tony Roma's, gave them tickets to a White Sox game, where neither Jacky nor Muriel would be caught dead, and that was the visit.

"Talk to me, Jimmy," Muriel chirps. In the background, the music is strings.

"I hate to bother you at your spa, but there's a bit of a problem with…"

"With Teddy," she finishes my sentence. "I'm so glad you and Nick are handling this. How bad is it?"

I tell her about the rent being in arrears, the cops' frequent arrests of Teddy's customers, and how word on the street is that Teddy is getting ready to run out on the situation.

"I try to do for my family when I can," she says. "I was hoping for better."

"Me, too," I say. "I sure don't want you and Jacky tied to some vehicle theft ring. And I know you don't want that coming back on the Dominos."

"That would be terrible. What can we do?"

"Nick and I will talk to him. If he needs the cigar money to run, maybe that's okay, but he has to shut down. Barstow's too close to Vegas. That kind of crap can bleed over pretty fast."

"You know that bitch Sally ran off with some biker a couple months back," Muriel says. "I feel bad for Teddy, but not at the expense of what we have, Jimmy. Too many of our people are hard-working, family people who need their jobs. Let's not let some chop-shop operation ruin everything for us."

"I hear you," I say.

"Jimmy, you and Nick handle this. Whatever you two decide. I don't want any of this crap coming back on us. Stay focused on the deal in the Bay Area. That's more important than whatever Teddy Bender is doing."

"We'll do our best, Muriel."

"Oh, and one more thing, Jimmy."

"Yeah."

"Jacky doesn't have to hear about any of this, capisce?'

"Capisce, loud and clear, Muriel. Enjoy your spa."

Chapter Three

Nick:

Jimmy leaves the donut shop to get Mike a Galloping Dominos shirt from the trunk of the Caddy. It's a nice gesture, a thank you to a guy for giving us information. I figure he's also going to do his best to phone Chicago about what leeway we have in handling Teddy Bender.

Mike fills our coffee cups and one of his own.

"Mind if I sit down?"

"Please," I say. "You the owner of this place?"

"Only the manager," he says. "I got talked into it when Bobby Krasny, the manager before me, got beat pretty bad one night, across the street."

"At Teddy's? What happened?"

"Motorcycle hoods didn't like his choice of music and his choice of women."

"What was it they didn't like?"

"Santana's music and Lucy Lee, Bobby's Chinese girlfriend. Some of that crowd over there is Aryan Brotherhood. Those boys are fresh out of the penitentiary at Pelican Bay. White power. They started hanging out over there a few months back. Bender's old lady ran off with one of them, some fat pig with Nazi tattoos. I quit going there when they showed up. So far, they stay on their side of the road, and I stay on mine."

"Probably a wise move," I say.

"Damn right. One of them has an attack dog. He brings it with him when he visits one of the working gals in the trailer outback. Teddy says it's a Presa Canario. I believe one of those dogs killed a woman in San Fran a few years back. The handler couldn't control it."

"Yeah," I say, "Or wouldn't control it."

Mike nods.

I look up and notice a bullet hole high up in the window, two booths over.

"Somebody take a pot shot at you?" I point to the hole in the glass.

"It happened a couple nights ago. We were closed. I noticed it in the morning when I came in to open up."

An SUV pulls into the donut shop lot and parks near the front door.

"I'm just hanging on here, Nick," Mike says. "My brother-in-law has a delivery driver job opening up next month in LA at a beer distributor. I'm just gonna walk away if the assholes across the road don't shoot me first."

The Aryan Brotherhood assholes, the attack dog, and the bullet hole send my alert level toward red. I check to make sure my Glock is tucked into the back of my belt.

A couple from the SUV walks into the shop with a little girl wearing a pink dress and matching sandals. I'm guessing she's about five or six. They look like a family on vacation, heading for Disneyland or Vegas.

"Daddy," the little girl says, "We should have some donuts here with a drink, and then we should take some with in our car."

"Good idea," Daddy says.

They sit in the booth that has the bullet hole in the top of the window. My mind flashes to my daughter Molly and our close call avoidance of the Route 91 Harvest festival in Vegas.

"Customers," Mike says. "Got to go to work."

He gets up from the booth, walks toward the couple and their daughter as Jimmy walks back into the shop, and hands him a Galloping Dominos shirt.

"Thank you," Mike says. "I brought you some more coffee. I left the pot on the table."

It doesn't take long for Jimmy and me to exchange what we've just found out.

I'm happy that Muriel has given us carte blanche to deal with Teddy. "She just doesn't want anything coming back on Chicago or Vegas," Jimmy says. "She'd like Teddy safely out of the picture if we can work it."

"Sure," I say. "We'll just go across the road and explain it all to the Hitler Youth Group."

Jimmy:

There's a part of me that wants to say, "Let's just cut to the chase. Drive across the road and shoot Teddy Bender. Case closed." Of course, we can't do that because Muriel's version of carte blanche implies a breathing Teddy Bender at the close of business.

So much with the "What-if-this?" and "What-if-that?" Has he turned into a Nazi? Is he taking a cut out of the chop-shop action? Or is he still the pathetic putz who tries to tell everyone he's big-time friends with show biz people?

I bet pathetic. You've got to be pathetic to have your old lady run off with "Fatso von Himmler" or whatever his name was. Although from the little bit I've seen of Sally, maybe "pathetic" should be replaced with "lucky."

Six months ago, when we stopped in on our way to Ojai, Teddy was pathetic. We had a small love letter from Muriel—six grand in a brown mailer. "A little boost to get his business moving," Muriel said.

It needed more than a little boost. Teddy was telling two old drunks at the bar how Al Pacino stopped in for a drink on his way to Vegas.

"Al is just a wonderful guy. Yeah, we go way back," Teddy said. "Dean Martin introduced us."

"Pacino," one of the old drunks said. "Didn't he used to play for the Dolphins?"

"Not in this lifetime," I said, strolling past. "Cold beer sounds good."

I headed for a barstool at the far end of the bar.

"Hey, good to see you, Timmy." Teddy walked over, wiping his hands on his dirty apron.

"It's Jimmy, not Timmy."

"Oh, yeah." He put the beer on the bar in front of me.

"This should take care of it," I said, handing him the envelope full of cash.

He looked inside at the money.

"This from Muriel?"

I nodded.

"I can use it," he said.

I looked around the bar.

He was right.

He could use it.

If he were smart, he could use it to walk out the front door and never come back.

In the corner booth, a fat woman was snoring with her head on the table. Her left hand was in a puddle clutching wet dollar bills. Broken potato chips littered the floor next to an empty beer bottle.

At the other end of the bar, a thin guy wearing a "Barstow Bug Busters" shirt was on his cell phone and maybe on his sixth shot of tequila. "You can have the car back, goddammit," he said. "All you gotta do is find it. I'm only three months behind on payments. What do you want fucking blood?"

Sally walked up next to Teddy. She had the look of someone always wanting more dope.

"Did Muriel send us some mad money, Honey?"

She took part of the stack of bills out of the envelope and stuffed them in her bra.

"Party time," she said, wiggling her tight jeans through the curtained doorway behind the bar.

Teddy followed her.

"Easy come, easy go," I said.

I waited for Nick to come out of the john. On the wall near the jukebox was an enlarged photo of Teddy and Sally standing in front of the Welcome to Las Vegas sign. An Elvis impersonator stood between them. An inscription done with a Sharpie read, "Viva Las Vegas, Luv Ya, Elvis!"

On the other side of the jukebox was a poster from the original Ocean's Eleven movie. Frank Sinatra, Dean Martin, and Sammy Davis, Jr. grinned at the camera. The good wishes from all three Rat Packers done in Sharpie resembled Elvis's scroll.

Nick came out of the john and headed over to where I sat.

"Where's my beer?" He asked.

"The help is in the back room with their party favors," I said. "The beer is warm and flat. I think there's a better watering hole down the road."

Nick stared at the fat woman snoring.
"The live entertainment ain't much, either," he said.

Chapter Four

Nick:

The air in Barstow is smoky from fires. Towns east of San Diego are
burning. Yosemite is on fire. There's another fire raging near the Oregon
state line. Authorities say they're worried about a spreading disaster.
I'm worried about a spreading disaster, too: Teddy Bender.
We're back in Jimmy's Caddy, doing a slow crawl past the back of
Teddy's. The road is busted blacktop and gravel. Two beat-up trailers sit
behind the bar in sandy soil. A few patches of high weeds and broken
bottles add to the ambiance. If the front of Teddy's is an embarrassment,
the back of Teddy's is an embarrassment ready to slide down a 20-foot
embankment.
"Jesus Christ," Jimmy says. "I believe what our friend in the donut shop
says. Teddy's is a problem we don't need. We were here six months ago.
The joint was headed for the dumpster then."
"You don't like deadbeat exterminators or fat ladies snoring?" I ask.
"Hey, at least they pay cash," Jimmy says. "It's the other shit. You got
hate crimes, stolen vehicles, hookers, and crooked cops all coming out of
Teddy Bender's. You want to know the real bitch? The minute he gets
busted, guess who he cries to for help? Vegas and Chicago. Suddenly,
we're involved. Some D.A. gets wind of that, and he's thinking interstate
crime. Our friend RICO enters the picture, and it's Bad Day at Black
Rock for all of us."
"You left out drug busts and health and safety violations," I say.
"Hey, dogfighting, too," Jimmy says. "Let's not forget man's best
friend."
"Worst part of this," I say, "Is that Teddy probably isn't responsible for
any of it, other than his being a putz who's too dumb to see he's in deep
shit."
"You're right," Jimmy says, "There's no way we can leave town with
Teddy Bender anywhere near Teddy Bender's Bar and Grill. He has to
leave permanently."
"Yeah, but he's family," I say. "We gotta treat him right."
"Right," Jimmy says. "He needs a new gig, far, far away from here."

"And far away from us," I add.

"Damn straight."

"There probably shouldn't be a Teddy Bender's Bar and Grill after Teddy leaves," I say.

"I was just about to say that" Jimmy says. "We can't leave Teddy's legendary establishment in the hands of someone who might draw the wrong crowd and still point the finger at our crew."

"So, this is a basic case of R&D?"

"Yes, relocation and demolition," Jimmy says. "We're lucky to be working in an organization that takes care of its members."

One of the ways the organization takes care of its members starts on Pulaski Road in Chicago. Each month, Fetcha Cell Communications sends out new burner phones from that location to key people in our group. Upon receipt of the new burner from FCC, the old one is destroyed. It makes for secure communications.

Anthony Stompanato, aka "Tony Stomps," answers his burner on the first ring.

"Nick, what can I do for you?"

"I'm in Jimmy's Caddy. We're in Barstow. You down in L.A.?"

"Yeah, just got done playing golf."

"Let me put you on speaker so Jimmy can talk."

"Hey Jimmy," Tony says. "What's up?"

Jimmy starts the list of what's wrong with Teddy Bender. Every time Jimmy says another topic like Nazis or dogfighting, Tony Stomps says, "Jesus!"

"Yeah, Jesus in spades," Jimmy says as he finishes. "We gotta get him out and get him somewhere where he'll be okay, preferably far, far away. Any ideas? Anybody owe us a favor?"

Tony thinks for a minute and asks, "He can tend bar, right? I mean, without fucking it up too bad?"

"Yeah, I wouldn't let him manage it, though," I say.

"Hell no, not from what I just heard about Barstow," Tony says. "My company just got done shooting some promo video for a guy who has a resort opening down in Cabo. We could work something there; tell him he'd be doing a favor for Chicago."

"There's another aspect to the situation," I say. "We don't want any trace of Teddy Bender left behind. It's an R&D situation."

"Gotcha," Tony says. "How soon?"

"Yesterday," Jimmy says.

"I'll call Bruno and get right back to you."

Bruno De Rosa is an innocent man. He was found innocent of the Major Dan's Steak House fire-bombing in Morton Grove, Illinois. He was also found innocent of the Club Diamond fire-bombing in McHenry, Illinois. They looked at him for the fire-bombing of Club Samba, outside Cincinnati, but later the witnesses realized they were mistaken. As far as the other arson incidents in Ft. Lauderdale, Miami, and Tampa, he walked there, too.

"I visit a lot of places," Bruno told investigators. "Just 'cause I travel there, don't mean things are gonna explode. Hell, I go to Disneyland and Dodger Stadium every chance I get. I love the fireworks displays, but that don't mean I engineer them. I'll say one thing about those places that exploded and burned. They were all ugly. Another thing, nobody ever got hurt in any of these fires, except insurance companies. And you know, I never met anyone who loved an insurance company."

Jimmy:

Tony calls back and tells us that help is on the way. He and Bruno are coming up from L.A. Can we hang out until they get to Barstow?

"Sure," I say. "It's Nick's favorite town. We're going to go tour Walmart right after we destroy our health at some fast-food dump."

"You got to have Bender ready to move," Tony says. "I want to get back to L.A. late tonight. I can put him up in my guest house until we put him on the plane to Cabo. I talked to our friend Carlos down there. He's okay with the bartender gig. He'll even put Teddy up in a small room at the resort. One thing, though, it would smooth things out if you comped him for a week at Dominos."

"He can have two weeks," Nick says, "As long as he leaves Teddy down there."

We find a decent restaurant that serves salads and seafood specials. Our waitress is Luann, a dark-skinned woman who Nick guesses to be six months pregnant.

"Good guess," she tells Nick. "We're starting our seventh month. I'm planning to work as much as I can. We just got transferred here two months ago from North Carolina. I'm glad we got out before the hurricane hit. My husband's over at the Marine base. He's an M.P."

"Does he ever tell you stories about his work?" I ask. "Bad hangouts where there's trouble all the time?"

"He does." She smiles. "There are a few places that are bad in town. Some are off-limits. Lots of gangs pushing crack and oxy."

"He ever mentions Teddy Bender's?"

"Oh yeah. That's the place where those motorcycle bums hang out. You with the DEA?"

Nick and I laugh.

"No, we drove by there. It looked pretty bad," I say. "We work for the Galloping Dominos Casino in Vegas. We're on our way to San Francisco."

"I hear they have great jazz up there. My husband Quincy has a cousin in Martinez. One of these days we'll visit. You sure you're not with the DEA? Quincy says he'd love to get the DEA to bust places like that Teddy's you mentioned."

We leave the restaurant after leaving Luann a forty-dollar tip, two Dominos golf shirts, and fifty dollars in Dominos chips.

"Instead of that tour of Walmart you promised me, maybe we should just drop in on Teddy's to get the lay of the land," Nick says when we're back in the Caddy. "We could sit for a beer, check things out and tell him we'll be back later with a love note from Muriel."

I like the idea, even though it means seeing Teddy and exposing us to his dumpy establishment twice in one day.

The unmanned cop car is still in front of Teddy's. The two motorcycles have been joined by a third. The beat-up Buick sits off by itself in the corner of the lot near the auto junkyard gate.

Inside, the place looks worse than it did six months back. Some of the furniture is busted and stacked in a pile off to one side near the jukebox. The posters on each side are still there, but someone has added to the Sharpie writing. The writing over Sinatra, Martin, and Davis reads, "Nigger Lovers!!" The lettering over the Elvis picture reads, "Faggot!!" The place smells of stale booze and a backed-up septic tank.

We sit at the far end of the bar from where the cop is talking to the bikers. At first, I figure the cop is asking them about stolen motorcycles. It turns out he is, but not like you'd think.

"We can move the Harley quick," he says. "I don't know about the Yamaha."

"It's Jap crap," a fat guy with swastika tattoos says. "We shouldn't waste our time with inferior races."

I see something move next to the fat guy's feet. It's a dog—a big dog with a heavy chain collar. I think it's one of the killer dogs Mike told us about. Nick sees it, too. I can see him casually touch the back of his shirt, his way of making sure the Glock is ready.

Teddy walks over. Before he can say anything, I say, "This is our first time in your town. Can we get a couple of beers? We need some directions to find Walmart when you have time."

He comes back with the beers.

"Hey, Timmy," he says, barely audible. "Did Muriel send me something?"

"Yeah," I say. "A ticket out of here."

"Hey, hand it over," he says. "I can use the cash."

"You'll get it later when you walk out of here for good."

"Walk out of here? Where would I go?" He looks over at the cop and the bikers.

"Those your partners?" I ask.

Teddy grabs a bottle of Jim Beam, pours a shot for himself, and downs it. "No, it's not like that. If I leave, they'll track me down. I know too much."

Nick leans forward.

"Here's the deal, Teddy. Chicago says you're leaving. You're being moved to a luxury resort. A friend of the family has a nice gig for you. When we come back, you're going to walk out that door and head across the street like you're buying donuts from Mike. No luggage, no bullshit. We'll pick it up from there."

"Yeah, but…" Teddy starts to say.

"No, Walmart," Nick says loud enough to be heard at the other end of the bar. "We're looking for Walmart, not K Mart." And then, under his breath, "You're not going to fuck this up, Teddy. If you do, I'll kill you."

Chapter Five

Nick:

Threatening Teddy is a good way to get his attention. I've just finished telling him that we're taking him out of his disaster of a bar and placing him somewhere decent, far away from the Aryan Brotherhood. I've not gotten to the juicy parts of his new workplace where he'll be tending bar poolside, attending to the needs of rich women in skimpy swimsuits, when he starts to protest.

"Yeah, but…" Teddy starts to say.

That's when I cut to the chase. He either cooperates, or I'll kill him. There's little room here for error. He's stuck in a bar where a crooked cop currently sits making deals for stolen motorcycles with modern-day Nazis. Somewhere in one of the back trailers is an active prostitution ring and a small meth lab. My best guess is that everyone here is armed and dangerous.

One of the Aryan assholes has brought his doggy to Teddy's. Puppy is of the killer dog variety featured in the real-life story of NFL hero Michael Vick. Quarterback Vick did time in the slammer for dogfighting charges.

Still, he was welcomed back to big-time football with open arms upon release from prison. Wife beaters, drug addicts, and sexual predators are regularly forgiven by the NFL Just don't take a knee during the National Anthem.

I look at Teddy, and I start to feel bad about threatening him. He's one of those sad specimens, a cross between Woody Allen and Lee Harvey Oswald. If he were a dog, he'd yap at you and then wet himself.

"I just get worried," Teddy says. He pours another shot of Jim Beam and downs it.

"Just take it easy," I say. "Everything's gonna work out."

I look to my left and notice an "Inspection Failed" sticker on the small kitchen counter. Spare stove parts are spread across the countertop. A note hanging on the range hood says, "Do not use fan, blows fuses." A cheap plastic bucket with dirty water inside sits near an open floor drain.

"Bandit at three o'clock," Jimmy says under his breath.

Sure enough. Officer Friendly has left his Gestapo meeting and approaches us.

"Barkeeper," I say to Teddy, "Give everyone a round of drinks on us. The LA Times is paying."

"L.A. Times?" Officer Friendly asks. "You were asking about Walmart? I couldn't help but overhear."

Up close, Friendly looks like everyone's idea of the nice camp counselor who does his best to hide his drinking problem until happy hour. He introduces himself.

"Ed Twilly," he says. "Been with the Sheriff for 12 years. What's the L.A. Times doing up here?"

"Bradley, Ben Bradley," I say, putting out my hand for him to shake. Twilly shakes my hand and quickly puts his hand back to rest on his gun belt.

"I'm glad you came over here," I say. "My partner Pete Hamill over here can't seem to find his way around your town even with GPS. We're supposed to meet some important people at Walmart for a big story. Say, can we buy you a drink?"

"Crown Royal with a Coke back," Twilly yells at Teddy, who's busy drawing beers halfway down the bar.

"What's the story?"

"Probably something you know about already," I say.

"Could be."

"This guy Spenser just took over at DEA in L.A.," I say. "They say he's trying to make a name for himself. You heard about him?"

"A little," Twilly says.

"Yeah, I know you can't say much to a reporter. You're probably in on the planning. All I know is they promised us a series of raids on places run by criminals. Drugs, hookers, you name it. Our problem is we can't find where we're supposed to meet this task force. It's supposed to go down around seven."

Teddy comes back with our drinks.

"Yeah, I heard about that guy Spenser," Twilly says. He downs his whiskey in one gulp and drinks his Coke. "The barkeep can tell you how to get there. I'm late for a meeting."

Twilly heads for the door. One of the Nazis, a skinny guy who looks like a victim on a drug poster, follows him.

"Where you going, man? I thought we was working out something."

"I got to go," Twilly says. "If you're smart, you'll go, too."

Skinny guy turns back to the table where all the Brotherhood was sitting with Twilly when we walked in.

"Wally, Pete, deals off for now. Let's go."

One guy stands up and heads for the door with Skinny Guy.

"Fuck you all," the fat guy with the dog says. "I'm staying."

Jimmy:

You gotta hand it to Nick. He knows when to threaten a wuss like Teddy, and he knows when to drop a line of bullshit on a crooked cop that clears out Teddy's bar. Well, almost clears it out. The fat skinhead in the "White Power" t-shirt and his killer dog are still sitting at the other end of the place. Mr. Skinhead is downing gulps from a bottle of vodka while the killer dog is lapping up beer from a schooner on the floor. Why Thomas Kinkade or Norman Rockwell never used such a heart-warming set-up for a painting is a mystery to me.

"Pete does this a lot," Teddy half whispers to us. "He's waiting for Alma."

"Oh yeah?" Nick asks.

"She's his old lady. She's busy with a john in the back trailer. They'll be leaving soon."

"What? He's waiting to drive her home?"

"Close," Teddy whispers. "She has to drive him and the dog. Too many DUIs. They pulled his license."

The large flatscreen tv has been playing silently above the bar. Some sort of a game show has people jumping up and down like they're fighting for the last toilet on a transcontinental airliner.

The news comes on with pictures of forest fires on one side of the screen and hurricane destruction on the other.

"Hey, turn up the fucking sound," Pete Skinhead yells.

"I can't," Teddy says. "The speaker system don't work."

Pete Skinhead gets to his feet and starts to stagger his way toward us. Then he turns toward his dog.

"Stay, goddamn it. Stay."

The dog snarls and settles down.

Pete makes it to a bar stool three stools down from us and plants himself.

"Get everybody a drink on me. Put it on my tab, Teddy."

"Sure, Pete," Teddy says.

"Look at this shit," Pete says, pointing at the screen. "Half the goddamn country is on fire, and the other half is flooded. You think those assholes in Washington care?"

"They only care when they want your vote," Nick says.

"They ain't getting one from me." Pete drinks from his beer. "Wanna know why? I'll tell you. I'm an ex-con. I can't vote, and you know what? I don't give a fuck."

"You ain't alone," Nick says. "A lot of people are fed up."

"No, I figured it out a long time ago." Pete takes a swig from his vodka bottle. "These goddamn bankers took everyone for a ride. Guess what? I went into their bank and pointed a shotgun at them. I took them for a goddamn ride."

"Yeah, till they grabbed your ass."

Freckled face walks in from the back door of the bar.

She's a short redhead with wolf's head tattoos on both forearms. An extra-large Harley t-shirt hangs down to just above her bare knees. She wears black motorcycle boots and has a large matching handbag slung over her shoulder.

"They threw Pete's ass into the slammer," she says. "Tossed the whole lot of them into Pelican Bay. Think any of them gave a shit for poor old Alma? Hell no. I had to hit the streets and go back to be a working gal."

She grabs Pete's beer and drinks the rest of it.

"Time to go, Sugar," she says. "Grab the beast. We gotta go buy dog food and condoms."

Chapter Six

Nick:

Jimmy, Teddy, and I are alone in Teddy Bender's Bar & Grill. The cast of characters engaged in white power, vehicle theft, and prostitution have all departed. It's time to get our shit together, get Teddy relocated, and get Teddy Bender's Bar & Grill obliterated. Our removal & demolition team is on the way. Tony Stomps is driving Bruno De Rosa up from L.A. to perform the exorcism, hopefully without casualties.

"We should make sure no one's in those trailers out in back," Jimmy says. "We need to secure the place."

Teddy takes me through the back door of the bar to look. The two run-down trailers sit in a sandy weed patch of broken beer bottles and fast-food wrappers. One trailer is for hookers to work from. Creaking floors, dirty carpet, and paintings of nude women on black velvet curtains supply the ambiance. The other trailer, Teddy says, was used as a lab in the Aryan Brotherhood's crystal blue persuasion business. Now it's just storage for miscellaneous motorcycle parts.

"They moved most of the acetone and the lab equipment to Idaho," Teddy says. "Sally went with it. Like, I give a shit. Can't say it was much of a marriage."

We lock up the trailers and go back to the bar.

Jimmy has locked the bar's front door and put the "Closed" sign in the small window facing the parking lot.

"I just talked with Tony," Jimmy says. "They'll be here in another hour or so. This could be a good time to gather what you want, Teddy. Once you leave, there's no coming back."

"Yeah," Teddy says. "How about telling me where I'm going? Or are you just gonna take me out and shoot me?"

"No way," I say. "Teddy, you're family. Muriel and Jacky care about you. They don't want you here having to kiss up to Nazis and crooked cops. They've lined up a nice gig for you in Baja at a new resort."

Teddy pours a shot of Jim Beam and downs it.

"Muriel and Jacky, you say they care?"

"Sure, they care. They worry about you."

I don't tell him that they worry about his pain-in-the-ass act showing up in Chicago or that Baja may turn out to be not far enough away from Muriel and Jacky. At least it's a step out of the country for now. Putting Teddy in Tierra del Fuego or Zanzibar would probably be more to everyone's liking.

"I'm the one what told Muriel about the house, you know," Teddy says. "One of my connections let me in on it. I told her a while back. She said she was gonna get you two to take care of it. I figure I'd get a taste from giving her a tip on that."

"Let's be a little more specific, here Teddy," Jimmy says. "House? What house?"

"Jesus. What am I, on the fucking witness stand?"

"Settle down, Teddy," I say. "Jimmy's just trying to make sure you're on the same page with us. We do a lot of confidential work for Muriel and Jacky. We don't have room for fuck ups."

Teddy pours another Jim Beam and downs it.

"It's the one in the Bay Area," he says "Old-timer I know came through here. He used to work at the Sands when Jack Entratter had it. I buy him a drink. Next thing he's telling me this story about the house and its history with Sinatra and some of the heavyweights, people Muriel and I are related to but maybe don't want to admit too much about."

Jimmy leans forward, looks around the bar, and looks at Teddy.

"You're sitting in a dump like this kissing up to the shit bags that just left. And you're worried about someone finding out that you're related to people who used to run bookie joints in Cicero in the fifties? I'm shocked. Next, you're going to tell us that you've been skimming out of your own cash register."

Teddy laughs.

"Hey, I do alright. I take care of myself. I never got word that you guys were coming to get me out of here. Sure, I was getting ready to run. You met Mike across the road. We got this gig lined up in L.A. in a few weeks. He's got a guy down there who can give us a beer delivery route down in Central. We been saving what we can on the side. Traveling money, a stake to get us going."

"That's just wonderful," Jimmy says. "How fucking heart-warming can you get? Your story will bring a tear to the eyes of every MS-13 gang member in L.A. Does Dominic's Sports Betting Emporium in Vegas have a line on how long you two will last before you get robbed or killed?"

Teddy shrugs and tosses both hands up. He pours another shot of Beam and downs it. He looks at the spot where the "Ocean's Eleven" poster hangs.

"Whatever you guys can do," he says. "I'm grateful. Everything's been falling apart on me. This ain't like I been running the Bellagio, you know."

Jimmy:

Trying to listen to Teddy Bender and work past his bullshit makes me regret going on this trip. I could be sitting at home in Vegas with my beautiful, smart wife, Cassandra. We could be roasting shrimp on the grill and watching our Labradoodle Zorro do laps in our saltwater pool. Nick is irritated, too, I can tell. This crap about Teddy looking for a finder's fee on the house has us both pissed. I can guess what happened.

Clancy Booker used to work for Jack Entratter at the Sands. He probably told a story about the house to Murray Bender. Murray lives in Ojai and teaches Noir Literature at U.C. Santa Barbara. Clancy and Murray have been working on a book about the old days in Vegas when Bugsy Siegel was running things. Clancy might have mentioned something about the house when he stopped for a drink at Teddy's on the way back to Vegas. The pisser is I can't remember much about this house deal. Muriel spoke to both of us on speakerphone before we left Vegas. She mentioned the house, I know, but she also mentioned a lot of other things. Muriel's hard to follow. Nick says Muriel walks sideways into a conversation and wanders out three paragraphs later, referring back to something she hasn't yet talked about.

We got a package on the house, FedEx-ed from Muriel in Chicago. It's unopened in the trunk of the Caddy. I figured we'd look at it after we got Teddy taken care of. I knew we'd be hearing more about it from Murray when we stopped in Ojai.

I didn't expect Teddy to be a move-the-mountain-to-Mohammed project. We could have just played dumb and followed orders. Give Teddy a box of Havanas with 20 Gs inside and move on down the road. Except that, too, would be asking for trouble. The minute Teddy got busted with the Aryan Brotherhood and friends, he'd have everyone in our crew worried about being implicated.

No, it was time to move Teddy.

"Time to grab whatever you want," Nick says to Teddy. "We're clearing out of here real soon."

Teddy gets busy in the small back room he's been living in. He packs some clothes and things into his set of matching luggage, two Target shopping bags, and announces that he's ready.

"Except for Frank, Dino, and Sammy," he says.

He walks over to the jukebox where the poster from the original "Ocean's Eleven" hangs. It's been written over with an angry scrawl: "Nigger Lovers!!"

It turns out the angry scrawl is on the glass covering the poster. Teddy removes the glass and rolls up the poster with the three autographs on it. "Good as new," he says. "And a valuable collector's item.":

"Those autographs for real?" Nick asks.

"Real enough," Teddy says.

Nick points to the framed poster on the other side of the jukebox.

"What about the other one? The one of you and Sally with Elvis?"

"Nah, phony baloney," Teddy says. "Elvis impersonator, phony bitch of a broad. I'm the only one real in the photo."

"Yeah," Nick says. "You're the real deal."

Chapter Seven

Nick:

We're sitting in Jimmy's Caddy in front of a Sandwich 2 Go joint. We finally got Teddy out of his run-down bar, locked everything up, and stopped to see Mike to ask him to stick around. We said we had a deal for him. Hell, we'd even buy him a sandwich and bring it back to the donut shop so we could talk about it.

"Large turkey, all the way on sourdough," Mike says. "If you're bringing beer, make it Beck's."
Before we call Tony, I give Teddy two c-notes and send him into the sandwich joint with our complicated order.
"Make sure you get it right," I say. "And keep the change."
Luck is with us. The line at the sandwich shop is almost out the door. It gives us time to talk on the phone with Tony without Teddy around.
"Is this guy sober? Does he have three heads? Is he dumber than Teddy?" Tony's voice comes barking out of my cell phone speaker. He's about thirty miles outside Barstow with Bruno.
We're talking about Mike, the Donut Clay manager, Teddy's proposed partner in the "Deliver Beer in an LA Barrio and Commit Suicide by MS-13 Gang" plan that the two have worked up.
"So, is Barstow an open-air nuthouse?" Tony asks. "This crap with Teddy, is it catching?"
"It's complicated," Jimmy says. "It's like one of those problems where the guy has a rowboat to cross a river, and he has to carry a chicken, a fox, and a sack of corn across, but he can only take one at a time. He can't have the chicken eat the corn or the fox eat the chicken."
"Yeah, I know that one," Tony says. "He takes the chicken over first, comes back for the fox, drops off the fox, picks up the chicken, rows back, leaves the chicken, grabs the corn, rows that to the fox, then rows back and gets the chicken."
"How'd you figure that so easy?" Jimmy asks.
"It's the same principles involved in money laundering," Tony says.
"Or financing a movie," Bruno says.
"Same difference," Tony says.

"Look," I say. "We know we can take Teddy all the way to Cabo and get him settled. We know we can take down Teddy's bar and reduce it to rubble. We've got that all planned, but if we leave Mike behind after we blow up the joint across the road, that leaves us in a bad position. We don't know what he'll do."

"We could shoot him," Tony says.

"Yeah, Teddy's friend," Jimmy says. "You want to take credit for that one? You want to talk to Jacky about why Muriel and her Cousin Teddy are so upset?"

"Oh, Jesus," Tony says. "Let me think a minute."

A minute of silence passes.

"You still there?" He asks.

"Yeah."

"This guy manages a donut joint. I guess he cooks. He must know something about dealing with customers."

"Yeah, he's a reasonable guy, friendly," I say.

"Shit. What have we got to work with? A little dinero could go a long way in greasing the wheels."

"I got ten Gs for you and Bruno to split," I say. "I know it ain't much, but it's worth it to keep Jacky and Muriel happy."

"Christ, the C4 could cost more than that," Bruno says.

"Yeah it could, but you never spent a nickel on it," Jimmy says. "Unless you're calling yourself Davenport Elko Engineering. I heard some of their supply has gone missing."

"Here's what I think, Nick," Tony says. "If you and Jimmy are offering us ten Gs, then I know that you're holding at least that amount as your taste. I don't blame you. I'd do the same thing, especially if I had to deal with Teddy. So, here's what could work: toss us another five and let us offer our guy in Cabo another comp week at the Dominos. He'll send some rich cholo up there, and you can make it all back, maybe more."

I look at Jimmy. He nods.

"You got a deal."

Jimmy:

Dinner at dusk at Donut Olay in Barstow is memorable. Teddy has managed to screw up everyone's sandwich order, but remarkably, there's more than enough food for everyone. The table is a wreckage of empty wrappers, beer bottles, and donut boxes.

Bruno stands up and belches a few times and announces that he needs to see the layout of Teddy's Bar & Grill so he can make things happen. Nick and Tony grab the keys and take flashlights across the road with

Bruno.

I get to explain the impending deal to Mike and Teddy. I'm hoping for a miracle that all will fall into place, and the two of them will accept our package as offered, without a hitch, and be on their merry way to Cabo San Lucas.

Mike beats me to the punch.

"Teddy tells me that you guys think our beer delivery job in the barrio might be a little dangerous," he says. "Is there a better way for us both to get out of Barstow? We're kind of desperate."

"Yeah," I say. "We have a business associate in Baja who has just finished building a new resort. He could use you two down there in barkeeping and food prep. The salaries will be paid in cash because you'll be listed as consultants. You'll each get a room and get your meals free at the resort. It pays better than beer delivery, and it's a hell of a lot safer."

"Wow," Mike says. "I love Cabo. Love that whole area down there. I was there a couple years ago. How soon can we go? I'm ready. I got all my stuff in the back room."

The front door to the donut shop opens. A man and a woman wearing motorcycle jackets walk in.

"Hey, what's the deal with across the street?" The man asks. "We were gonna go in and have a drink, but it's got a closed sign. Something happen?"

"Some kind of electrical problem or gas leak," I say.

"We thought we saw flashlights through the window," the woman adds.

"Yeah, I think they're trying to fix things."

"No problem," the man says. "Plenty of watering holes in this town."

The two get back on their Harley and leave in a loud cloud.

"I get the drift of what you guys are doing across the street," Mike says. "It makes sense. No trace of Teddy Bender's name left behind. No Aryan Brotherhood hangout to tag him with. It all goes."

"It's the best we can do," I say.

"Yeah," Teddy says. "It's just that we need that done on this side of the road, too."

It's the old good news/ bad news routine.

The good news is that our two heroes Teddy and Mike, have plenty of money. So, they won't need pocket money for their trip. My first guess on that topic is, of course, they've been skimming out of both cash registers.

"True enough," they both say. "But there's more."

"You've been over-ordering supplies on credit and boosting them out the back door for cash, right?"

"Yeah, but…"

"But that ain't all?" I ask.

"Follow us," Mike says.

The bad news part is in the back room. Mike lifts a canvas tarp off a large pile in the corner. Cans of acetone are stacked five feet high.

"It's from across the street," Teddy says. "The Brotherhood was moving the meth-making supplies to Idaho. We just moved a few cans at a time across the road. They never caught on. We moved some of the crystal meth across, too."

"Where's that?" I ask.

"It's already gone," Teddy says. "We found a buyer for it. Guy named Manuel Rose. He was head of the Knight Ravens Motorcycle Club. They bought most of it. They wanted to buy the acetone, too, so they could set up their own lab."

"So, what happened? Why hasn't this guy Rose bought it?"

"He did come by," Mike says. "He'd ride his bike up through that rough trail in the back and knock on the back door. He wanted to avoid the assholes across the road as much as he could."

"Don't blame him on that," I say.

"Two days ago, there's a knock on the door," Mike says. "Sure enough, it's Manuel Rose, looking like warmed-over shit. He's higher than a kite, and he wants to sample more of the meth we sold him. We don't have but a few leftovers. His boys took most of it. 'Don't matter,' he says, 'Gimme it.' So he goes out the back door to toke up. I go to wait on a couple customers. When I come back, I see that we got a big problem."

Teddy motions me over to the walk-in cooler and opens the door. A blast of cold air clouds my vision for a few seconds. Then I see it. To the left is a large trail bike complete with knobby tires. To the right is another canvas tarp. Under the tarp is the body of a black man wearing a black leather jacket that proclaims "Knight Ravens M.C., Barstow, California."

Chapter Eight

Nick:

Barstow is one surprise after another. Some are good, some not so. Bruno tells Tony and me that he's surprised Teddy's Bar & Grill is still standing.

"There's so much wrong with this place that I'm surprised it hasn't gone up in flames on its own," Bruno says. "The electric is in terrible shape, poorly grounded, exposed wiring. That strange smell is a combination of sewage and gasoline. I figure gas is leaching into the septic system from the chop shop next door. I see they have a gas pump and maybe a medium-sized tank buried under it. Probably hasn't been inspected in years."

Our tour of the area behind Teddy's reveals more. Large cans of acetone covered by a tarp are stacked under each trailer. There are at least a dozen cans under each trailer. In addition, a 250-pound propane tank, half-filled, sits between the back of the bar and the trailers.

"You don't need C4 for this job," Bruno says. "A tossed cigarette could do the honors, probably take out the chop shop next door."

I look at the darkened street. The only light is coming from the donut shop. Failed businesses in run-down storefronts line the street.

Tony sums it up: "This street could use a few fires."

Across the street is another surprise. Unfortunately, this one isn't so good.

I stare at the dead body of Manuel Rose, the head of the Knight Ravens Motorcycle Club.

Teddy and Mike ramble on about their stack of acetone cans, their cleverness in skimming cash out of Teddy's and the donut shop, and how the Ravens' esteemed leader came to o.d. in the back of Donuts Olay.

It looks like the bike is stolen, too," Bruno says. "The locks have been busted, and its ignition is hot-wired."

Jimmy and I need to talk," I say. "Everyone cool it. Eat some donuts, have some coffee while we decide what we're doing here."

Bruno and Tony grab some donuts and coffee. They sit in the booth with the bullet hole in the window. Teddy sits on a stool at the counter, talking with Mike as he makes fresh coffee. Jimmy and I are back in the booth we sat in this morning when we first walked into Donuts Olay, which is starting to seem like several years ago.

"Any idea what the odds are that we can pull this one out clean?" I ask.

"Don't forget to factor in a stolen trail bike, a dead soul brother, and the fact that the Knight Ravens could show up any minute looking for the acetone, the bike, and their esteemed leader."

"We could take the body out the back door along with the bike," Jimmy says. "Take them down the road somewhere and dump both in some high weeds."

"Yeah, we could," I say. "Thing is we still have to torch both Teddy's and Donut Olay to cover up for all the skimming and thievery. The acetone in the back could help with the torching. That, though, brings on suspicion of arson. Once they start looking into that, the cops start looking for Teddy and Mike as the prime suspects. If we don't get them out of the way fast, it can all come back on us."

"Yeah," Jimmy says. "Who the hell else is around to blame? The Aryan Brotherhood will disappear fast once they hear about their playhouse going up in flames and investigators sniffing around."

I'm about to answer when the loud whoop-whoop from a sheriff's patrol car comes from Teddy's parking lot across the road. A flashing blue light casts a glow on everything.

"Sit tight," I yell. "Everyone play it cool. We haven't done anything they can prove."

The patrol car makes several fast circles in the lot, scattering loose stones. Finally, it straightens out and screeches tires as it bounces out of Teddy's lot and crosses the road to Donuts Olay, where it comes to a sudden stop in front of the door. It whoop-whoops a couple times and goes silent. The driver's door opens. Officer Ed Twilly steps out and staggers through the door to Donuts Olay.

"Gimme cuppa coffee," he says to Mike. "Gonna pour some brandy in it. Nightcap."

He takes a small bottle of B&B out of his pants pocket and opens it, looking at Teddy sitting on the stool next to him.

"Cheers," he says. "Why the hell ain't you open? So, you get scared off by some smart-ass reporters with a phony story about some raid?"

He takes a swig of brandy and looks straight at Jimmy and me.

"Oh, there they are. New York Times, was it? Buncha shit. Yeah, a bunch of shit."

"LA Times," I say. "Looks like you missed the raid."

"Yeah. I missed it," Twilly says. He turns toward Mike. "You see any fuckin' raid. Huh? You see any fuckin' raid, Jazzbo? Where's my fuckin' coffee, Sambo? We don't allow your kind across the street no more, do we? Ah, fuck it, I'm leaving."

Twilly stands and stumbles against the counter. He puts the brandy bottle up to his lips and guzzles it all down. He heads toward the door but only gets two steps before he falls face-down onto the floor with a crash. He's out, cold.

The radio clipped on Twilly's shirt squawks: "Officer Twilly, are you 10-7 or 10-8? Repeat, are you 10-7 or 10-8? Officer Twilly, respond, please."

"Jesus, old Mayor Daley was right," Jimmy says. "The police aren't here to create disorder. They're here to preserve it."

Jimmy:

"Basket case," Tony says from his kneeling position next to Twilly on the floor of Donuts Olay. "He's still breathing. I think he's pissed in his pants. What do we do now? Should we turn off his radio?"

"No," Nick says. "I think we can use him. He might just be the hero that saves our asses."

I look at Nick. He's smiling that crooked smile of his that says the world may be nutso, but there's still a silver lining to be found if you know where to look.

"In chaos is opportunity," he says. "We have to move fast."

The next few minutes are a blur of activity, with Nick directing the players. He tells Teddy and Mike to put all their luggage into Tony's car, get into the back seat, and stay there. He turns to Bruno.

"We need the acetone sprinkled around both places, and I'm going to want a half-filled can of acetone out here in the parking lot. So, we'll torch both places right before we leave."

Bruno nods and heads across the street to Teddy's.

"Jimmy, you and Tony get Twilly back in his squad car, passenger side, and back the car up, so it's near the road, away from the fires. Then slide Twilly back into the driver's seat."

Getting Twilly into the car is no fun, but we do it. All the time, I'm wondering what the plan is all about, but I can't think beyond the moment. So, I'm telling myself that any plan is better than none, which is about all I'm capable of coming up with.

We slide Twilly over to the driver's seat and turn to walk back toward Donuts Olay. That's when I notice that Nick's been busy. The trail bike with the knobby tires is on its side on the asphalt halfway between Twilly's squad car and the donut shop.

"Get over here," Nick yells. "I need help with something."

The something turns out to be the dearly departed leader of the Raven Knights Motorcycle Club, or at least what's left of him. We drag him out and toss his body over the bike.

Bruno is back from across the street and is back in the donut shop, pouring acetone around the floor. He comes out and hands Nick a half-filled can of acetone. Nick wipes off the handle and puts it in the hands of the deceased Manuel Rose.

Nick turns to Bruno.

"Are we ready to burn?"

"Yeah, we got puddles of accelerant. All they need is a match."

"Good, one more detail, and we're cruising."

Nick heads over to the squad car and comes back with Twilly's service revolver. He stands about ten feet away from the dearly departed Manuel

Rose and fires two shots into Rose's chest. Then, he heads back to the squad car and opens the driver-side door. He unbuckles Twilly and drags him out of the car, letting him fall to the pavement. Nick wipes the revolver clean and puts it in the hands of the passed-out Twilly. "Everyone get mobile," he yells. "It's time to burn."

Chapter Nine

Nick:

A stream of flame races toward Teddy Bender's Bar & Grill on one side of the road. Another stream of flame speeds toward Donuts Olay across the street. Both streams shoot through each establishment's open front door and run into a motherlode of the volatile liquid. A bright flash and a loud "Whump!" come from each side of the road.
"Got to go now before the propane tanks blow," Bruno yells.
Tony drives off with Bruno, Teddy, and Mike aboard his Escalade. Jimmy and I follow in Jimmy's old El Dorado. I look back at orange flames lighting up the night. A strange glow covers a bizarre tableau. A cop car with blue flashing light sits on the edge of the Donuts Olay parking lot. Next to the driver's door, Officer Twilly is unconscious on the busted asphalt. He holds his service revolver in his hand. Twenty feet away is the body of Manuel Rose with two bullet holes in him. He's sprawled across a stolen trail bike. Behind him, Donuts Olay is crackling, smoking, and getting ready to explode.
It's time to hit the highway.
On the way to Victorville, I parcel out cash into large envelopes. Fifteen Gs go to Bruno and Tony for their help in removal and demolition. I put three grand in an envelope for Teddy, his taste for whatever he thinks he's done on this house deal that Muriel has been touting, but neither Jimmy nor I seem to know much about.
"What a day," Jimmy says as we drive along I-15 in the dark. "I hope this means that we're done with Teddy Bender. That was a lot of shit to go through just to please Muriel."
"I know," I say. "I don't like having to shoot people, even if they're already dead. Maybe I'm starting to get old."
Jimmy laughs.
"No, I get it. I didn't like the idea of adding any more shit into the air with the fires, but what else could we do? Start a flood?"

"How'd we get stuck in this shit?" I ask. "Dealing with Nazi creeps? Starting fires? I thought we're supposed to be respectable crooks, hanging around the casino and making rich dentists feel like they're Robert Fucking De Niro while we take their money."

We follow Tony's car into a Denny's parking lot. He heads over to the side of the building by the dumpsters and puts it in park.

"Anyone gotta take a leak, do it here against the wall," he tells his passengers. "Get right back in the car. This ain't no two-hour layover."

I hand over the envelope for him and Bruno.

"I already got our two refugees a flight tomorrow to Cabo in the afternoon," Tony says.

"Here's your taste on the house deal," I say to Teddy. "It's still too early to know where that deal ends up."

"Sure," he smirks, taking the envelope. "I'll stay abreast of the deal when I talk with my cousin Muriel."

"You do that," I say. If he talks to her enough, I think she'll be shipping him off to Burma.

Everyone wets the back wall of Denny's and gets back in their vehicles.

"We're off to LA," Tony yells through his open window. "We'll stay in touch."

"Talk soon," I yell.

They head for I-15 and LA.

"What now?" Jimmy asks.

"There's a Hilton nearby. We have reservations. We can go there and collapse."

Jimmy:

Two tough guys on the move, we manage to find the Hilton, order a pizza and a six-pack, and collapse into our beds. Morning finds us both awake at six, slurping on coffee and ready to watch the early news.

"Firefighters in Barstow had their hands full overnight when a suspicious blaze thought to be arson broke out in several buildings in an industrial area. A donut shop, an auto-junkyard, and a bar were totally destroyed in the blaze. Police are saying that quick thinking on the part of Officer Ed Twilly of the Sheriff's department prevented arsonists from destroying more of the area's businesses. Twilly was able to shoot one of the alleged arsonists who was in the act of pouring liquid accelerant in an attempt to spread the destruction. Officer Twilly reportedly lost consciousness from toxic fumes. He's been transported to County Med Center, where he's listed in fair condition."

"A great American hero," Nick says. "Toxic fumes from brandy and Crown Royal don't bother Ed Twilly."

The tv camera does a slow pan showing the rubble that's left of Teddy's and Donuts Olay coupled with more commentary.

"The man Officer Twilly shot is believed to be a Knight Ravens Motorcycle Club member, a primarily African-American club. The Ravens reportedly have been in conflict with an Aryan Brotherhood gang that hangs out in the fire area. In other fire news, officials near Yosemite have...."

I click the set off. Thanks to Nick's clear thinking, we're in the clear.

"It was just a crazy notion," Nick says. "Either they'd make Twilly a hero or have him arrested for manslaughter and being drunk on duty. Them selling the story like they have tells you a lot about how law enforcement thinks in Barstow."

We manage to get cleaned up and work our way back to Denny's for a decent breakfast. Soon we're on the road to Ojai when my cell phone rings. It's Cassandra. At least that's what the caller i.d. says. Instead of my husky-voiced wife, a more diminutive voice comes on the speaker.

"Uncle Jimmy, this is Molly. Is my daddy there with you?"

"He's right here, Sugar. We're on speaker."

"Good morning, Honey," Nick says. "What's going on?"

"Go ahead, tell them," I can hear Cassandra in the background.

"Don't be bashful." Now it's Dawn we can hear in the background."

"I'm going shopping with Mommy and Aunt Cassandra. We're going to look for a car you can plug into the electricity in your garage, Uncle Jimmy. Aunt Cassandra says she's tired of the stinky gas-guzzler you're making her drive."

"He's just awful, isn't he?" Nick asks. "She should go look at a Tesla."

"Momma was hoping you would say that," Molly says. "She wants a plug-in car, too."

"And she should get one, too," I say. "You three ladies should go and have lunch in some expensive restaurant while you're car shopping, and your daddy will pay for everything."

"We will," Cassandra says. "How are things? Have you finished with Barstow?"

"I hope so. We're headed for Ojai."

"And the better Bender," Nick says."

"Give Murray our best," Dawn says. "He's a lovely guy."

"We'll let you go, for now, boys. Take care. We'll talk later," Cassandra says.

Chapter Ten

Nick:

Our drive takes us away from the smog-filled country, and soon we come into blue skies. I notice Jimmy looking restless behind the wheel like he can't get comfortable.

"Hey, what's the hurry?" I say. "Come on, I'll buy you a donut."

We stop a few miles short of Ojai for a mid-morning coffee break at a café. Another look at the contents in the FedEx package will help us both before we see Murray. The restaurant has tables that can seat eight. Jimmy requests one of the large tables, explaining to the waitress that we need to spread out some papers on a house deal.

"I know what that's like," Joann says as she takes our orders. "Me and my husband just closed on a house. All that paperwork was a nightmare. Now we're wondering if we have enough fire insurance."

We start out with coffee and banana cream pie. The coffee smells delicious, and the pie slices are tall and tempting.

"I shouldn't be eating this shit," Jimmy says.

"Shit? Why the hell did you order it?"

"Don't get me wrong," he says. "It's delicious. I just shouldn't be eating it."

"Yeah, me too," I say. "Cassandra will probably blame me for leading you astray."

Jimmy shakes his head and growls.

"Jesus, Nick, look what's happened to us. I remember years back when I was with my first wife. You really were a bad influence on me then. All night drinking, getting into bar fights, ending up with bimbo broads. So, what the hell happened? Look at us. We've stooped to worrying about a slice of banana cream pie."

"Things change," I say.

"Are we just getting old?"

"No, we're just taking care of our health. Look at the bright side. At least you're not drinking decaf."

"Yeah, life in the fast lane." He grumbles.

We open the FedEx package and try to make sense of it all.

"This one lists the various owners of the house Muriel's interested in," Jimmy says. "It starts with a Chester and Rose Golan who sold the place to Teddy Swoboda back in 1925."

"I wonder how Chester and Rose got ahold of it," I say. "You don't suppose there's some dead Indians buried in the backyard, do you?"

33

Jimmy laughs and continues with what's on the paper.

"Swoboda quit claims it to Oscar and Lacey Bender in 1927. We know that Oscar dropped dead in that year. Lacey puts it into a trust controlled by her but naming her heirs as directors of the trust upon reaching maturity."

"She had five kids with Oscar, right?"

Jimmy sips some coffee and nods.

"I think that all the Bender kids didn't make it," he says. "The two boys got killed in the war. So far as I know, neither had any kids. I know that one of the daughters died young, leukemia. I think she was twelve."

"So? Who's left?"

Jimmy flips through the mass of papers and finds what he's looking for.

"It's a 1950s filing with the state regarding directors of the trust. There's a Barbara Bender Santoro and a Carole Ann Bender as directors, along with Lacey Bender. Barbara and Carole were listed with San Francisco addresses. Lacey's address was listed here as Cicero."

"Lacey's long gone to that great bookie joint in the sky," I say. "That leaves Barbara and Carole. They still around?"

Jimmy eats some banana cream pie and looks up at me.

"I think Barbara is Muriel's grandmother. Couldn't say whether she's around or not. I've always tried to avoid those family dinners that Muriel and Jacky love to host. As far as Carole goes, I think she's the one who ran with the West Coast Mob and the Vegas bunch. If she's still around, she'd be, I don't know, Maybe eighty, eighty-five?"

"We should head for Murray's," I say. "He knows these people better. They're part of his family."

I leaf through the photos from the FedEx package as we drive toward Murray's house. Sinatra has a drink in one hand and a blonde in the other. Don't know who the blonde is. Could it be Carole? Barbara? They're standing in front of a large fireplace. A double-barreled shotgun hangs over the mantlepiece.

The next photo is of Jimmy Stewart with the same blonde in the exact location. I wonder if he's using the same glass that Sinatra used.

Another photo and another star. This time, it's Robert Mitchum standing between two blondes. Again, it's the same fireplace and the same shotgun. He's holding each of their hands, and they're each holding a drink. The blonde on the right is the same as the one in the photos with Jimmy Stewart and Sinatra.

"Christ, whoever these women might be, they sure knew how to connect with some of the top names," I say.

"Yeah," Jimmy says. "Makes you wonder what kind of dirt they had on those guys."

Jimmy:

I was happy to be heading toward Murray's. He was one of the few relatives of Muriel's I could stomach for any length of time. As far as I could tell, he and Muriel were the only two members of their family with any sort of class. Muriel had managed an Ivy League education. Murray was a university professor.

The rest of Muriel's family were more like Teddy Bender. I had a long list of choice Bender relatives I had bailed out of jail on Jacky's midnight call to ask for help. Junkie cab drivers, semi-pro hookers, pickpockets, and road-rage warriors were all fruit from a less than kosher tree.

Murray, though, was a charming guy, a friendly sort. He was also the driving force behind one of the featured events we brought to the Galloping Dominoes, which became popular with both the out of towners and the locals.

"Noir Fest" was a three-day gathering of writers, filmmakers, actors, and a wide swath of the public who loved the old hardboiled detective stories. At first, I was skeptical that the proposed convention would draw a decent crowd, but my skepticism was quickly put away by Murray's hard work and creativity. We were wall-to-wall with guests that first weekend. Murray had an annual winner going.

"It's all recycled material," he jokes. "Old actors, old movies, old directors. We try to take all that and turn it into something everyone can have fun with."

Some of the fun was the "Talk Like a Tough Guy or Dangerous Dame" contest.

Hundreds of contestants did their best in front of our cameras. Later they saw their work on the large screen in our theater and our websites.

There were serious panel discussions about why everyone liked Noir books and movies. In addition, there were current authors doing Noir in their books to sign copies of their latest attempt at the bestseller list.

A thousand Noir hats, t-shirts, and sweatshirts would get tallied up on the Dominos registers, and even our restaurants and lounges would get into the spirit of the weekend by having their décor and employees adopt some measure of a nineteen-forties crime opus.

No, I was happy to be heading to Ojai to see Murray. I was delighted we were heading into someplace closer to the ocean that didn't have smoke as the air's main ingredient. And I was happy that Murray had a place we could stay and maybe relax overnight.

I needed to lie down. I was tired. And I was tired of seeing blood in the toilet. This trip really was becoming a pain in the ass.

Chapter Eleven

Nick:

We arrive at Murray Bender's house and are greeted by his beautiful dark-haired lady, Annie. She announces that Murray is at the campus but will be back around dinner time.

"He has a few meetings," she says. "There's an excellent chance to get more funding out of the administration for expansion of his department. He says to make yourselves comfortable, relax and be prepared to spend the night in one of the guest rooms. He's looking forward to talking with you boys."

Annie directs us to the guest room and tells us that we'll be having lunch at the poolside. Do we want Caesar chicken salad, BLT club with fries, or a cheese and fruit plate? Will we drink coffee, beer, lemonade, or iced tea?

"Gee, it all sounds good," Jimmy says. "Could we have all of it?"

"Sure," Annie says. "Murray said you guys would be hungry and thirsty."

"Hey, wait," Jimmy says. "I was just kidding. The salad will be fine with lemonade."

"Jimmy's not used to polite company," I say. "We just recently got him paper trained. I shouldn't have left his muzzle in the car."

She laughs and tells us not to worry. Her smile says that life can sometimes be good if you give it a chance. She'll bring the food and drinks out on a serving cart, and we can take any or all of it. If we want to swim, there are extra swim shorts in a drawer she points to.

A quick dip in the pool feels great, and soon Annie wheels out a lunch cart as promised. She sets us up in a shaded area near the poolside bar. A flat screen tv hangs over the bar.

Annie hands the clicker to Jimmy and says, "Have at it. There're news channels and sports. Whatever you want. I think there's some baseball on."

She walks away, and we're on our own with an enormous supply of food and drinks and the most comfortable poolside chairs anyone could dream of.

"Pretty nice," Jimmy says. "Nice to see Murray's doing so well. Annie's a beautiful lady. I hear she's a part-time history instructor at the university."

"How'd you find that out?" I ask.

Jimmy laughs.

"That's one of the few things I can remember from our phone call with Muriel before we left Vegas. She said she had her doubts about Teddy, but Murray had it all together. I think Annie's working on her doctorate."

"I'm impressed."

"About Annie? Yeah."

"No. How you could remember stuff about Murray's girlfriend and let all the stuff about this house deal slide by."

"It's a special filter I have," Jimmy says. "Most of what Muriel says comes out ass-backward. I always figure that somewhere along the line, I'll run into a responsible adult who knows what's going on."

He flips on the tv. A news channel is showing a video from Yosemite. Firefighters are working hard in hundred-degree heat, trying to fight the smoke and burning trees that seem to be everywhere. Though we're hundreds of miles from the scene, a scent of smoke comes into the pool area.

"Jesus," Jimmy says. "Are we that close to the fire?"

"We get that every now and then," Annie says, coming back into the pool area. "I don't think it's anything nearby. It's just that the large fires in the state produce a lot of smoke. It's all got to go somewhere. The off-shore winds drive it in our direction."

"Maybe if you change the channel to the ballgame, we'll start smelling hot dogs and beer," I say.

The game is about to start as we tune in. The two play-by-play guys are staring into the camera, offering their baseball expertise to the unsuspecting public. One look at the two Armani suits, and I'm set for Jimmy's harangue.

"Will you look at those two yoyos," he says. "Who in the hell gets dressed in a suit to go watch a ballgame. Christ, they've even got vests on. Don't they know that they're the punchline in a joke: 'What do you say to a loser wearing a three-piece suit? Will the defendant please rise."

We watch the game as we eat a wonderful lunch. Annie sits next to us and sips on an iced tea.

"There's something about baseball that fascinates me," she says. "I think it might be the traditions and maybe how it's always been a part of American life. Even football announcers use baseball terms to describe the action: going for the home run for a long pass, bringing in a relief pitcher for changing quarterbacks."

"Yeah, I know," I say. "Politicians do it, too. Someone described one of our illustrious presidents as being born on third base and telling everyone he hit a triple."

Annie's laugh is mingled with the gentle snore coming from Jimmy.

"Is he okay there? She asks. "Should we turn down the set?"

"No, he's happy just like that. He's been busy, had a lot on his mind. Just keep talking and enjoy the game with us. He might wake up if anything big happens."

Jimmy:

The poolside lunch coupled with a ballgame and the pleasant tones of Annie get the better of me, and I drift off into a beautiful nap as the first inning gets underway. I almost surface a few times when I hear Annie laughing about something Nick says, but I love the nap too much to come awake.

I wake when a new sound enters my consciousness, an unmistakable African American baritone voice owned by the one and only Clancy Booker.

"Hey, lawyer man, you gonna wake up and join the living? Tell us some of your truer-than real-life stories about the criminally insane element? Or are you tired of discussing Nick's family tree?"

Annie and Nick laugh, and I rub my eyes and try to focus.

Clancy sits across the table from me, and I can see that he's been busy. His plate has a pile of chicken bones on it. Next to him is a glass half-filled with his favorite on ice. A bottle of J.T.S Brown bourbon is beside it.

I decide to give him some shit.

"Clancy, did Annie card you on the way in here? Ask about your age? She doesn't want to get in any trouble, you know."

"Yeah, she asks about that at the door. I tell her I'm twenty-one times four and maybe a little change, but I'm in fine shape and actually brought my own bottle. Drove all the way from Vegas this morning. Like to get an early start. The air over there no bargain today. California offering free samples of lung cancer, shipping it to Sin City."

"I worry about that," I say. "Cassandra has problems with bronchitis. This smoke is bad for everyone."

"Jimmy, you got to take care of that beautiful lady. She wrote some nice things about Murray and me when we did the Noir Fest."

"Yeah, I know."

"Little bit of smoke coming out of Barstow this morning when I passed through," Clancy says. "Could be maybe Murray or Muriel be filing a missing person report about their dear cousin. Or you boys got it under control?"

"Teddy's safely relocated," Nick says.

"What about the soul brother donut guy across the road? He and Teddy had some scheme going. Don't know what it was, but I can tell when things aren't kosher, detrimental to our family interests."

"Yeah, they got out together," I say. "We got them out with their loot and sent them south of the border."

Clancy sips from his glass and looks at us.

"So, are you telling me that Manuel Rose gave up his sad-ass motorcycle gang and took off with Teddy for parts south?"

"Manuel Rose? I thought the donut guy was Mike Robbins," Nick says.

"Uh-uh," Clancy says.

"Are we talking about some guy who looked like Morgan Freeman on a bad day?" I ask.

"That's Manuel Rose," Clancy says. "That Mike guy was some junkie that mopped the floor."

Chapter Twelve

Nick:

Clancy Booker's truths can cut deep. We sit with him, listening to the stories of how things were before everyone realized that places like California and Vegas were cutting-edge playgrounds for hip and cool people. Want to know about lynching in the California sun? He tells us about how a mob broke into a jail in San Jose in 1933 and took their prisoners to a nearby tree for "crowd justice." He also tells us about the die-hard Southern sympathizers. They proudly displayed the Confederacy's stars and bars well into the 1950s in the now liberal haven of Santa Cruz.

"Yes, I've always wondered about how people can ignore their history," Annie says. She pours more coffee into my cup.

"People always want to hope for the best," Clancy says. "Think about it. They stand in line around Christmas so their kid can sit on the lap of some old drunk wearing a Santa outfit. You think anybody like that wants to believe that sunny California was once a lynching capital where hundreds of Blacks, Chinese, and Mexicans just disappeared? Some got the end of a rope, others got a .45 slug and kicked into a ditch."

Now, he's telling us that the guy we left with two bullets in him in front of Donuts Olay isn't Manuel Rose, the Knight Ravens motorcycle gang leader but some flunky junkie who mopped the floor between hits of meth. The whole thing has me disjointed mentally.

My first reaction is I shot the wrong guy. But no. That's wrong. I mean, it's right, but I shot him after he was dead, on ice for a couple days. I didn't kill him. He did that to himself if we can believe Teddy Bender and Manuel Rose. They stole the dead guy's identity, and we fixed it, so they could ride off on an airliner to Cabo. Manuel Rose became Mike Robbins. If anyone should get credit for shooting Mike/Manuel, it should be Officer Ed Twilly, the hero-drunk from the sheriff's department in Barstow.

I'm doubly pissed at Teddy for being a 24-carat jerk in the first place and for leading us astray on his escape to Mexico after we burned down half of a run-down industrial area.

There's another troubling aspect to this whole situation. I don't like shooting people, even when they're dead junkies.

We don't run that sort of an organization, I tell myself. That's the way it used to be back when Jacky's old man and Muriel's people used to run with the Outfit. I'm not saying we're angels. Most of what we do is legit. We probably stack up pretty well next to the politicians who can't wait to turn a profit from "serving" the people.

I understand when Clancy Booker gets going on how things used to be when people would take the law into their own hands. I don't like mob violence or vigilantes, but then I stop and ask myself, "What am I? Am I exempt? So, Nick gets to shoot dead people and hang the blame/credit on a crooked cop? Nick gets to commit arson with his buddies? And now Nick is pissed because a shiftless bum like Teddy Bender lied to holier-than-thou Nick?"

Does everyone think they have a license to be their own law? Is it because things we used to count on are falling apart? Building inspectors take bribes allowing a hell hole like Teddy's Bar & Grill to stay open. Crooked cops get involved in drugs and stolen vehicles. White supremacists are happy to set up their half of a race war on one side of the street while a Black motorcycle gang does its part across the road. Where are those wonderful politicians then? Is there any wonder why people are arming themselves? Or running away?

The pungent smell of smoke wafts into the pool area.

"Damn, is that nearby?" Clancy asks?

"No, I don't think so," Annie says. "We get that when there are off-shore winds."

"Maybe that shifted it away from Vegas," Clancy says. "It was bad this morning."

Jimmy stands up from the table.

"Be back in a little while," he says. "I need to make a call."

"He looks a little worried," Clancy says as Jimmy leaves.

"Yeah, he's probably calling Cassandra to see how she's doing with the air pollution," I say. "That bronchitis is a real bitch with all this smoke."

"I hear you," Clancy says.

Smoke, I think, is only part of Jimmy's worries.

Jimmy:

The phone rings once, and I hear laughter and splashing water.

"The air here has cleared up," my wife says as she answers my call. "We just got in a few minutes ago from car shopping, and we're out at the pool watching Molly and Zorro do crazy dives. I'm going to fix big salads for us, and I'm giving Zorro that doggy bag from Ribs by Gus that you keep forgetting to eat."

"It was too rare," I say. "I sent it back. They over-cooked it. I didn't want to raise a fuss. Gus is good people, you know."

"Don't say any more," Cassandra says. "I know the whole story. Besides, this phone might be bugged."

I laugh. It feels good talking to this woman who understands my crazy lifestyle and the shorthand language I use.

"Any good news?" I ask.

"We're renting a couple electric cars from the Nissan dealer to see how we like driving them. Dawn has one for her and Nick to evaluate, and you get to play test pilot on ours. Ours is deep blue and very comfortable.

We have them for a couple weeks. We drove around with Zorro in the back seat. He loved it when it started to hum. Very comical bark-along, him and Molly."

"I'll bet. Anything else?"

"Your doctor called. He says you don't have anything life-threatening unless you're planning to die from hemorrhoids. He suggests what I've been suggesting, better diet, more exercise, and quit referring to people as pains in the ass."

"Some people really are," I say. "We just got done with one, Teddy."

"You've made it to Murray's?"

"Yeah, Clancy is here. He drove in from Vegas. We had a nice lunch, and we're spending the night. Hope to get some info from him and Murray about this crazy house deal that Muriel wants us to look at in the

Bay Area."

"That must be the place she's always bragging about when she talks about how her family used to entertain show business royalty at their chateau. Makes you wonder what royalty was doing with a bunch of knee-cap busting bookies and protection racket bums, doesn't it?"

"You have a theory about that?"

"They were probably slumming or maybe just playing royalty between mob hits."

"Cassie, I love the way you think."

"It comes from hanging out with the likes of you. You're not mad about the electric car, are you?"

"No, I'm looking forward to it. I think we could teach Zorro to drive it while we sit in the back seat and watch him try to run over cats."

Chapter Thirteen

Nick:

Jimmy comes back to the poolside with a grin on his face. I figure he made a phone call to Cassandra. He usually feels better after calling her. There were times in the past that I might have kidded him about having a hot babe stashed in our guest room. And there were times when that wouldn't have been a joke. But, since he met Cassandra, remarks like that are off the table. To paraphrase that old song, he's got it bad, and for him, that's good.

Clancy Booker is holding court around the white plastic table, dealing out hands of Oh, Hell to Annie, me, and himself. Oh, Hell is a card game, the object of which is to take an exact number of tricks from the cards dealt. If you take more than you bid, you lose. If you take less than you bid, you lose. You have to be right on the money. If it sounds tame enough to you, beware. Another name for the game is Screw Your Buddy.

Clancy claims he's won Oh, Hell tournaments, and I believe him. One thing about Clancy is he doesn't bullshit. He doesn't have to. His life has been one of excitement and success, a far cry from his growing up dirt poor on the west side of Vegas in the forties when being black was more than an inconvenience, as he puts it.

"Hell, it was damn dangerous," Clancy says as he shuffles the cards.

"You could say it was illegal to be black in Las Vegas back in those days. If you came to the white side of town, you'd better have a good reason for being there. I was lucky. I had parents who cared, and they were lucky too. They both had jobs that the white side of town could benefit from. My mama worked on costumes for the showgirls, and my dad was a sanitation engineer. He picked up the garbage from the casinos and fancier homes."

Annie looks at her cards.

"I'll bid three," she says. "Tell us your story about the piano."

"I'll bid four," I say.

"I want to be in the next game," Jimmy says. "Yeah, tell us about the piano."

"Dealer bids four," Clancy says. "Okay, the piano, but first a splash of J.T.S. Brown OTR, on the rocks, my friends."

Annie pours.

Clancy sips and begins.

"My dad pulled up at one of those fancy homes in the white neighborhood. This guy Vito Fontana comes out of the garage and wants to know if my dad can haul a piano for him. He'll give him twenty bucks if he can get it on the flat-bed stake-truck they used to haul the trash. My dad looks at his partner, who happens to be my uncle Roger. He gives a shrug and says, let's go take a look. Maybe we can do it."

Clancy takes another sip and continues.

"They go inside and discover it's a small Steinway, a beautiful instrument. Well, we can get it on the truck and tie it down, my dad says. How far would we be going? This guy Vito says, I don't care, as long as you get it out of here. You can use it for firewood if you want. Turns out he's got some bimbo showgirl for a honey. She thinks she can sing and thinks she can play the piano. Wrong on both counts, the guy says. I'm going to tell her that the company had to recall that model because it was giving people cancer of the fingertips."

"I love that story," Annie says.

"That's outrageous," Jimmy says. "If anyone other than you told that, I'd say they were bullshitting."

"Well, I would, too," Clancy says. "God's truth, that's how the kids in our family started to learn music. There were a couple old-timers that gave us lessons. My brother Joe, my cousin Roger Jr. and my sister Clara all learned, and we all went on to have decent careers in music. My Uncle Roger would tell us to play the hell out of that piano. He'd tell us that he didn't break his back getting it into our house so we could put family pictures on it."

Jimmy:

I listen to Clancy's piano story.

I've heard versions of it many times before. The story varies. It's all true, but sometimes you hear more about Vito Fontana and his problems with the opposite sex. Some of the more is not for the squeamish. It seems that Vito not only didn't think twice about hauling off Steinways into another part of the desert, he also didn't think twice about disappearing persons of interest, girlfriends included. Sometimes he'd do this on orders from the bosses. Other times, he'd get the urge and do it for himself.

He did it once too often, and that was the end of Vito, so they say. It seems that Vito was sharing the affections of a lady named Sherri Lo Casta with a South Jersey gambler named Frankie Tortoni. Frankie wasn't aware of this until Sherri let it slip one night that Vito was some kind of a loser as a lover. Or, at least, she told Frankie that that was what she heard from some of her friends. Frankie, being no dummy – he at least knew how to count cards at unsuspecting blackjack tables – figured that Sherri had first-hand knowledge of Vito's approach in the bedroom. Something had to be done.

Frankie had heard about Vito's talent for disappearing people. So why not give him the job?

They talked about it and reached a price, including an unmarked burial plot in the desert. Vito was pleased to get the work and also to get his pain-in-the-ass Sherri out of his life. What could be better? Sherri would be gone, and the extra cash from Frankie would be helpful. He should have used that extra cash to repair the broken rearview mirror on his DeSoto. He would have noticed Louie "Bulldog" Bacon following him out the road to Boulder City if he had. "Bulldog" had Silvio Tortoni with him. It was over quick.

Before Vito could get out of his car to grab Sherri and kill her, "Bulldog" pulled up and shot both of them. Silvio did his part by pouring a gallon of gasoline into the car and tossing in a match but not before getting Frankie's money out of Vito's pocket. The story goes that the newspaper had a headline that read: "Lovers Die in Flaming Auto." I guess the heat got so intense that it melted the lead bullet slugs.

Clancy looks up from his drink and smiles.

"You know that house that Muriel has you boys checking out up there north of San Francisco used to be a hangout for Vito and some of his friends. The ladies in the Bender family knew all about showing those guys a good time. I remember those times. I was there strictly to play the piano and pour the drinks. You wouldn't believe some of the stuff that went on up there."

"I'd believe just about anything about the Benders," Nick says. "I'll tell you this, Murray's the only one of the Benders that isn't messed up in some way."

Clancy sips some more from his drink and looks at Nick.

"Muriel's alright, I have to say, but sometimes I have the devil of the time trying to understand what she's trying to say."

"I think she's perfected that act to the point that it's taken over her brain," Nick says. "I think it started when someone told her she might be required one day to testify in court about what she knew about certain business deals."

"I heard of that," Clancy says. "Don't they call that the scatterbrain defense?"

Chapter Fourteen

Nick:

Clancy leans back in his chair and sips from the JTS Brown in his rocks glass.

"Babble-On, that's the way I first heard the name of that place north of San Francisco that the Benders bought. You know, like babbling, talking about nonsense. Then I heard that it was supposed to be Babylon, like that ancient city in the Middle East. There were jokes about the Bender gals. Some of the wise guys called them 'The Whores of Babble-On.' Never to their face, of course. Guys were hanging around like Vito Fontana, who looked for excuses to kill someone who would say something like that."

The pungent smell of smoke drifts into the pool area. Is it from Yosemite, where things are far from being in control? Or is it spreading from something we've caused in Barstow? I'm about to say something about it when Murray Bender's Mercedes pulls into the driveway and parks behind Clancy's BMW.

"There's a small brush fire behind the golf course," Murray says as he enters. "Couple acres. Looks like the fire department has it under control." He kisses Annie and gives Clancy a brief shoulder rub.

"We don't have to hightail it to the ocean to save our skins?" Jimmy asks.

"Not unless you want to drown in the high surf that's forecast for tonight. Hey, glad you guys got here. You take care of my wayward cousin in

Barstow?"

"He's headed to Cabo. First, Tony Stomps got him a gig down there making Mai-tais for rich women with loose halter tops. Then, he conned us into helping him get some motorcycle gang leader out of the country."

"Sounds like Teddy, alright," Murray says.

"I was just giving Nick and Jimmy what little wisdom I have left about the notorious Babble-On house up there in Marin County," Clancy says. "Whatever you can add to the mix will be most welcome, I'm sure."

Murray sits next to Annie and takes a sip from her iced tea.

"It's quite a place. It's big. It hangs over the side of a canyon up in Fairfax. On one of those winding roads, you have to pull over to let people come from the other way pass through. It has kind of a Frank Lloyd Wright look about it. It's beautiful. Big wooden beams, inlaid Mexican tiles, wrought iron, and chandeliers. On a clear day or night, the view is magnificent. But, when it's foggy, it's the kind of a place that will give you the creeps, or, I don't know, maybe it's the people you run into up there that give you the creeps."

"I second that," Clancy says.

"You go there a lot?" Jimmy looks at Murray, then at Clancy.

"Carole, the old lady, is hard to be around," Murray says. "You'd think that a place like that having a lot of history would get a guy like me hooked on exploring it. I mean, many of the people I talk about in my noir studies were guests up there. I've tried several times to delve into some of the old stories, but it always seems that if you go beyond saying things like, 'Gee wasn't Joe E. Lewis a great entertainer' or 'That Sinatra sure could sing,' you're violating the we-don't-talk-about-that rule."

"Clancy might be one of your best sources," Annie says. "He saw some of it up close."

"Yeah, up close," Clancy says, "But not too personal. I was the go-to nigger in those days. Mix the drinks, play the piano, shut up. They had a small room for me to sleep in on the lower level of the house. It was next to a shed that held yard tools. If you stepped too far out the door, you'd go rolling down the steep canyon trail. You could walk it during the day if you were careful. A lot of overgrowth and rattlesnakes, they'd tell me. So don't go there."

"Sounds lovely," Jimmy says. "You suppose it's still like that?"

"If Carole's still running the show, I don't see why not. That's her personality – keep people in the dark, keep them scared of what they might find. It's not only what's going on with the house. It's what's going on in her head. The first night I stayed there, the canyon-side lights on the house flash on, and a gunshot breaks the silence. Then another shot and another. Finally, the lights go off, and it's silent. The next morning. I'm told by the cook that Carole often tries to shoot raccoons and possums. She doesn't want them digging anything up out in the canyon."

Jimmy:

The more I hear about Babble-On or Babylon, the more I regret getting involved in another of Muriel's good ideas. This was supposed to be a simple business trip to the Bay Area.

We had some business with the billiard table maker. There were some singers to look at for possible lounge acts at the Galloping Dominos. If everything went as planned, we would fly our wives up for a weekend of shopping at antique shops and eating at Italian restaurants in North Beach. I could imagine the taste of the beautiful ravioli and cannoli.

I could also see this wonderful experience getting shoved under the bus while once again we tried to bail out Muriel's sorry ass.

"Cheer up," Nick leans over and half whispers to me. "The way things are going with the forest fires, maybe the joint will burn down before we can get there, or with what we learned from Bruno in Barstow, we could become burn-it-your-selfers."

The conversation turns toward what Murray and Clancy have planned for the next Noir Fest in Vegas. They mention some prominent names they have lined up, and soon we're sitting in Murray's video theater, eating dinner and watching some classic films of the forties.

I excuse myself after "They Drive by Night," explaining I have some legal papers to look at concerning Babble-On.

I lay everything out on my bed in the guest room. All the legal papers, notes from Muriel, and photos of the people who supposedly hung out in the house are a mixture of rogue's gallery, iffy legalese, and gibberish.

Then, finally, it starts to come clear. Carole wants to get rid of the place for a price. She's hyping Muriel about how much family history the home has and how it fits into a Chicago couple's lifestyle who just happen to own a casino in Vegas.

I get another feeling off the mess on the bed. If I'm betting, I'm saying that Carole is over-selling the deal. She wants to take the money and run and leave Muriel and Jacky to deal with what's left in Babble-On.

A part of me says go to see the house and then tell Muriel that it's not a good deal, that it's a headache. Forget it.

But then I think about what might be left there. Was Carole just shooting at raccoons and possums at night? Or was it something or someone else? What was it she was trying to prevent them from digging up on the canyon slope?

47

Nick wants to have a look. I can't disappoint him, can I?

Chapter Fifteen

Nick:

Jimmy returns from the guest room to watch some more clips from the noir show that Murray and Clancy will bring to Vegas. Some of the clips feature actors in obscure roles in less than stellar movies. It's a before and after presentation. First, you see the likes of Lee Van Cleef playing a heavy in a gangster film, then you see him in "High Noon" and "The Good, the Bad, and The Ugly." Similar treatment has Jack Webb and Harry Morgan playing cheap hoods, then you see Webb in "Dragnet" and Morgan as Colonel Potter in "MASH."

"Noir films, many of them the B movie variety, were great training grounds for actors and producers who later made it big in television and major films," Murray says. "Cheap meant work fast and be ready to come back the following week to work fast and cheap in another cranked out opus for the bottom end of the double feature at the local theater. It was an easy transition for some into weekly TV shows."

"A lot of those types were guests up at Babble-On," Clancy says. "Some were happy to get a free meal and a few drinks. They weren't exactly making big money. I guess it was just another place to connect."

"Connect with the ladies, too?" Jimmy asks.

"Hard to find a lady in that group. Lots of women, though." Clancy grins.

"It was a lot like improvisation, the way they produced the shorter noir films," Murray says. "They had to crank them out fast and cheap, so they used every trick they could find, even filming real crime scenes so they could insert them into some of their films. Of course, the actors didn't make much, but if they were good enough, they'd find work the next week in another noir film being cranked out down the street."

I hear what Murray is saying, and it strikes home in my own life. I didn't work in films, but I remember living hand-to-mouth, week-to-week when I worked as an organizer for the Teamsters union. Money was scarce.

That was when I met Jimmy, a hot-shot lawyer, just out of a third-rate law school. He was chasing ambulances and looking for the next judge who would look the other way on drunk driving cases in exchange for an honorarium.

We might have gone on that way for the rest of our lives – a couple of cheap hustlers playing for nickels. Then we met Jacky. He had a problem that needed fixing. His old man had been deep into the rackets, a close friend to the boys in Cicero who ran the Outfit. The old man didn't want his kid involved. There were legit businesses that he wanted the kid, Jacky, to have, and he wanted the kid protected from the Outfit guys who would try to muscle in and get him involved. In short, he needed the likes of Nick and Jimmy, who could smell the Outfit coming from miles away. So, who gets a gig like that? They sure didn't give out degrees in that at De Paul. Maybe we were doing the Chicago version of what Murray says about Hollywood in the forties and fifties. There was no job description, no rules. You just made it up as you went along.

"A couple guys who went through that starving noir period learned a lot and got really big on what they learned." Murray says. "Jack Webb hit it big with the original Dragnet, not the watered-down later version. The original version had little money and a production schedule that demanded a complete show each week. He couldn't afford elaborate sets, and there wasn't time for the actors to learn their lines. What could he do? He went to extreme close-ups, where you couldn't see much of the background. Then he wrote the actor's lines on cue cards. One take, no re-shoots. And you know what? The public loved it. The crooks all seemed stupid or half crazy, and the ratings went sky high."

"That's right," Clancy says. "Other producers were trying to make the crooks sound like Sir Laurence Olivier or Richard Burton. But, damn, real-life ain't like that."

I look at Jimmy. He's laughing and nodding his head.

"Another guy who picked up on that was Clint Eastwood," Murray says. "He was in some goofy movies as an extra or bit player. He saw it up close. One take, and you move on. If you have a good story, you don't need Hamlet's soliloquy."

Jimmy:

We're getting ready to turn in when my burner phone rings. It's Jacky.

"Where you guys at?"

"Murray's. We're heading out in the morning. What's up?"

"You guys where you can talk?"

"Yeah," Nick says. "We're in the guest room at Murray's. Everyone else has turned in."

"I had a talk with my better half, and she tells me you're handling that place in the Bay Area for her. I want you guys to be careful. That can be a dangerous crowd that hangs out up there. They're not all retired show biz people."

"What? You think it's a bad idea?" Nick shrugs at the phone.

"No, I'm not calling you off. I want this to happen. There's something up there in that property that's valuable to a lot of people. I'm not sure what it is, but I've heard stories about people who have disappeared trying to get hold of it. It could be something that turns out to be an embarrassment for people in Muriel's family. We don't want that. Do we?"

"No, no," Nick says, and I'm thinking embarrassment? Does he mean embarrassment, as in Teddy Bender and his fiery escape to Mexico with the black motorcycle gang leader?

Or is he referring to the drunk cab drivers and cheap hookers in the Bender family that I had to get out on bail, back in the "good old days?"

"Yeah, we'll do what we can to make things go smooth," I say.

"I know you guys can handle it," Jacky says, and I start to wonder how many J&B Scotches he's had. It's after midnight in Chicago. I picture him sitting out on his 19th-floor balcony at 1040 Lakeshore Drive. I can hear the traffic on the Drive, and maybe it's only my imagination, but it seems like I can hear the waves crashing onto Oak Street Beach. I'm guessing he'll sit there until he falls asleep or kills the bottle. Muriel's been on his case. That's for sure.

"We'll keep you posted as we find things out," Nick says.

"Okay, boys. Watch your backs." He clicks off.

I look at Nick.

He doesn't look worried. He just seems pissed.

"Fucking Muriel," he says from his bed. "Better turn in, Roomie. There's a hell of a game waiting for us up in Fairfax."

"Yeah, or maybe it's just another cheap B movie." I roll over and turn out the light, wishing I was home with Cassandra.

Chapter Sixteen

Nick:

Smoke and sirens are making me panic. I'm fighting my way through my smoke-filled house in Vegas, looking for Dawn and our four-year-old daughter Molly. Sirens are blaring, and lights are flashing in an alternating yellow, red, and blue pattern.

"I knew it would come to this," I manage to choke out."

"There's a fire nearby," Jimmy says, and I hear him as I come awake from my nightmare. We're not in Vegas but at Murray's house in Ojai. I'm relieved that we're not fighting a house fire in Vegas, but now I wonder if we'll have to fight a house fire here.

I slide the vertical shades open and open the sliding patio door. Two fire trucks are speeding past the house toward an orange glow somewhere not far away. Not far enough. A police car runs behind the two vehicles. Smoke begins to make its way into the room. My watch says it's four in the morning.

I shut the sliding door, switch on the bedside light, and turn to say something to Jimmy like, "Let's get a move on," but then I stop with the words jammed in my mouth.

Jimmy's standing there in his boxer shorts and t-shirt. There's blood all over his shorts and trailing down his legs. A quick look at the sheet on the bed reveals more blood.

"What the hell?" I say.

"I don't know. I don't know," Jimmy says. "This happened once before a couple weeks ago. Cassandra hustled me off to the doctor later that day."

I'm standing there with my mouth open, trying to think of something to say.

"Does it hurt? Are you in pain?" I finally manage.

"No, but Jesus, look at this mess. I think it's stopped bleeding. Murray's gonna kill me with this. What the hell can I do?"

"What did the doc say to you?"

"They ran some tests. They think it's hemorrhoids."

"Tell you what," I say, "you get in the shower, get cleaned up. I'll take care of Murray. Grab one of those hand towels to take with, just in case."

I slip into my clothes and head out to the great room to see if anyone's around. Annie is coming out of the kitchen with a cup of coffee in her hand.

"Lots of excitement," she says. "Murray and Clancy just took off to follow the flashing lights to the fire. We think it might be the one they were trying to put out yesterday. Stuff like that's been happening pretty often, lately."

"I guess it woke you up," I say.

"We sleep kind of funny since the fires started to get out of control all over the state. There's coffee out there already brewed. Help yourself. Lots of food. Anything I can get for you?"

I look around the beautiful house. But, unfortunately, there's danger up the road. A sudden wind shift, and this house could be ashes.

"What are the plans if...?"

"...if the fire burns us out?" She half-smiles and half grimaces. "We'll get out what we can. There's help at the university. They've already told us we can store some of our possessions in a field house there, and we have some grad students who will help. They're good people. We often have them over for dinner and drinks."

I pour some coffee and sit on a stool by the kitchen countertop.

"Do you have any of those big black trash bags?"

"We do. How many do you need?"

"Two be alright?" I smile.

"No problem." She goes to a small closet and drags out two large bags.

"This will be a big help," I say.

"Let me know if you want more."

I sip some coffee and head back to the guest room with my bounty.

Jimmy:

A hot shower does wonders. I'm cleaned up and alert. Best of all, I'm not bleeding out of my ass. My main concern is how to deal with the mess on the bed. I don't feel like confessing to the world that my ass is bleeding over hemorrhoids. It's got to be one of the least sexy things you can come down with.

There's another side to having hemorrhoids. It's a plus, actually. It beats the hell out of having cancer which is what I've been worrying about. But I'm together right now. Cleaned up and ready to hit the road toward the Bay Area. There's just that mess with the bedsheets and how to explain it to Murray and Annie.

I shouldn't have worried. Instead, as I exit the bathroom, I see Nick hard at work, stuffing sheets into a big black garbage bag.

"It's all under control," he says. "The blood didn't go through to the mattress cover. We're taking all the evidence with us."

"What are we telling Murray?"

"Just enough," Nick says

"Just enough?"

"Yeah. Don't you get it? Murray's into all that noir stuff. It will be just like out of one of those B movies he's always talking about."

"What do you mean?"

"You hand Murray a couple of C notes and tell him we had to borrow a couple large plastic bags and some sheets that Nick has plans for. It's important. It's also important that that's all he knows about it. Tell him we don't want anything coming back on him or Annie."

I stand there looking at Nick. Okay, I'm dumbfounded. Part of me thinks this guy is the biggest screwball on the planet. On the other hand, who would come up with such a hare-brained scheme?

And then, I think again. He's doing all this for me. He knows that I don't want to proclaim to the world that I have a bleeding ass that destroys bed linens. He's already weighed the alternatives. Do I want to be known as "Hemorrhoids Man" or the mysterious guy who needs garbage bags and sheets to wrap up something that's better not to know anything about?" Murray and Clancy get back to the house and report that the fire is contained. For now, it's more smoke than fire. We sit to a quick breakfast and load the Caddy with our stuff, two black bags included. I hand Murray the two C notes and tell him about needing the black bags and the sheets for something Nick has to take care of.

"That's all I can tell you," I say. "That's all you need to know."

Murray gets a sly look on his face, smiles, and says, "Sure, I get it. But, you guys, be careful. Stay in touch."

We drive out toward US 101 to head north.

"Everything okay, so far?" Nick sips his coffee. "No pain in the ass?"

"You're the only one I know," I say.

"I'll put it on your tab," he says.

We both laugh.

Chapter 17

Nick:

The Caddy moves along toward Santa Maria. The hillsides are overgrown with tall weeds and thick bushes. All of them have turned brown and dried out. Last winter, when it rained, all this vegetation was healthy and green. Now it's just fuel, waiting for the first spark. If it burns, houses, cars, and people will die. Then, when the winter rains return, mudslides will take their toll on what's left. So much for 'California Dreaming.'

We sip what tries to pass as coffee from a fast-food joint and grumble as we go.

"You had to pay for this shit?" Jimmy asks. "This reminds me of that clip that Murray showed us last night."

Murray showed us a couple dozen clips, but I know which one Jimmy is talking about. We've been friends for years. Most of the time, I can finish his sentences for him, but I try not to do that. It gets creepy. Jimmy is talking about a clip from the original Dragnet TV show, which had a shoestring budget about twice the price of the bitter cups of java we're both bitching about.

"You don't mean the drunk on his way to Pismo Beach who gets stopped at the police checkpoint, do you?"

"I do. Where in the hell they get that guy? It's supposed to be police drama. The cops have traffic blocked and check cars for a fugitive when this goofball shows up, loaded to the gills. Instead of the cops arresting the guy, they give him a cup of coffee to try to sober him up. Nice try."

I start to laugh. It is a brilliant piece of television. The drunk keeps asking if "this is the road to Pismo Beach," and going off about his friend Claude who told him to drive from LA to Pismo Beach in the middle of the night to get some clams. While he's yelling about "that dirty Claude," the coffee spills out of his mouth, his glasses start to skid off his nose, and the cops, instead of arresting him, just park him off the side of the road and let him belch and slobber it out of his system. It's a show-stealer. What starts out as drama turns into comedy.

"Big difference in those days," Jimmy says. "Cops had a short-wave tube radio that maybe worked, maybe not. There weren't any breathalyzers. I don't even know if there was a DUI law other than drunk and disorderly. It was the charming fifties. People were more on their own, not tied into the Internet all goddamn day."

"You saying it was better?" I ask.

"No, I'm saying it was different. People didn't have to worry about answering their damn cell phones 24 hours a day. Look at us. We're cruising along. Next thing you know, our pleasant drive gets interrupted by Muriel or Jacky wanting to know if we've made it to Babylon or Babble-On, whatever the hell the place is called. We're just like that poor drunk in search of clams."

Our pleasant drive comes to a traffic slowdown outside Santa Maria. A flashing sign says that Highway 101 is closed north of San Luis Obispo due to smoke from the forest fires. The alternate route north is Highway 1, the Coastal Highway. I open my window and quickly close it again. Even though we're thirty-five miles from the detour point, the smoke is thick and doesn't have the fireplace smell of burning pine. Instead, there's a scorched plastic and oil flavor to it.

People's houses and cars have burned.

Another part of the scent is burnt flesh. Death is in the air.

"You know what this means?" I ask.

Jimmy looks ahead at the long line of traffic heading for the Coastal Highway.

"Yeah, we're on a slow crawl toward San Francisco."

"You left out the best part," I say. "We're on our way to Pismo Beach."

Jimmy looks at me and shakes his head.

"Yeah, Nick. Maybe that old drunk is still sitting on the side of the road. If he is, I'll bet he has better coffee."

Jimmy:

We crawl through Pismo Beach. It's a nice town that's changed a lot since it was mentioned in Dragnet in the 1950s. It's a lot bigger than it was then. There's definitely more traffic today and more smoke in the air. The wind is out of the northeast, and it's coming from one of the major blazes, maybe Yosemite, maybe closer.

"Maybe this traffic will thin out, and we make it into Monterey or Carmel for the night," Nick says.

"Yeah, or maybe we'll get stopped at one of those Dragnet roadblocks."

"Negative thinking," Nick says.

"Call me negative but look at what we've had to put up with. A simple drop-off of money in Barstow led to us burning down part of the town and hustling Teddy and some outlaw biker out of the country, probably on phony passports. The goddamn fires keep chasing us. We had a taste of fire at Murray's. Now, we have it again. Rather than cruising up 101, we're crawling along on Highway 1."

"True," Nick says. "What else?"

"I'm sitting on a hand towel shoved into my shorts, so my ass won't bleed like it did on Murray's sheets. At any minute, we're either going to get a phone call from Muriel with some whacked-out instructions about the mysterious house in Fairfax, or one from Jacky, telling us that we better find something up there that's buried in that canyon full of rattlesnakes and rats."

"Boy, you sure know how to recap a ballgame," Nick says. "You could be on Sunday Night Football."

"Yeah, sure, wiseguy. I could be the one who tells it like it is. I could talk about the absurdity of fans living on the edge of poverty worrying about a league run by billionaires who employ a bunch of millionaires. But, instead, we should all worry about poor Tom Brady or Drew Brees? The NFL is probably trying to figure out a way for fans to buy tickets with food stamps."

Nick laughs.

"You'd last about a minute on Sunday Night Football, Jimmy. But damn, it'd be one hell of a good minute."

My burner phone rings.

"What did I tell you," I say to Nick. "Muriel, or our noble leader Jacky." But I'm wrong.

Tony Stomps is on the speaker.

"I talked to my guy down in Cabo. He wants to know why Teddy and his asshole friend never showed up. I had Bruno check the airline. Turns out they never got on the plane. Now we look like fools."

"Any idea what they might be up to?" Nick asks.

"Yeah, could be. Bruno drove them down to LAX. He says they were both high on something. They were talking crazy about going to the Middle East and digging up something valuable. Bruno asked them what was so valuable. Was it Egyptian treasure? 'No,' Teddy says like he's all doped up. 'It's buried family treasure in Babylon.' Any ideas?"

I look at Nick. He looks like he wants to strangle someone.

"Tony, you were right about Teddy," Nick says. "We should have just shot him."

Chapter Eighteen

Nick:

As we sit in northbound bumper-to-bumper traffic on Highway One, I'm on the phone to Murray to see if he knows what Teddy knows about the house in Fairfax.

"If he's relying on info from me, he doesn't know much," Murray says. "I told him once about the movie stars that used to hang out up there, but I never gave him the address. The fact is, I don't know the address. I kind of know how to get there, but it's been years."

Clancy cuts in.

"That's about all I told him. If he's got his eyes on doing something there, he's got to find it first. The best bet is he might hang around Fairfax and wait for you and Jimmy to show up. It's a small town, pretty laid back."

I thank them both and ring off.

"Muriel opened her big mouth to him," Jimmy says. "She probably told him about buying the place. He coupled that with Clancy's story about gunshots in the night into the canyon so animals wouldn't be digging out there."

"Right," I say, "So Teddy shoots his mouth off to the resurrected Manuel Rose, and in their junkiest of dreams, they figure that the crown jewels are buried out there."

Jimmy's quiet for a minute as traffic begins to clear, and we pick up speed along the Coastal Highway.

"Are you saying that you're convinced that the crown jewels aren't buried out there?" Jimmy asks.

"No, I ain't saying what it is, if anything, is buried out there. Jacky seems to think there is, but he doesn't know what it might be. He wants it found, that's for sure."

"Agreed," Jimmy says. "Think about this, though. The people who have the house want to get rid of it. They want to take the money and run. Have they already dug up what we're trying to find? Or are they trying to leave somebody else holding the bag? Maybe whatever's buried up there isn't anything anyone should be digging up."

We roll past San Simeon and the Hearst Castle. The spectacular views of the ocean and rugged terrain are marred by smoke coming out of the northeast. This area which is known for afternoon coastal fog has been changed by the fires. The fires have created their own weather system, and it stinks.

"I'll say this about Muriel's family," Jimmy says. "They never let morality get in the way of making a buck. They say that when the Benders and the Swobodas boarded the ship to come to America in the 1890s, they left Hamburg as Jews and arrived in New York as Roman Catholics. They knew that Chicago was a Catholic town. If you wanted to make it, you had to wear the right uniform."

"Pretty quick conversion, eh?"

"And quick to convert back when it suited them," Jimmy says. "When it started to get close to college time for Muriel, someone in the family found out that Vassar was looking for diversity candidates. Presto. They dragged out their Jewish roots, and Muriel was soon on her way to Poughkeepsie."

"Not bad, but I got to say, I'd probably do the same for Molly," I say. "I mean damn, you do anything for your daughter."

Jimmy is silent.

I've put my foot in it, and I wish I could take the words back. I was with him some fifteen years back when the news came that his daughter Rachel and her mother were killed in a terrorist attack in Paris. It was devastating news, and now I feel like shit. I'm trying to figure out what to say when he clears his throat.

"Nick, you're the best friend a guy could ask for. You helped me get through it back then. The closest I have to a daughter now is your Molly. Cassandra and I both think the world of her. Believe me, we'd do damn near anything to see her succeed. I don't know if I could pull off a conversion on a boat trip from Hamburg, but I'll bet Cassandra could."

"Christ, now you got me choking up," I say, and it's true. This crazy bastard has become the brother I always wished for as a kid, although I never expected I'd get a brother who knew how to bet the over-under on a Bears/Packers game.

What else can I do? I have to reach over and sock him in the arm. Jimmy laughs and continues his story about Muriel's family.

"Lacey Bender was all about money. The family bought marginal properties in Chicago. One of them was an old gymnasium on the north side in a German neighborhood. When the Bund, the Nazi front group, got going in the thirties, Lacey got them to rent out the place for their meetings to idolize Adolf. She even had a couple of her boys selling beer to the crowd. I don't think they ever caught on that their money was going to a Jew. It was strictly business."

Jimmy:

We finally make it to the city by the bay in the late afternoon. The sky is orange from the fires to the east, and there's a warning out that the air is so bad that people should stay inside. Of course, a lot of people are out just to see how bad things really are.

After checking in at our hotel, we head to the 19th floor and the Top of the Mark lounge.

"Not much of a view this evening, gents," our barman Danny says as we order. "It's smog, pure and simple. We'd love to blame it on our friends in LA, but in all honesty, it's homegrown, coming down from around Chico."

We order beers and a snack plate.

A fat guy sitting near us enters the conversation.

"I drove in from Sacramento this morning. It was brutal. I thought I'd get relief when I got to the city, but no way, Jose. If anything, it seems worse here."

A woman on the other side of us joins in. She's about two tokes over the line.

"You think that horse's ass in the White House will do anything to help? Hell, no. He hates California. We're too smart for the likes of him. Where you guys from?"

"Vegas," Nick says.

"Great place to have some fun," she says. "You guys work in a casino?"

"No, Ma'am, we work for Alcoholics Anonymous. We're here on a recruiting mission."

"I'll drink to that," she says.

Three drinks and some good laughs later with the fat guy and the woman, we're exhausted and ready to watch tv from our room. It's been a long haul. I figure I'll try to call the contact number for the house before I turn

in. Maybe, I think, someone will answer. To my surprise, someone does.
"Good evening, this is Carole Bender. What can I do for you?"
"This is Jimmy Cox, the representative for Muriel...."
"Oh, you're Muriel's lawyer. She said you'd be coming. Are you in town, Honey? You want to come up tonight, have some drinks, have some fun before we get down to business?"
"Kind of tired tonight. Just made it into SF," I say. "Could we get together tomorrow for a chat? We'd like to get a good look at the place."
"We? Who's we?"
"I have our architect with to look over the structure," I say. "His name is Nick."
"He sounds like quite a man, Honey. I'm looking forward to meeting him. Can you come about three?"
"Sounds good."
"We'll be waiting. Good night Mr. Cox."
I ring off and turn to Nick, who's been listening on the speaker.
"That old broad sounds like she's still running a whore house up there," Nick says.
"Yeah, or that's the impression she wants to give."

Chapter Nineteen

Nick:

Jimmy and I are sitting in a bagel joint about six blocks downhill from our hotel. It's called the Lox, Stock, and Bagel. It's seven in the morning, and we're here to meet someone. You could ask, "How did this come about?"
At five am. my burner phone announces that Jacky is calling. He's the only one I know who has Nixon saying, "I'm not a crook...we can get the money," instead of a ring tone.
His opening line is, "I don't trust any of those whores in Fairfax that you're about to deal with. I got someone you need to meet. They'll meet you and Jimmy at Lox, Stock, and Bagel at about seven-fifteen. The name's Charlie Lynch. Someone you can trust."
We hear the name Charlie Lynch and Jimmy and I both roll our eyes. The name has drama attached to it, not necessarily in a good way. We both know three Chicagoans by that name.
One Charlie Lynch is a federal judge known to solicit "contributions" to

a mysterious wildlife charity he says he chairs, but no one can quite trace what its name might be or where it might be headquartered.

Another Charlie Lynch is a black militant who has almost been convicted of major drug trafficking six times. His famous quote on those matters is, "Almost don't mean shit, motherfucker. All I do is supply party favors." The third Charlie Lynch is a red-headed Irishman who deals in top-quality audio gear. His company can sell a top-of-the-line turntable that wholesales at $2,000 for the low price of $1,200. Similar deals can be had on speaker systems and amplifiers. How does he do it?

"We do it on volume, Nick. Volume and rebates. It's a funny business. Most people don't get it. Were you paying with cash, Visa, or Mastercard?"

Jacky assures us that his Charlie Lynch is none of the three we know. "Just hang around. I described what you look like. Charlie's got some info on Fairfax, and don't worry about any fee. I've got it covered."

Seven twenty rolls into seven twenty-five, and soon it's seven-thirty. We look around. No one's coming through the door of Lox, Stock, and Bagel. We've already consumed onion bagels with lox, blueberry bagels with cream cheese, and something called a pretzel bagel. It's time to leave. Charlie Lynch is a no-show.

We stand and head for the door.

"You guys leave, and Jacky's going to be pissed," someone yells.

I turn. In the far back booth sits a thin woman who looks like Jacqueline Kennedy would have looked had the former first lady made it to eighty. She's wearing a simple black dress with pearls, and she's grinning to beat hell. Next to her is a guy who looks like he once was half the Chicago Bears' offensive line.

"You must be Nick and Jimmy," she says. "Come sit down. I'm Charlie Lynch, and this here's Porkchop."

Porkchop smiles and offers his massive right hand to both of us.

"We know Jacky and Muriel from Puerta Vallarta," he says. "Their villa is next to ours. We've taken them sportfishing on our Hatteras. We go for marlin. They put up a hell of a fight."

Charlie fakes a vicious bite on Porkchop's arm, and he laughs.

"They're not here to talk about sport fishing," she says. "They want to know about Babylon—what they're about to deal with."

Porkchop nods.

"That bunch up there. Troubles go way back with that crew."

Charlie sips her coffee and nods.

"I used to be in law enforcement up there," Porkchop says. "Don't ask me why. I guess the boys in charge thought because I played football for Cal and had three years with the Niners, that I'd be a great cop. Go figure, huh? I wasn't bad once I caught on to what I could let slide and what I couldn't."

"He was great," Charlie says. "One look and I knew I had to have him. I was in talent management. That's how I came to know some of the crew that hung out at Babylon. One night, there was a party that got out of control. Carole Bender had grabbed a rifle out of the closet and was shooting at something down in the canyon."

"Yeah, some of the neighbors were complaining," Porkchop says. "I happened to get the call. I went there and told her to knock it off. If she stopped shooting the rifle, I could let it slide. Otherwise, I'd have to confiscate the gun and take her into the station."

"What happened then?" Jimmy asks.

"Believe it or not, she starts giving me lip. Don't I know that she has big-time guests? These are powerful people in Hollywood, she yells. I look around. There's Old Blue Eyes. He's got his hand on the ass of some floozy, a Marilyn Monroe wannabe. Over in the corner is that singer with a really deep voice. Next to him is that guy with the freckles that played in all those old kid movies. They're passing a banana-size joint between them."

Charlie grins.

"That's when I stepped in. I said to Carole, Honey, your ass is hanging out all over the place. This nice policeman is trying to do you a favor. Be nice to him. Stop shooting and take care of your guests. They don't want any trouble. They're here for a good time."

Porkchop laughs.

"Next thing you know, I'm the one having a good time. Carole slips a couple of C-notes into my hand and says she's sorry that she just got carried away and maybe saw a snake near her property line. I slip the money into my pocket, and as I do, Charlie comes up and kisses me one of those kisses that ricochets all over my body."

Charlie looks at Jimmy, then at me. She has a grin that says it all.

"I saw this charming young stud. He looked like a keeper. I knew he was fifteen years younger than me, but that didn't mean shit. I had fifteen years more of experience, and I knew how to use it."

Porkchop tosses both hands into the air and smiles.

"What can I say? I'm probably the happiest guy on the planet."

Jimmy:

It doesn't take long for me to start liking Charlie Lynch and the unforgettable Porkchop. There's a quality about them that says they've told convention to take a walk. She's a fit 80-year-old white woman who

61

brags about nude sunbathing.

Porkchop, the three-hundred-pound black Buddha, has a different take on it.

"I got a built-in tan already, but if Charlie wants me to run around nude with her, I play along. I told her I'd do it if she got into weightlifting with me. She can press 125 pounds. I can do two hundred more than that. We both do more than our own body weight. Not bad."

Charlie leans forward and looks at us.

"Porkchop thinks you want to hear about all our secrets. What you boys really came here for is to find out what we know about Babylon. Well, listen close."

"Yeah, Babe," Porkchop says. "Cut to the chase. I worked on one of those interagency task forces when I was in law enforcement up in Marin County. Mostly it was about what the plan was for earthquakes and fires. It got into crowd control at various events ranging from drunks at sports events to rioting and firefights during civil unrest. In a way, it was a fool's errand, trying to figure out how to evacuate people during an emergency. Hell, the roadways weren't even working right during so-called normal times."

"They wanted him to go out and measure traffic," Charlie says. "Real geniuses."

"I would have done it, but then something came up that saved me from all of that. They needed help straightening out the 'Persons of Interest' files. These had been compiled since the twenties, and they were scattered about in different forms. Some were typed, some handwritten on legal pads. They came in large cardboard boxes. Guess who I find in one of the boxes? Lacey Bender and Carole Bender."

"A whole file on them," Charlie says. "Tell the boys, Honey."

"I can guess," Nick says. "Whoring, making book, loan sharking? That's what built the family fortune."

Porkchop laughs.

"Yeah, that was in there. So was an unregistered agent of a foreign country and suspicion of espionage for Lacey."

I look at Nick. Has his jaw hit the table? Will his eyes get any wider? He looks at me and laughs.

"Slimy bitch," he says.

"Tell us more," I say.

And Porkchop continues.

"She was working both sides of the street during the thirties and into the forties. She collected money for the America First groups that wanted the country to keep out of European wars. That group ranged from basic Republican conservatives to outright American Nazis. At the same time, she was collecting for labor groups, socialists, and communists. The FBI had her down as a Stalinist for a while."

"It wasn't out of the goodness of her heart," Nick says. "She was taking a healthy cut out of the proceeds, you can be sure."

"Yeah," Porkchop says. "Working the vig."

"That's not hard to believe," Nick says. "Between the two of us, we've spent a ton of time bailing the various Benders out of fixes."

"No surprise there." Porkchop shakes his head and looks at Charlie.

"There's something else," Charlie says. "Tell them about the people who disappeared, the ones they lost track of."

Chapter Twenty

Nick:

Porkchop puts a thick file folder on our table in the back booth at Lox, Stock, and Bagels.

"While I was straightening out the 'Persons of Interest' mess at the law enforcement interagency headquarters, I also discovered a top-of-the-line photocopy machine. I got good at taking pages of interesting entries out the door folded inside of my San Francisco Chronicle. None of the crime solvers who worked with me ever wondered how the newspaper got so fat by the end of the day."

Jimmy laughs.

"You walked it out, right past them? No problem?"

Porkchop gives a deep laugh and hugs Charlie with his left arm.

"No problem. I wasn't sure what I might do with the info, but I knew it might come in handy sometime. Even if I just used it to embarrass these undercover cops who claimed to be defenders of liberty. They were tracking ballplayers and comedians like they were Russian spies. Some taxpayer money went to a hotshot investigator who followed the Forty Niner's kicker to report how many beers he had after the game. Awful things were going on, mainly in the heads of these cops. The Giants' shortstop was sending $300 home to his mother in Nicaragua each month. Shocking stuff."

"Those were in the reports?" Jimmy asks.

"Yeah, along with bra sizes of women newscasters and where men on local tv were getting their hairpieces."

Jimmy turns and looks at me.

"Jesus, don't we all feel better knowing that our police are making the world safe for tits and bald heads? It's a damn good thing that the feds were on top of their game, keeping us from stumbling into Iraq and Afghanistan."

"You left out Syria and Yemen," Porkchop says.

Charlie shakes her head.

"It's damn embarrassing. It used to be something to be proud of to say you were an American. Back in the fifties, we were still the heroes. We were the ones who had defeated Hitler and Tojo. Now, we're just bullies. We're the new Roman Empire. We can't go a year without a war."

"That's why we spend most of our time in Mexico," Porkchop says.

"The air there is cleaner," Charlie says. "When strangers ask, I tell them we're from Canada."

Everyone is silent for a minute. Outside, a fake cable car busload of tourists goes past Lox, Stock, and Bagel. Bells on the ride jingle in rhythm.

Porkchop slides the file folder toward Jimmy and me.

"These are the people who have disappeared after having contact with the ladies up at Babylon. Charlie and I never had any contact with them at all. Take these and use them if you can."

We finish our coffee. Soon the four of us are out the door. Charlie and Porkchop are headed to SFO for their flight back to Mexico. We're headed toward Jimmy's Caddy when Porkchop stops us.

"You're going up there to Babylon. I hope you're carrying."

We nod.

"I wouldn't be taking these wheels," Porkchop says. "That's a tricky road up there. Maybe need an all-wheel-drive car. They rent them over on Van Ness. Best advice: be watching your asses."

Jimmy:

Back at our hotel, we wait in the lobby for the rental company to deliver the Jeep. A quick glance at the names in the file folder reveals exciting characters, but how they fit into what we're dealing with doesn't register in any meaningful way. The fact is we don't know what's supposed to happen up at Babylon, except we're supposed to find out what's been buried out in the canyon.

"Jesus," Nick says. "You don't suppose that these people are buried up there, do you?"

I'm about to answer him when my cell phone rings. The familiar tones of Tricky Dicky get cut off quickly as I answer.

"That son of a bitch Teddy called Muriel and got her all upset," Jacky says. "He told her that he's tired of getting cut out of what's rightfully his. He claims that you guys along with Tony and Bruno burned down his bar and tried to sell him into slave labor at some farm in Mexico."

"That's bullshit," Nick says.

"Of course, it is. He's nothing but a blowhard. Now Muriel's all upset. I got Eddie Scarponi driving her down to her shrink's office."

"Tony tells us that Bruno took Teddy and his friend to LAX, but they never got on the plane," Nick says. "Best guess now is they're headed up here to Babylon. That's bad news all around. Teddy's friend runs a soul-brother motorcycle gang. He and Teddy were hustling meth out of the donut shop across from Teddy's bar."

"Son of a bitch. I'd like to wring his damn neck."

"Me too," Nick says.

"I don't think they know where the house is," I say. "They know it's in Fairfax. Our best guess is that they're probably going to hang around up there hoping to spot my Caddy and follow us to the place."

"Yeah, so?"

"So, we're renting another vehicle to go up there. We talked with Porkchop and Charlie. Porkchop says a four-wheel-drive Jeep could come in handy on the canyon roads."

"Yeah, I like Porkchop. He's sharp," Jacky says. "I'm just wondering if Teddy didn't somehow get the address of Babylon out of Muriel when he called her. She was rattled. It's her goddamn family. The only good one is Murray. The rest of them are walking embarrassments. Muriel has tried to live them down, put them in the past. It's unfair. She goes to Vassar, gets a degree, gets her masters at Northwestern, but in the end...."

"I hear you, Jacky," Nick says. "All that exposure to something better in life just points out more how shitty the rest of the family is."

"I know that too well," Jacky says. "My own family left a lot to be desired. I know my wife pretty well, too. I think she sees Babylon as a place she could be proud of. Famous movie stars and musicians used to hang out there. I see it a little differently. I think some bad shit went down up there."

"No one's got a monopoly on bad shit," Nick says.

For a moment, there is silence.

I look at Nick. He shrugs.

"You're right, Nick," Jacky says. "You boys, be careful up there. Keep in touch."

Chapter Twenty-one

Nick:

We get into the rented four-wheel-drive Jeep in front of the Mark Hopkins Hotel. Jimmy pulls out into traffic and heads not for the Golden Gate Bridge and Fairfax but for somewhere south. I'm about to inquire when he offers his theory on our present situation.

"Nobody knows shit. We're supposed to take all their muddled crap and come up with a plan that will please Jacky, Muriel, and that old bat Carole in Fairfax. We're supposed to pull off a house deal, dig up whatever or whoever is down in the canyon and keep Teddy Bender from showing up and ruining everything. Shit. We don't even know what everything means."

"You left out the black motorcycle gang drug pushers," I say. "I won't ask you where you're taking us right now because you'll probably come up with some off-the-wall answer."

Jimmy shakes his head and weaves us through traffic, headed south on Van Ness.

"That goddamn Muriel," he says. "If she heard you were going to Hell, she'd want you to bring her a snowball on the way back. Jacky, if he heard about it, he'd want the damn snowball gift wrapped for Muriel."

"So, is that where we're headed now? Is your ass on fire again?"

"Might as well be. SOMA. That's where we're headed. You can't say the South of Market Street district anymore. You have to say SOMA. Just like you can't say Museum of Modern Art. It's MOMA. In New York, it's SOHO for South of Houston Street. It's cute. It's hip. Mainly it's putting image over fact. SOMA is a high-crime district, but it sounds cute. The suckers go for it. They get robbed or worse."

"So, we're going there to get us robbed?"

"No. It's where Moses has his shop. We need to get something done on this trip besides chasing ghosts in Fairfax."

We turn off Mission Street and head down a narrow street full of small shops and car repair places. Jimmy pulls the car into a small parking lot in front of Truthseeker's Billiard Supply.

"You're going to like this place," Jimmy says.

He's right, of course.

Moses Truthseeker greets us at the door. He's a thin black man who has seen more than his share of life. Behind him are a half dozen of the most gorgeous pool tables you'll ever see.

"Jimmy, so good to see you. This must be Nick. I've been expecting you. Please." He motions with his cigar toward the tables. "Please check them out. I think you'll find they're what you've been looking for."

Like crazed kids, Jimmy and I play the tables. The slate is flawless, the cushions are alive, and the leather and wood surrounding the velvet turn them into works of art.

Jimmy looks up at me as he's about to break to start our third game.

"What do you say? Isn't this what we've been wanting? We can put them in the Diamond Room just off the main corridor at Dominoes."

I nod.

"And we each get one for our rec room?"

"With balls, cues, racks, the whole shebang," Jimmy says.

"We can deliver the whole shipment in three weeks," Moses Truthseeker says. "We have most of the tables in our Daly City warehouse. Our techs will install. In fact, I'll be down to watch over the process. I can help you set up a tournament at Dominos. There are some fine players in your town, and I'm sure we can attract more from all over the West Coast."

I'm about to say something when the door opens with a jingle. Three men enter. On the hottest day of the year, these guys are wearing leather jackets and ski masks. They're carrying baseball bats.

"We're here to collect for the Latin Pharaohs," the fattest guy of the three says. "So, take out your wallets and put them on the table, or maybe Julio here has to do a home run on your head."

I look at Moses Truthseeker.

He's scared. He's getting out his wallet.

I look at Jimmy. He nods.

We both toss our wallets onto the pool table.

The fat guy motions for Julio to pick them up.

"Thank you, gents, for your donation to the Latin Pharaohs," Fat Guy says.

He's about to turn to leave.

"Aren't you interested in our jewelry?" I ask.

"Jewelry?" Fat Guy walks up close to me.

I pull my Glock out of my pants' back and shove it into Fat guy's face. Jimmy has his Glock on the back of Julio's head.

The third Latin Pharaoh stands frozen near the door.

"Drop the bat, or I'll blow your fucking head off," I yell.

The bat drops to the floor.

"What are we going to do with this trio?" Jimmy asks. "They're not very smart, wearing winter clothing on a day like today."

"You're right. We need to help them adjust."

"What do you mean?" Fat guy says.

"Take off your ski masks and your leather jackets."

"Those heavy boots and those Levi's look too hot," Moses Truthseeker says.

"Damn right. Shirts and underwear, too." Jimmy waves his Glock toward the guy standing frozen at the door.

"Hey, wait a minute," Fat Guy says. "Can't we work this out, Man? We weren't going to hurt you."

"Okay, tell you what," I say. "We'll let you walk out of here with your clothes on if you promise to never come back and try to rob us."

"Okay, yeah, okay," Fat Guy says.

"In exchange, we're going to shoot Julio and the guy at the door, okay?" Fat Guy looks at both of them, then at me.

"Uh, yeah. I guess so. Okay."

"You motherfucker," Julio says. "You're worse than pig shit, Miguel."

"I have to object," Moses Truthseeker says. "I don't want any blood or pig shit getting all over these beautiful tables. Can we go back to taking all their clothes and tossing them out of here?"

"You could shoot Miguel and let the two of us walk," Julio says.

"I go for that," the guy at the door says.

"We should put it to a vote," Jimmy says. "There's six of us involved here. Let's take a vote. If you're in favor of throwing these three out into the street with no clothes, raise your hand."

Fat Guy, Julio, and the guy at the door raise their hands.

"Those in favor of shooting them raise your hand."

Jimmy and I raise our hands.

I look at Moses Truthseeker.

"What do you say? Are you going to vote?"

"I'm on the fence. I don't want blood all over the place. We'd have to get rid of the bodies. That would be expensive to clean up. Also, the price of ammunition has to be factored in. Plus, extra work. There's a dumpster down the street, but you could hurt your back trying to get this fat guy in there."

Compromise works in the end. The Latin Pharaohs leave with copies of the Chronicle taped around their waists. We tell them they have a ten-minute head start before we call the cops.

They take off bare-footed and bare-assed, running toward the Mission District.

We have their identification, phone numbers of their girlfriends, and twenty-five bucks in cash. Their clothes get unceremoniously deposited in the dumpster down the street from Truthseeker's Billiards.

We shake hands with Moses after handing him a check from Dominos.

The tables will be moving toward Vegas.

Jimmy starts the Jeep rental and heads north toward the Golden Gate. "You were right. I really like Truthseeker's," I say. "The tables are beautiful."

"To say nothing about the intellectual crowd that hangs out there," Jimmy says.

Chapter Twenty-two

Jimmy:

Driving Nick through San Francisco on our way to the Golden Gate and Marin County becomes a strange trip in itself. Nick can't resist calling all the girlfriends of Miguel, Julio, and Hector. He tells them how the three Latin Pharaohs got beat up and robbed of all their clothes at that gay bar they like to hang out at in the Castro district.

"Si, claro, Chica," Nick says, "Estan maricones. Ay, caramba!"

After exhausting all the phone numbers, he realizes that coffee and some sourdough bread would be good to have on the road to Marin. Of course, there's a place in North Beach that he can run into and get the treats while I circle the block.

"It's right down the next street," he says.

But somehow, it isn't.

"It was here a couple years back. Go left and take a right. I know another place."

He hops out of the car in front of a café.

"Go around the block and pick me up," he says.

Any chance at parking is nonexistent, and a traffic cop is pretending to be a Rottweiler.

I move into the mess ahead, where a utility pole has fallen onto a Muni bus.

"You got to turn left and keep moving," the Rottweiler says.

Good trick. Turning left gets me stuck behind traffic in a narrow alley. Several minutes go by, and traffic starts to move with horns blowing behind me. Part of the problem is a large funeral procession coming through Chinatown. I decide that turning right might solve my problem, but that gets me blocked by another funeral procession coming out of North Beach. The Catholics and the Buddhists are competing for the Funeral of the Day award.

I look to my left and notice a prophet standing on the corner. He's wearing a Jesus outfit complete with sandals, a beard, and a robe. His large sign on a shepherd's staff reads, "Death is only the beginning." I try to ignore the prophet, but it grabs hold of me, this thought of what? Reincarnation? Rebirth?

It's upsetting me because I almost believe in it, except I'm skeptical. I feel it, but maybe I don't trust my own feelings. I don't even know how I'd bet it if I was sitting in Dominic's Sports Betting Room in Vegas, and it came up on the giant board. What would the odds even look like: "Reincarnation five to two against?" Would I take the plunge? Bet a double sawbuck on it just to be in on the action?

See, it has to do with crossing the Golden Gate Bridge. I've crossed it before, but I could never tell you truthfully how many times I have, or for that matter, about the time I probably died while crossing it.

I grew up in Chicago. Never left the neighboring states until I was in my late teens, but as a kid, I had this recurring dream of crossing a giant, orange-colored bridge in the back seat of a car. The fog was all around in this dream. The car moved along, and then the dream would suddenly end. I asked my parents about where the bridge was. Had we gone someplace like that when I was a small kid? They said no. Nothing like that in Chicago. It was just a crazy dream I kept having.

Then I came to San Francisco as a young adult.

That first time, I stood by the Golden Gate Bridge, and I knew I had been there before. This was where the foggy drive had happened.

Or had it? As the joke goes, was it déjà vu all over again?

Years went by, and I pretty much put it away, bringing it up only when others discussed weird dreams and such.

That would have been it, but then tragedy struck. My wife Martha and daughter Rachel were killed in a terrorist attack in Paris. I went completely off the rails. Jacky had Nick watching me 'round the clock, attempting to get me to the point where I could deal with their deaths. Finally, Jacky shipped me to a rehab center in Elkhorn, Wisconsin. I needed professional help. I needed some way to deal with it all, an approach I could buy into.

I was telling my lament to Doctor Raj Singh, the shrink at Elkhorn.

"It's like they've never died," I said. "Both my wife and my daughter were so filled with life and adventure. Hell, I was the stick-in-the-mud. They were off to Paris and Rome, then Israel. Me, I had to stay home and take care of some minor court cases. Shit, I could have gone, but instead, old Jimmy here had to keep the books up to date."

"You feel guilty," Singh said. "Had you gone with, you would have been a victim, too. What sense does that make?"

"I loved them. I would have been with them."

"And where is that, Jimmy? Can you tell me?"

"I don't know, but I know it's not all cut and dried. It's like I can almost feel them coming back to life. They were so vital. So full of life."

"And you think that people come back from the dead? They get reborn?"

"Maybe. Maybe I have," I said. "Maybe I remember a bit of who I once was."

Singh listened as I told about crossing the Golden Gate Bridge as a child in the back seat of a car. Driving through thick fog, the recurring dream always came to a sudden end.

I didn't know what to expect when I finished my tale.

"Does telling me that story make you feel better, Jimmy?"

"It does if it means that somehow my wife and daughter have lived on. If my dream is what happened to me in another life before I became me."

"Neither of us can say that's what happened, but we can hope," Singh said. "And because we are wise, we can see the dream for what it can be, a useful tool, a means of both acceptance and recovery. If you let go of your wife and daughter, they will be free to move on. Perhaps just as the child you may have been, moved from that life to the one you are in at present."

We did several months of that conversation. I began to feel better, like I could handle being Jimmy Cox and get back into the swing of life in the wild game called Chicago. I wasn't cured, but I was better. In some ways, better than I had ever been, able to move on to another marriage, friends, and a career I was happy about.

"Hey, move your ass. You're blocking traffic." The Rottweiler cop is waving at me.

Horns behind me are blowing.

I see the break in the traffic on Columbus, and I pull ahead and turn back to where I dropped Nick. He's standing in front of the café, holding a large carry-out bag.

"They didn't have any decent sourdough bread," he says as he jumps in. "I got us coffee and some pastries, a Napoleon and a Bismarck."

"That's fine," I say.

"Think of that," Nick says. "Two big shots from France and Germany alive again as gooey bakery goods."

"Yeah," I say. "What are the odds on that?"

Chapter Twenty-three

Nick:

We drive through the smog-filled air and onto the Golden Gate. The color of the air is almost a match with the color of the bridge. Both are orange. California is still on fire. Traffic is moving, and I'm hoping that fresh air is up ahead in Marin. Jimmy looks a little nervous behind the wheel.

"Smooth ride," Jimmy says. "Looks good, huh?"

"Jesus, Jimmy," I say. "This ain't the time you're going to die on the friggin' bridge. That was when you were a little kid, remember?"

He grumbles.

"I guess I told you about my dream about the bridge, huh?"

"Yeah, it only comes up when you get drunk enough."

"That bad, huh?"

"No, I respect what you think happened to you. Forget about it. You know I always got your back."

"Yeah, I know."

We sip coffee and move along in the traffic.

"We should look at this file of people that went missing up at Babylon," I say. "Maybe we know some of them."

"You read, I'll drive."

I flip open the folder that Porkchop and Charlie gave us.

Four people are in it.

The first is Dieter von Ritter. His photo shows a muscular man in a polo outfit. He's holding a martini in his left hand, a polo mallet in his right. There's a scowl on his face. The date on the back of the photo is May 1938.

I read the short file on Dieter.

"Racecar driver and airplane daredevil, von Ritter hung out with the Hollywood set and the Bay Area jazz scene until his sudden disappearance in June of 1939. A frequent visitor to Sausalito and other towns in Marin County, von Ritter was believed to be in touch with the German consulates in Los Angeles and San Francisco. Promoting himself as a representative of a European film production company, von Ritter had contact with Hollywood film executives and automotive and aeronautic manufacturers. He was known as a big spender and a ladies' man. Naval intelligence suspected he was tracking ship movements out of the major ports on the West Coast."

"So, do you think that Dieter bought the farm in Babylon?" Jimmy asks.

"He seems like just the type that would be hanging around with the Benders."

"Hell, for all we know, he could still be alive, living in that room next to the tool shed where Clancy used to stay," I say. "Old Dieter maybe just doesn't go out much. We should ask about him. Maybe his monthly rent is one of the perks in the house deal."

We're off the bridge now and headed through the Robin Williams Tunnel.

"Now, this guy's a tunnel?" Jimmy asks. "Didn't he used to be a comedian?"

"Yeah, in his former life."

"Yeah, very funny. Who else you got in that folder?"

"An old Chicago legend, Philly Petrillo."

"Big Philly, or Little Philly?"

"Jesus, Jimmy. Pay attention. This file is about people who disappeared. Big Philly fell off the radar back in the late fifties. Little Philly's still doing time for beating up Senator Scott's kid with a tire iron."

"Yeah, I never liked him."

"Little Philly or Senator Scott's kid?"

"Take your pick. What does it say about Big Philly?"

I take a deep breath and hit the highlights that Bay Area crime solvers have put together on Phillip Anthony Petrillo, Sr.

"Truck hijacking, burglary, operating an unlicensed liquor establishment, running a house of prostitution, and here's one they could never prove: theft of weapons from the Illinois National Guard."

"That's a famous whodunit," Jimmy says. "They came in by crashing trucks through the gate, overpowering the guards and making off with machine guns, mortar launchers, and grenades, cases of them. They hauled off the loot in large produce trucks supposedly stolen from Scalera's Wholesale Provisions. They think Big Philly was involved?"

I read more from the file.

"Suspected of being the organizer, Phillip Anthony Petrillo, Sr., according to informants, shipped the stolen weapons to the Port of New Orleans, where they were transferred to a sea-going vessel or vessels and shipped to one or more Caribbean nations. Cuba and the Dominican Republic are the suspected destinations."

"That sounds like Big Philly," Jimmy says.

I resume reading the Big Philly report:

"It goes on to say that Petrillo relocated to the San Francisco Bay Area in 1957. He associated with Hollywood film people, West Coast gangsters, and known associates of Rafael Trujillo, dictator of the Dominican Republic. Petrillo was last seen June 6, 1958, entering a lavish home in

Fairfax, California."

"You think Big Philly buried any of the weapons up there?" Jimmy asks. "Maybe some of his ill-gotten loot?"

"Or, hell, maybe even Big Philly himself is part of the canyon," I say. "Wouldn't that be a nice conversation starter if Jacky and Muriel buy the place and have their housewarming up there? 'Oh, and here's the final resting place of Big Philly Petrillo. We had Nick and Jimmy dig him up to make sure it was him. Of course, the boys were kind enough to bury him again.'"

"Yeah," Jimmy says. "Be careful not to step on any of the land mines or rattlesnakes."

I pick up the following report and read it.

"Alexi Komarovsky aka Alvin Comaro aka Mickey Saturday, a suspected agent of the USSR. Disappeared in 1948 around the time of the closing of the USSR Consulate in San Francisco. Last seen in Fairfax, California. Believed to be involved in attempts to purchase information on weapons development, nuclear and non-nuclear. Komarovsky is rumored to have been in possession of gold bars seized in fall of Berlin, 1945."

"Nice," Jimmy says. "Anybody else?"

"Dannielle Leroux," I say. "Actress, drug addict, sometimes prostitute. Member of the German Bund USA during the 1930s. Member of the Communist Party USA during the 1940s. Girlfriend of Dieter von Ritter during the 1930s. Also dated Alexi Komarovsky in the 1940s. Whereabouts are unknown. Last seen in Fairfax, California at a private home in 1948."

"You got to hand it to the Benders," Jimmy says. "They don't discriminate when it comes to having people over."

"Or suddenly disappearing them," I say.

Chapter Twenty-four

Jimmy:

We pull through San Rafael on our way to Fairfax. The air has cleared, and it's a pleasant summer day as we drive slowly down Fourth Street. It's a street filled with interesting shops, the kind of avenue I'd love to stroll down with Cassandra.

Dawn, Nick, and especially four-year-old Molly would be good company. There are lots to do and good excuses for spending money on ice cream, expensive clothes, and restaurants that offer meals from countries all over the world. Our whole crew would love it, I'm sure. Instead, though, we're headed to Fairfax to check out Babylon. It's more of Muriel's bullshit spilling over into everyone else's good time. We've taken precautions before our arrival.

The four-wheel-drive Jeep is a flat white color that doesn't look like the traditional Jeep. It seems like a small SUV that a realtor might drive. We rented it under assumed names, so whatever goes down up at Babylon might not be traced to us. My Illinois driver's license says Robert Lewandowski. Nick's says Donald Lewandowski. According to the address listed on both licenses, we live in a basement flat on Milwaukee Avenue in Chicago. Our landlord is Stan Kowalski, who runs the Polka Palace tavern on Milwaukee Avenue, not far from the dump he rents to us.

Has Bobby or Donny ever been to the basement flat? No.

Have we ever met Stan Kowalski? No.

Does he even exist?

It's been said that he does.

Whoever Stan Kowalski is, we are told that he'll pay the bills on the credit card we're using. He'll stumble into the Logan Square Savings Bank, and using broken English, he'll pay cash. No check, no trace. No Bobby. No Donny. Isn't capitalism wonderful?

We pull into a grocery store lot to check if we're ready for Fairfax. Nick's got his canvas hat with a wide floppy brim on his head. Aviator sunglasses cover half his face. A blue polo shirt and khaki pants top his white running shoes.

"Christ," he says. "With these get-ups, we could be anybody."

"Do I look as anybody as you?" I ask.

"You're almost the mirror image," he says. "Except my anybody is a bit more continental than yours."

Fairfax soon appears, and we pull into downtown and park to get our bearings. Babylon is somewhere up one of the hilly roads. A look at our map shows streets resembling spaghetti tossed against a wall. A look out the windows of our Jeep offers more confusion.

Signs on a bistro wall state, "Make Love, Not War!" and "Get Out of Viet Nam." Graffiti written above the signs state, "The Only Dope Worth Shooting is Nixon" and "Love the One You're With!"

"What the hell did you do?" Nick asks. "You take a wrong turn and drive us back into the sixties? I thought we were looking for Fairfax, not Haight Ashbury."

It turns out that Fairfax, or at least a sizeable portion of it, is the sixties.

Straight-haired bra-less women with tie-dyed t-shirts stand next to shirtless guys in jeans and sandals. Peace symbols are abundant, as are Egyptian ankhs hanging from ears and dangling from necklaces. The smell of marijuana is thick. Downtown Fairfax is a contact high complete with beads and flowers in the hair. Jimi Hendrix music pours out of doorways, and any moment I figure the ghost of Abbie Hoffman will appear.

Instead, another ghost shows up. I see Teddy Bender walk out of a shop through the rearview mirror and turn away from our Jeep. Another ghost follows. Manuel Rose trails Teddy to a black Cadillac Escalade.

Nick sees them, too.

"Hang on a minute," he says as I'm about to leave the parking spot. "Let's see if they've got anybody else with them."

We wait for several minutes. The Escalade sits with its engine running. "They're waiting for someone or something," Nick says. "Maybe they're waiting for us to show up in your Caddy."

"Or maybe they've been waiting for the cavalry," I say as two motorcycles roar up next to the Escalade.

"I know you're going to say that I'm guilty of racial profiling," Nick says. "But I'm going to stick my neck out and say that those two guys are members of the Knight Ravens Motorcycle gang."

"No, I'd say we're both morons if we choose to hang around here." I put the Jeep in gear and pull out of the parking spot.

"Good move," Nick says. "Let's go see what Babylon is about."

We watch behind us to see if the Escalade moves. It doesn't. Teddy has reached into a cooler and is handing out beers to the two motorcyclists. We've gotten past a hurdle.

Surprisingly, it isn't hard to find our way up the canyon walls along the winding roads. The hard part is staying on the narrow pavement. For the most part, the ride is along a 12-foot-wide-road. Oncoming traffic means pull over, back up, or try to squeeze through without hitting a tree on one side or going over the edge into a deep dive to the bottom.

"According to our info, we should be getting close to Babylon," Nick says. "The road plays out in a little bit and comes to a dead end."

That's when we see it.

Babylon.

For all the crap we've gone through to get here, I have to say that Babylon is a thing of beauty. The house stretches out on the canyon side of the road, hanging over the sloping ground on steel girders. Large wooden beams and turquoise-colored shingles on the roof add to its striking looks. A large concrete apron in front of the house looks like it can hold ten cars. In the middle of the house is an open courtyard with a

Mandarin-style roof covering it.

"Jesus," Nick says. "I expected some shit house, ready to fall over a cliff."

I'm about to pull into the driveway when I see it. An unmarked white panel van is pulled off to the side. Two men are wearing orange vests and carrying what looks like surveying equipment. Down the road, another unmarked white panel van sits. Two more men in orange vests gather equipment out of the vehicle's back.

I drive slowly ahead and pass the second van.

All the equipment, including the vests and the hard hats, looks brand new.

"What do you think?" Nick asks. "Feds? FBI? State's Attorney?"

"Maybe, if we're lucky," I say. "The Benders did a lot of people dirt in this place. Somebody else besides the Feds knows that."

"Yeah," Nick says. "The Nazis and the Russians, according to our files. I don't think it's Big Philly Petrillo's people. They wouldn't get caught dead driving a white panel van."

Chapter Twenty-five

Nick:

It's a short trip to the end of the road past Babylon. We pass two luxury houses and find ourselves staring at a wall of boulders and scrub bushes. We make the U-turn and sit like a couple tourists poring over their map of Marin County. It's a big map and very useful for staring out over the top of it to see what the boys in the white vans are up to. It turns out they're just as interested in us. All four are giving us a look, wondering who we are and what we're up to.

"We could hoist a flag of truce and have you walk over and ask them who they really are," Jimmy says. "I'd go, but I'm busy driving our getaway car."

"Yeah, I'd do it, but I'm a little weak on my Russian and not too good on the German. As far as speaking the Big Philly Petrillo dialogue, I'd have to charge you extra."

"Besides that, you got any other big ideas?" Jimmy asks.

"Yeah, let's assume that whoever they are, they aren't ready to move. If they were ready, they'd already been in the house and gone with whatever they came for. Maybe they're in the same boat that we are.

They're looking for something, but maybe they're not quite sure what it is. They've probably got surveillance equipment aimed at the house. We could just go in and play dumb."

"That, we're good at." Jimmy puts the Jeep in gear, and we head for the driveway in front of Babylon.

The house is beautiful. It stretches out eighty feet on each side of the main doorway. The first floor is built from a combination of cedarwood and turquoise-colored ceramic tile. The second floor has an open space in the middle with a mandarin roof above. A lighter-colored wood and red tiles dominate this level.

The large double doors in the center of the house open as we pull in. Two guys dressed in Marin Security uniforms step out and motion for us to enter.

"You da Chicago outta Vegas guys," the thinner of the two says. It's not a question. We either are, or we're in deep shit.

"Yeah," Jimmy says. "We're here about the house."

Thin guy motions with his head to follow him. The other guy stays behind and locks the front doors. We hear piano music as we climb the stairs taking us up to the second-floor open area. Somebody is playing "The Lady is a Tramp" and humming along.

If Steinway makes a bigger piano, I've never seen it.

The woman playing it is thin and old. She's dressed in a black suit with a jacket, white blouse, and a large gold chain around her neck. Her grey hair is fashionably styled, and she starts to ad-lib new words to "Lady" as we walk into the room.

"Here comes Chicago, it's Jimmy and Nick,

By way of Vegas, now isn't that slick?

Make a good offer, and I'll make it stick.

Don't take this lady for a tramp."

She plays a few bars more and then stops.

"Shit. I can't think of any more words. I must be getting old. Julius, get these boys a cold beer. It's damn hot today. This goddamn place is about to catch on fire."

Julius, aka the thin guy, heads for the bar behind the piano.

"I'm Carole Bender," the woman says. "In case you haven't figured that out. You must be Nick and Jimmy. I think I might have met you years ago in Chicago, maybe at Muriel and Jacky's wedding. Jesus, that was a lifetime ago. I think I was running around with Dominic Aldarisio in those days. Big blowhard dago, had Club Alabam before Jacky took it over."

"Yeah, of course," Jimmy says.

I nod.

Julius comes back and hands us each a beer.

"Julius, for Christ's sake, give the boys a frosted mug," Carole says. "Where the fuck are your manners?"

She runs a few bars of "Ain't Misbehavin'" on the piano.

Julius comes back with the frosted mugs.

"Take a walk, Julius," Carole says. "We're gonna talk some business."

Jimmy:

Carole Bender is a cut-to-the-chase woman.

"I don't have time for bullshit," she says. "I'm getting older, might have a few good years left, but I don't want to spend them taking care of this place. It was fun in the day, but that day has long gone away. Now, I just get rubberneckers coming by trying to see the house where Frankie got laid? Hitch got drunk?"

"What about those bozos out front with the vanilla vans?" Nick asks. "They don't look like rubberneckers. They ain't surveyors. Who are they?"

She looks around the room and out at the valley past where we sit along the railing.

"They're part of the legend. The one that doesn't want to go away."

"Must be more than a legend," Nick says. "I heard it was real enough for you to be shooting at it. Let's hear it. We didn't come here to get jerked around."

She reaches into her small purse and pulls out a cigarette.

"I more or less grew up here with the old lady, Lacey Bender, running the show. I was just a kid, but there must have been some bad shit that went down. I was in therapy for years, couldn't sleep, had nightmares when I could sleep, a real mess. Later, when I got to drinking, some of those fears and nightmares almost became real."

"So, you're having a party, and in the middle of it, you grab a rifle and start firing at something down in the canyon," Nick says. "What the hell were you shooting at?"

"I don't know. Ghosts maybe. Part of the nightmare was buried down there—something valuable, but something that would turn into a terrible thing. I'd surround myself with people. Throw large parties. I didn't want to be alone. Then I'd make the mistake of looking out down there. I'd see something moving, and I'd freak out, grab a gun, and fire at it. I think I killed a possum once. I felt like shit the next day."

Down in the canyon, a light breeze moves through rustling scrub weeds and bushes.

"I hired people to go down there and have a look," Carole says. "They whacked down some weeds and blazed a few trails you could walk on. No one found anything weird. I've even searched the house for something. Didn't even know what I was searching for. In the end, I found nothing. I even asked people who stayed here if they had anything weird happen to them. You know, Frank was pretty into extrasensory stuff. He had a long thought about it and said no. Except then he said he thought something was rattling me, a memory I couldn't quite bring to the surface."

"So, this legend?" Nick asks.

"You throw a few parties where the shooting stuff goes down, and word gets around," Carole says. "Lacey's reputation got around. She was mobbed up with no doubt about it. There were a lot of you-know-the-types hanging around. Plus, all the show biz people. Everyone knew there were hot broads up here for the price. There had to be something hidden out back on the property. People just don't open fire for no reason."

"So now, you want to leave, sell the place?" Nick asks.

"Yeah, I'm done. I have maybe five or six good years left. I saved some money. I want to travel, see some friends in Europe. Hey, when I die, Muriel's supposed to get the house. I want her to have Babylon. I've had it appraised. Six million is about right."

Nick and I both look around the large open area. Pictures of movie stars enjoying themselves at Babylon cover the walls. Several autographed guitars are mounted to wooden beams. A look toward the canyon shows just a hint of fog coming in.

Carole goes on with her story.

"Muriel could just wait until I die. She and Jacky could have it clear and free, but there's space for a few challenges to that transfer if you read the papers on it. One part of the agreement opens the door to Murray Bender getting a slice, and worst of all, there's Teddy and his trashy wife, who I hear has run off with some motorcycle bum. I don't want that to happen. I'm willing to clear out now for half the appraised value. I'd drop two hundred thousand to Murray. He's a nice guy. I'd leave a dollar to Teddy the bum just to keep it kosher. Three mil from Jacky and Muriel, and I'm off to Paris."

"And what about the legend you leave behind?" Nick asks.

"That's the best part of the deal," Carole says. "We'll let the word out that wild old lady Carole took all the mystery stuff with her when she went."

Chapter Twenty-six

Nick:

Carole takes us on a tour of Babylon. It's impressive. There are eight guest rooms which she refers to as suites. Each suite covers about eight hundred square feet. All have large bathrooms, wide-screen televisions mounted on the walls, and private decks with hot tubs, overlooking the canyon below.

"Lacey Bender made a lot of money in her day with the bookies she ran and the other whatnots," Carole says. "She put a good chunk into this place. It was an obsession, some say. One of my shrinks said it had something to do with over-compensating, a way to make good come out of all the bad that came first."

"Yeah, we heard some of the stories," Jimmy says. "We're wondering if the surveyors out on the road aren't from one of the groups she might have crossed back in the day."

"You could go ask. You think they'd come right out and tell you?"

"No, I know they're not for real, though," Jimmy says. "Real workmen don't go around with everything clean and new. It looks like they came right out of the showroom. Hell, for all we know, maybe they're clones."

"Clones, clowns, it doesn't mean shit to me," Carole says. "I got friends. That's where Julius and Fatso come from. Marin Eversharp Security. You heard of Mary Ashford Stevens?"

Jimmy looks at me. I give the noncommittal shrug and turn back toward Carole.

"She the one that writes those sexy novels about rich bitches on the make?"

"I didn't know you read great literature," Carole says.

"I only read the covers."

"So, who's this Mary Ashford Stevens?" I ask. "How does she fit in?"

Carole takes a long drag on her cigarette and winks as she lets out the smoke.

"I introduced her to her husband, David Rockwell, the financial wiz. One of his properties is Marin Eversharp Security. The security guys are a gift. They're here around the clock."

"So, Rockwell turns out to be a decent guy," Jimmy says.

Carole pats Jimmy's arm and laughs.

"No, it's just that his wife can be a first-class bitch if he doesn't toe the line."

The tour of Babylon continues past oil paintings of famous entertainers.

Jimmy Stewart's portrait hangs next to Kim Novak. Rita Hayworth is next to Frank Sinatra. Cary Grant hangs beside Eva Marie Saint.
"All these people hang out at Babylon?" Jimmy asks.
"That's the story," Carole says. "I can't vouch for all of them."
She waves her hand toward the paintings.
"They're hanging out here now, though."
We walk through the kitchen, which is well-equipped with the latest appliances that would be at home in a medium-sized restaurant. Everything is clean and shiny.
"Everything you see in the house stays here for the new owners," Carole says. "The paintings, the furniture, appliances. Hell, even the linens. I'll just be taking my personal stuff. You can tell Jacky and Muriel that they can make up any tales about whatever mysterious stuff I removed from the house before I left."
We come to a large room off the kitchen. Papers are spread out on a table.
"Take a look at the plat map," she says. "I'm going to have Fatso walk you guys down there so you can see where the surveyor stakes are. I had it done a few months back, and if you're wondering, it wasn't by those yahoos out in the street."
We walk over to the window facing the canyon. There's a pathway coming out of the center of the house toward the canyon below.
"The lot starts out wide up here at the road and narrows down as it heads to the canyon floor," Carole says. "There're pins down there as permanent markers. Most of it, after you get beyond ten feet from the house, is unbuildable. It goes down pretty steep."

Jimmy:

We get a good look at the rest of the house, and I have to say I'm impressed. Everything is beautiful and well taken care of. I can see Jacky and Muriel holding court in the place, and I know my wife would enjoy being a guest. Hell, I'm already enjoying it.
Fatso, whose name turns out to be Gary, is more muscular than fat. I ask him if he likes guarding Carole and Babylon.
"Hey, compared to Fallujah, this is a piece of cake," he says. "I was there when we swept in with the Iraqis. I'll take Fairfax any day."
He takes us down to the pathway coming out from underneath the house. I can see that this is pretty much how Clancy Booker described it to us.

On one side is a small guest room with your basic toilet, shower, and sink. Across from it is the tool shed with essential yard tools. We stop there at Gary's direction.

"We'll each take a machete to hack a way through any brush you might want to see past," he says. "Carole always says the machetes are for killing rattlers, but I haven't seen one down there. Julius says he has, but he's a little hyper at times. He's a bit of a bullshitter, too."

"Yeah? How so?" Nick asks.

"He likes to brag about his connections. Talks about being tight with David Rockwell, the boss of our outfit."

"Is he?" I ask.

"Yeah, Rockwell bought us lunch once down in Fairfax. It was change of shift. The new crew was coming on to guard the house. I think Rockwell was tired of listening to his old lady, Mary Ashford Stevens bitch to Carole about their lousy seats at the opera. He just wanted an excuse to get away. It was a good lunch, but good old David talked more into his cell phone than he did to Julius and me."

"Hell of a guy," Nick says. "You're probably lucky. You didn't have to listen to him."

"I'm starting to like you guys," Gary says.

We head down the pathway. Most of it is dirt and dusty gravel. I'm thinking that it's an occasional stream bed for run-off from the road above. On each side of the path are high weeds and brush.

Gary hacks away at some weeds and motions for us to follow him. Off to one side is a small marker embedded in concrete.

"This is the marker for the southeast corner of the property," he says. "I think it was placed there back in the '20s. The other one, the southwest, is over here."

We follow as he hacks his way through more brush, and soon, there it is. "You can see how the lot narrows down from the street side," Gary says. "It's two hundred feet along the road. Down here, it's eighty feet."

Nick points to a large concrete cylinder sticking up in a tall patch of weeds.

"What's that?"

"It's part of the property," Gary says. "You'll see on the side it was cast in 1928."

Sure enough. Stamped in the concrete, it says, "BABY LON, 1928."

The top of the four-foot-tall cylinder has an iron grating over it. We look over the side and find ourselves reflected in standing water.

"I figure it was part of an elaborate drainage system someone had the bright idea to install," Gary says. "You see a lot of concrete stamped with the year 1928 around town. That was the year before the

Depression. All those big plans went down the drain. Hell, there's an abandoned subdivision toward the ocean with all the sidewalks laid out and poured. All it is now are weeds. No roads. No houses. Nice old sidewalks, though."

We make our way back toward the house.

"Great tour, Gary," I say.

"Yeah," Nick says. "Maybe you could spice it up a bit and charge money. You could throw a rubber snake out of your pocket and hack it up with the machete."

"That would be fun," Gary says. "But I don't see myself working here much longer. Carole wants to get out and enjoy what she's got left. My understanding is she's trying to convey Babylon to family members."

"Yeah, some folks we work for," Nick says. "Anything else you can tell us so they can go ahead with decision making?"

Gary looks back at the canyon and then up at the house.

"The house is in great shape. It's Carole I worry about. She's carrying something around in her head that won't let go of her. We do the security. A big part of that is keeping Carole company. We listen to her sing. We play chess and cards with her, and sometimes she tells us stories about the old days, but you know? You can listen to the old tales, but you don't get very far asking questions about them."

"What happens if you ask?" Nick says.

"She says, 'I'll tell you more if I ever figure it out.' That's usually a sign to mix her another drink."

Chapter Twenty-seven

Nick:

We find Carole sitting in an oversized wicker chair on the deck overlooking the canyon back inside Babylon. She motions for us to sit down and has Julius grab us a beer. He remembers the frosted mugs this time. I notice something has changed from an hour ago. Her large telescope mounted on a tripod is gone. Carole's large binoculars are still on the table in front of her.

She gives me a sly look and winks at me.

"You're a good detective, Nick. You notice when something's changed, something's missing."

"Yeah, you give up on trying to find little green men?"

Jimmy notices it, too.

"The telescope. I was going to ask about it. Can you see anything through the fog around here?"

"You mean the smog," Carole says. "Look at this orange cloud of shit rolling in through the canyon. That's California burning. That's people's lives down the drain, up in smoke."

"Still got the binoculars at the ready," I say.

"Yeah, for closer work than galaxies and men from Mars."

She sips her whiskey and continues.

"I got into looking for answers in the cosmos awhile back. I wasn't finding them down here. On a clear night, I could scan the sky forever. I mean that. You look at stars millions of light-years away, and you're looking at forever. Something was disturbing about that and, at the same time, comforting. We're all just little people, throwing our dirt around. We really are stardust."

I look at Jimmy. He nods.

"A lot of truth in that."

"We've seen some sights in the night sky outside of Vegas," I say. "Beautiful stars and strange things that make you wonder if those stories about Roswell, New Mexico, and Area 51 aren't true."

Carole smiles and sips from her glass of whiskey.

"I decided to give you guys the telescope. Muriel says that you'll use it. You're both married to women smarter than yourselves, and one of you has a gifted daughter. Anyhow, I packed it up into those two black cases. Consider it a gesture of goodwill or call it an old lady getting rid of stuff and not wanting to answer questions from geeks on Craigslist."

"That's wonderful," Jimmy says. "We'll use it for sure."

"I'm glad," Carole says. "I just wanted you to know that people and things aren't always what they seem to be. Whatever wild things you heard about me, maybe only half are true. I don't want to go out of Babylon without doing somebody some good. Keep that in mind. I know you've got some thinking to do, and you'll certainly be discussing this deal for the house with Jacky and Muriel. If you can get back to me in the next few days, I'd like that."

We start making motions to leave when two people enter.

"Stay just a bit longer, boys," Carole says. "I want you to meet Mary Ashford Stevens and her husband, David Rockwell."

We do the stand-up, shake hands, and smile bit. Soon everyone is sitting with a fresh drink in their hands, supplied by Julius, who does his best to bow and scrape for the Stevens-Rockwell duo.

It's clear that dear old Mary Ashford Stevens is the power behind Rockwell. She has that overly friendly demeanor of an aging prom queen congresswoman running on the pro-life/NRA prayers-in-school ticket. On the other hand, Rockwell has all the charm of a third-rate midnight news anchor from Tulsa.

"Nick and Jimmy are part of my Chicago family," Carole says. "We've been having a visit. They're part of the group that owns the Galloping Dominos Casino in Vegas."

I look at Mary Ashford Stevens. Something about too much smile quickly plastered onto her mug tells me she wasn't expecting to run into the likes of us. On the other hand, Rockwell seems like he doesn't know what's going on, or he's waiting for a cue from wifey, so he'll know what the party line is.

"Fact is," Carole says, "The whole group of us came off the rough streets of Chicago and Cicero. We're all quick learners. We know how to use the right knife and how to swear at waiters in French and Italian."

"How nice," Mary Ashford Stevens says.

"Yes," David Rockwell nods.

I glance at Jimmy. He's calm, but I know inside the wheels are turning. Some part of this game has changed. I'm waiting for his move, his way of politely asserting our position.

Everyone sips their drink, then Jimmy speaks.

"We'll be bringing up two more members of our crew from LA to verify the integrity of the construction and to video the property before finalizing Chicago taking over Babylon. We'll let you know when they arrive, Carole. Probably tomorrow in the afternoon."

Rockwell suddenly wakes up.

"Whoa, Carole, you're going ahead with the deal with…."

"It looks pretty good, David," Carole says. "You can tell by looking at these boys that they're serious."

"Well, so were we," Rockwell says. "Six million asked? I offered five, five."

"Yes, I know," Carole says. "There's quite a difference between your money and Chicago money."

"How much difference?"

Mary Ashford Stevens reaches over and pats Rockwell on the arm.

"It's not about how much, darling," she says. "Chicago money is different. Now don't be all upset. I'm sure we'll have time to visit with Carole before she leaves Babylon. I don't think she's going to leave tomorrow. Besides, we'll be visiting her in Hawaii at her new home."

"You better count on it," Carole says. "I'm planning on that."

"Well, we are too," Rockwell says. "You've certainly talked about going there enough. I'm sure it will be fine."

"She's been telling us about the beaches," Jimmy says.

I catch a wink from Carole.

I figure it's time to move on.

We drain our drinks, pick up the two cases with the telescope parts inside, and head for the door.

"You'll hear from us tomorrow," Jimmy says.

Gary, aka Fatso, helps us out the door. The Jeep is where we left it. Outdoor lights are coming on as the sun starts to set. A pickup truck from Marin Eversharp Security pulls into the drive. Two German Shepherds are on the back.

"They bring the dogs in at night," Gary says. "Heinrich and Himmler. Rockwell's old lady's idea. She'd love to see them draw blood."

"Think she'd like to sic them on one of the so-called surveyors across the road?" Jimmy asks.

"Can't say," Gary says.

He looks toward the white vans where the four men are gathered.

"Rockwell and Mary Ashford Stevens don't seem to care much about those guys."

We pull away from the house and begin working our way down the narrow canyon road. Long shadows and steep inclines have us both on alert.

I start to think about Babylon and BABY LON, Paris and Hawaii, the telescope promising the universe, and the orange clouds from fires destroying the earth.

"Looks like we have a lot to think about," I say.

"Yeah," Jimmy says. "We can start by thinking about those two vans following us."

Chapter Twenty-eight

Nick:

Jimmy's right. The two clean, white vans are following us. A glance through my side-view mirror tells me the "surveyors" are close behind as we work our way down the narrow canyon road.

"What's your best guess?" I ask.

"They either want to follow us, rob us, or kill us," Jimmy says. "Or maybe all three for the price of one. I don't think they're headed to the local watering hole for happy hour."

I hear "rob." I start to connect the dots. The group following us watched as we left Babylon with two heavy black bags holding the telescope and its tripod. We also had a packet of property documents.

Jimmy gets it, too.

"We walk in with nothing but our good looks and waltz out carrying god knows what. Fact is, we don't really know. We saw the papers in the property package. The telescope? We saw it standing there. Then we saw it gone. Next thing, it's gift-wrapped for us to explore the heavens, according to Carole. Haven't we seen this before at Penn & Teller shows?"

"Think it's a setup?" I ask.

"Maybe or maybe something else. Maybe she was hoping we'd get out with whatever's in those bags. Would you trust David Rockwell or Mary Ashford Stevens?"

The white van is right behind us, blowing its horn. The driver wants us to pull over to the right. The guy riding shotgun really holds a shotgun. He points it at us and then motions to pull to the right. The problem is there is no right. Pulling to the right means going to the canyon floor, quick time. It's either road or nothing.

I pull my Glock and start to wonder what the Jeep offers in cover from bullets when Shotgun Guy supplies the answer by blasting out our rear window.

We swerve right and nearly go over, but Jimmy pulls us back to the road. "Nick, you okay?"

"Yeah, just glass fragments. You?"

"Getting by."

Shotgun Guy is lining up his next shot, taking his sweet time like Tiger Woods waiting for the gallery to kiss his ass before he putts.

Big mistake.

I aim, and I fire, spending the whole magazine on the front of the van. Shotgun Guy drops his head out the side window and dangles his hand toward the canyon below. The driver follows by turning his bleeding head and dropping toward Shotgun Guy. The van bumps and sways on its own and then follows Shotgun Guy's pointing hand. Two small trees growing out of the canyon's rocky sides are no match for the van and its passengers. It bounces once off a rock outcropping and plunges to the canyon floor.

Van number two stops. Both men get out and look over the edge to where van number one took its dive. One guy picks up the shotgun and fires it toward us. He misses.

Jimmy keeps the Jeep moving toward downtown Fairfax.

I keep looking back for the second van to come after us. I load another magazine into the Glock and wait.

Nothing, yet.

We pull into a small side street and park. We both have cuts from glass fragments thanks to the shotgun blast taking out the back window. The interior is a mess with the back seats and the roof liner getting most of the shotgun blast.

"Nothing we can't live through," Jimmy says. "Damn good thing we got full coverage on this thing."

"Hey, it's a rental. Looks like the brake lights and the taillights are still intact. We could tell them we gave a ride to a hitch-hiking bear."

We decide to keep moving. Van number two may be coming down the road. We need to get to somewhere safe where we can get organized and find out what's in the black bags.

Flashing lights from cop cars greet us as we pull into downtown. Are they on the way toward Babylon? Are they coming after us for the extreme road rage up the hillside?

No.

Turns out the cop cars are parked near the Escalade that Teddy Bender and Manuel Rose drove into Fairfax.

Jimmy:

I'll say one thing about Muriel's family: Their get-togethers are never dull.

So far on this trip, we've had the helping hand for Teddy Bender turn into arson and mayhem in Barstow. We had an enjoyable time with Murray Bender and his lady in Ojai, where we enjoyed stories about old detective movies and entertaining stories about Vegas from Clancy Booker.

The follow-up to that was meeting Carcle Bender and touring Babylon, or is it BABY LON? But That wasn't enough. No, the Great Oddsmaker always has more excitement in mind for Nick and Jimmy. How about a chase down a mountain with gunplay? And a van plunging to its death in the canyon below? All that excitement. What more is in store? Comedy relief, maybe?

Blue lights are flashing from the three, no four, wait, make those five squad cars surrounding the Escalade that Teddy Bender and Manuel Rose drove into Fairfax. A heavy-set blonde woman is struggling to get away from a cop who's holding her. She's trying to punch and kick Manuel Rose and doing pretty well at it. Manuel has a hard time defending himself. He's handcuffed and sprawled over the hood of a police cruiser. One of Fairfax's finest is holding him down.

"That piece of shit stole my purse," the woman yells. "He stole my stash and my roll. I had five hundred in there."

The two Raven Knights that motorcycled in earlier are on the ground. They're also in handcuffs. A cop holds a plastic bag half-filled with white powder. The bag is big enough to hold a head of lettuce.

"All this crazy action," Nick says. "Where's Teddy? Did they haul him away? Is he in one of the cruisers?"

We finally spot Teddy face down on a park bench, half a block away. The remnants of two six-packs are strewn about the bench, and Teddy is busy sleeping it off.

"What a loser," Nick says. "He brings the circus to town, and he forgets to go and see the show."

I look back at the scene by the Escalade. The cops have now handcuffed the blonde woman and placed her in the back of a squad car. They've tossed Manuel Rose into another. Even the two Raven Knights get separate squad car back seats, a tribute no doubt to their standings on the social scale.

A cop blocks traffic from the road we just came through. Lights flash, sirens go woo-woo, and the squad cars start to pull out of the space around the Escalade.

I put the Jeep in gear to head out on the tail of the cops.

"Good move," Nick says. "I think the second car back from where the cop stopped traffic is a white van. If it's who we think, they're looking for us."

We get in line behind the police cavalcade with its lights flashing. Everyone pulls over to let us get past. Then they get back on the road behind us. I look through the cracked rearview mirror. If there's a white van back there, it's at least ten cars back.

Sir Francis Drake Boulevard moves well past Greenbrae, but our Jeep with the missing rear window and roof liner hanging in tatters is an easy one to I.D.

"The ferry," Nick says. "We ditch this thing there and grab the ferry back to town."

We strip the Jeep of all our packages and papers after we park in a far corner of the lot. The Larkspur Ferry Terminal is busy, and soon we're standing with the crowd waiting to get aboard.

Nick turns to a guy wearing a Giants sweatshirt.

"Could I ask a huge favor? Our rental got stolen, and I need to call and report it, but my phone was in the car when it happened."

"Sure, have at it," the guy says, handing over his phone."

Nick fumbles with the rental papers and finds the number.

"This is Donald Lewandowski from Chicago. That car we rented has disappeared. I think someone stole it with all our luggage."

He listens for a moment and gives me a wink.
"No, we're taking the bus back to our hotel, but we might need to rent another car tomorrow. We have some serious business to handle."

Chapter Twenty-nine

Nick:

We're standing on the dock at the Larkspur Ferry Terminal, waiting for the ramp to be put in place so we can board the boat and make our way back to downtown San Francisco before any of the white van crowd can find us. I'm keeping an eye on the parking lot as I hand the phone back to the guy wearing the Giants sweatshirt. So far, no van. Maybe they aren't chasing us. I turn and thank the guy for the use of his phone.
"Hey, thanks. That was a big help."
"That's rough, getting your rental car and your luggage stolen," the guy says.
"Yeah, it is, but I think we're covered."
Jimmy interrupts and points to the parking lot.
"I believe those guys in the white van are the same good-time Charlies we met in Fairfax. They look like they might be trying to find a place to park near that beat-up Jeep in the far corner."
It's them all right. The tall guy who grabbed the shotgun off the road and fired it at us is unforgettable. He has the look of a zombie.
His fat partner gets out of the van and unleashes some rage, kicking the side of the Jeep. He spits at the windshield for extra effect.
They get back in the white van and start toward the terminal dock where we're standing.
The gate to the ramp leading to our ferry opens, and the crowd begins to shuffle on board. The white van makes its way down the last aisle of parking and gets stuck behind a car waiting for a pickup truck to move out of its parking place. The fat partner jumps out of the driver's side of the van and starts yelling at the guy trying to move the pickup.
Zombie Guy gets out and yells something to everyone in sight. Are these two guys going to bite someone?
I reach back and pat my shirt, feeling for my Glock tucked in the back of my pants. I don't want it to come to that, but who knows what these guys will do.
Will they fire into a crowd?

Will I have to drop them?

Who the hell are they, anyway?

Who are they working for?

The crowd moves onto the ferry in what seems like slow motion. Jimmy, me, and the Giants Sweatshirt guy are the last to get on as the guy with the ramp shuts the gate and pulls the ramp away from the vessel.

We begin to move away from Larkspur, accompanied by the bon voyage speech from Zombie Guy, who, pardon the expression, has just missed the boat.

"You motherfuckers," he yells from outside the turn styles. "We know where you're going. We're going to meet you Downtown and get you good."

His fat, red-faced partner shakes his fist at us.

The ferry moves out. We wave to Zombie Guy and the red-faced fist shaker.

"They're a lot of fun, aren't they," Jimmy says.

"Dodger fans," the Giant Sweatshirt guy says. "How stupid can they be. They think this boat is going to dock Downtown. What do they think? We're going to walk to the ballpark?"

"Yeah," Jimmy says.

He gives me the noncommittal shrug and a questioning look that asks, 'where in the hell is this boat going?'

It doesn't take a rocket scientist to figure it out. A good look at the crowd tells you that they're all Giants fans. Sweatshirts, jackets, hats, banners all proclaim this is a Giants crowd. Turns out we're on the slow boat to the ballpark. Our newly acquired friend in the sweatshirt tells us how it works.

"Usual ferry service to Downtown S.F. is fast, but this one goes slow, so we get docked at the rear of the ballpark just before the first pitch. Enough time to grab a brewski and get to your seat."

Why so slow?

"Well, there's a full-service bar on the ferry. They like to make a buck, too."

As predicted, the rest of the ride is slow and alcohol fueled. The fun begins to break out after the second drink. A crowd near the front of the boat starts singing, "Take Me Out to the Ballgame." The rest of the group joins in. As the song ends, a guy wearing a Giants uniform jumps up and starts a chant. "Let's go, Giants. Let's go, Giants!" The crowd goes nuts. Soon they're yelling, "Beat LA! Beat LA!"

I can see Jimmy's lips moving, but I can't tell what he's saying. It's too loud. Finally, it quiets down as we pull into the ferry slip at AT&T Park.

"I was going to call Tony Stomps in L.A.," Jimmy says. "I had to give up. It was too loud to talk. We need to get him and Bruno up here, but I knew he'd go nuts if he heard all that Beat LA cheering. He loves his Dodgers."

Jimmy:

I feel tempted to go into the ballpark with the rest of the crowd from the ferry. Just losing ourselves in a summer-time night game with hot dogs and beers sounds like a great escape, but then I think there's another escape we need to take care of out there. Nick's taken to calling them "The Fat Fuck and The Zombie."

My inclination when I first hear that is to laugh, but then I stop and think. These two are out to kill us. What's our best move? What was their move? This chess game has high stakes attached to it.

Let's say they got back into their white van in Larkspur and hustled over the bridge to the SF Ferry Terminal. They had all kinds of emergency cones to put up. Parking wouldn't be a problem. Did they get there before the next ferry from Larkspur arrived? Did they find no Nick and no Jimmy and then figure out that the boat went to the ballpark? Are they waiting somewhere around here, outside the stadium?

We're standing just off the dock on the promenade next to the ballpark entrance. Do we enter the ballgame? Or do we head for the front of the park and hope we don't get shot waiting for a cab?

"I know what you're thinking," Nick says. "Follow me."

He grabs both bags of telescope parts, if that's what's really in the bags, and hustles off to a service kiosk.

The young woman behind the counter is friendly.

"My name is Jenny. How can I help you?"

"It's my friend," Nick says. "We were going to take in the game, but he's not feeling so hot. He has a heart condition. In fact, I'm carrying his medical equipment in these bags. I just want to get him home safe. Is there any way we can get a taxi to come back here to take us to his home? I'll be happy to pay extra for it if there's any charge."

"No, sir," she says. "There's no need for any payment. Just a moment." She turns and punches a few buttons into her phone. She speaks into the phone and turns back.

"Your taxi will be here in just a moment. The Giants are happy to take care of you and your friend. We hope he feels better."

"Getting safely home means more to me than you realize," I say.

Before she can finish smiling, a cab pulls up, and a driver hops out and opens the side door for us. We get settled inside, and soon we're headed for the street.

"Where we going, gents?" The driver asks.

"California and Powell," I say. "Could you drive past the front of the park? There were some people we were supposed to meet. Maybe they're still looking for us."

"Two guys in a white van?" They've been asking around for two guys carrying bags like you've got. Want me to find them?"

"No," Nick says. "We'll take care of them later."

Chapter Thirty

Nick:

The cab pulls away from the ballpark. Soon we're making our way along the Embarcadero, heading for our hotel. There's something about our driver. He seems overly attentive towards us.

"Looks like you might be missing a good game," he says. "Giants and the Dodgers, always a good one."

"Yeah, sometimes you got to do what you got to do," I say.

We move along through traffic for a minute.

"Too bad you couldn't connect with your friends," the cabbie says. "They were looking all over for you guys."

"Too much crap in the air for us," Jimmy says. "Fucking pollution."

"Yeah, I know," the driver says. "Your friends were worried about you."

I decide to throw a curveball.

"How well do you speak French?" I ask.

"How's that?" The cabbie asks.

"Our friends Armond and Francois don't speak any English," I say. "They always have a hard time when they come to the States – two black guys from Martinique."

The cabbie does a slight flinch.

"I don't speak it," he says. "Another driver down there knows French. I guess he figured out what they were saying."

I look at Jimmy. He shrugs. It's another case of somebody trying to bullshit us. Only this guy is in it for more than bullshit. I'm thinking he's going to call our white van friends as soon as he drops us off. I'm betting there's a c-note or two being waved in his direction by the Zombie and the Fat Fuck.

"I don't know if I gave you the address," I say. "It's the Fairmont Hotel, room 801. Geez, I guess you don't need the room number, come to think of it. Just drop us off in front."

"Sure thing." He smiles and shuts up for the rest of the ride.

We grab our bags and exit the cab at the Fairmont. I toss too much money at the driver, and we head for the lobby. I watch as our cabbie takes off down California Street. We wait a minute and hot-foot it across the street to the Mark Hopkins where we're registered.

"You got all this shit figured out?" Jimmy asks.

We're back in our hotel room, and there's a lot to be worried about. The white van guys are probably on their way to the Fairmont, looking for Jimmy and Nick. Was it our scintillating personalities that made us so popular with the Shotgun Zombie and Fat Fuck set? Or was it whatever we were carrying out of Babylon in the two black bags designed to hold a telescope and a tripod?

I'm about to open the bags when my cell phone rings. It's Tony Stomps. "This house deal," he says, on speaker, backing into the conversation at a leisurely stroll. "Bruno and I have been wondering about it."

"Yeah," I say.

I roll my eyes at Jimmy and look at my watch while Tony takes forever to get to the next sentence. There're two guys in a white van on their way to kill us and a couple black bags that need opening. Tony, meanwhile, seems like he's sipping a mint julep at poolside on a warm afternoon. He meanders along with the next sentence.

"Bruno says that when he took Teddy Bender and his friend to LAX, they kept bragging about some guy in the house deal that was tight with tough-guy actor Tucson Rivers, you know, Mr. Hollywood Gun Fanatic, the private militiaman? Anyhow, some name like Rockway or Rockwell ring a bell?"

"Yeah, David Rockwell. He's some kind of financial wiz. He's married to that writer Mary Ashford Stevens. We met them earlier today, up at Babylon. I don't trust them. They seem to be shadowing Carole Bender. She wants to sell the place to Muriel for three big ones. Rockwell and Stevens have offered double that, but Carole isn't interested."

"Jesus," Tony says. "You two sure know how to pick 'em. Mary Ashford Stevens, bitch of the world. The only thing good she ever did was marry that asshole Aaron Ross and take most of his money when she divorced him. He went from big-shot Hollywood producer to working on 'Bowling with the Stars.'"

Jimmy looks at his watch, looks at me, and grabs the phone.

"Look, Tony. It's like this. We got trailed by two white vans when we left Babylon. A guy in van number one tried to get us with a shotgun. Nick unloaded a magazine, and the van went over the cliff into the valley. Van number two followed us to the ferry. We got on. They just missed the boat. They got a line on us at the ballpark, and we're pretty sure they're on their way up here to try to kill us and take whatever it is in the two black bags we walked out of Babylon with. Fact is, we might be in deep shit. Do I have to say it?"

"You're at the Mark Hopkins?"

"Yeah."

"We're flying up tonight."

Jimmy:

California Street at night is beautiful. Cable cars make their way past the newspaper vending machines we're standing behind. Despite the smog-filled air from the wildfires around the state, people are out enjoying the city. It's been a half-hour since the cabbie dropped us across the street at the Fairmont. The white van hasn't shown up, and we're beginning to think that our taxi driver was just mouthing off.

"It would have been so good if they showed, and we could get them out of our hair," Nick says. "That cabbie never connected with them."

I'm about to say, "Let's go back upstairs and see what's in the black bags," when Nick sees it.

"White van going slow, looking for parking," Nick says. "If it's our boys, they won't do valet parking. They want to get in, shoot, and get out."

Sure enough, they park in a corner no-parking zone next to the Flood Mansion. There's no mistake. It's Shotgun Zombie and the Fat Fuck. They head for the Fairmont and stop halfway to check their leg holsters.

"Timing is everything," Nick says.

We cross California Street and head for the van just as our would-be killers enter the front lobby of the Fairmont.

A Slim Jim gets the van unlocked.

We're in and hot-wired in a few seconds. We've got their ride.

"Gee, I hate to leave them stranded without transportation," Nick says. "Maybe I can help."

He dials a number on his cell phone.

"Yeah, Police? Two guys with guns drawn just ran into the lobby at the Fairmont. They said something about killing somebody in room 801."

He looks back at me and then speaks again into the phone.

"Yeah, I just saw them go in, a fat guy and a thin guy that looked like a zombie... My name? David Rockwell."

We pull the van out of its illegal parking spot and head into the Russian Hill neighborhood to another illegal site on a darker street. The dome lights in the van's cargo area reveal the new plastic hard hats and the white coveralls we saw our friends wearing earlier near Babylon. Whatever surveying equipment there was must have gone into the other van and maybe went down into the canyon with it.

A large, unmarked cardboard box sits in a corner next to a heavy-duty two-wheeled hand truck. A smaller plain cardboard box sits beside it. Nick opens the larger box. Stacked inside are four sets of protective coveralls specified for the nuclear industry. Below the coveralls is a large metal canister. It's empty. Next to it is a lid that can be tightened down with screw latches. The nuclear materials warning sign is on the container and the cover.

I open the smaller box. A Geiger counter and contamination badges are packed next to face shields and protective gloves.

"Shit," Nick says. "This is starting to look like it might be above our pay grade."

We drive back toward California Street and our hotel, stopping a couple blocks short of our destination. The boxes fit neatly on the wheeler. We look like a couple of salesmen bringing in our samples as we head toward the Mark Hopkins lobby.

A doorman steps in front of us.

"Big trouble across the street at the Fairmont tonight," he says. "Cops caught two guys with guns trying to break down a door on the eighth floor. The security over there sucks."

"Wow," Nick says. "Anybody get hurt?"

"No, they were lucky," the doorman says. "Here, let me get an elevator for you, fellas."

Chapter Thirty-one

Nick:

A young mother and her daughter run toward our elevator as the doors are about to close. I hold the button so they can get on. The woman carries three shopping bags while the little girl is holding her new toy, a plastic version of a pond, complete with birds that somehow move around on the shiny surface.

"It's not a real pond," the five-year-old blond know-it-all announces to Jimmy and me. "The birds are magnets, and the water is a mirror."

"Clara, please settle down," Clara's mother says. "We've had a long day of shopping."

"It's okay," I say. "I have a four-year-old at home that beats people at Blackjack."

"Clara plays Poker with her dad. I think he owes her a few dollars."
Clara's mother laughs.
"She'd fit right in with Molly," Jimmy says. "Nick and Dawn's daughter.
I'm her Uncle Jimmy."
"Nice to meet kindred spirits," Clara's mother says.
They get off on the floor below us with their packages.
"Makes you think about what's really important, doesn't it?" Jimmy
asks. "Cute kid out for a day on the town with Mom. Meanwhile, we're
out dealing with creeps and killers."
We enter our suite and put down our bags.
Jimmy parks the two-wheeled hand truck carrying the radiation safety
equipment next to the bathroom door.
It's been a hell of a day.
Room service gets a call. Drinks and dinner are on the way.
The television has the late news, and much of it comes from the hotel
across California Street. An excited woman news reporter stands in front
of a group of police cars with their blue lights flashing.
"Two men are reportedly shot dead by San Francisco police officers as
they try to force their way into an eighth-floor suite at the hotel. Police
spokesman Angelo Castro says both men were armed with automatic
pistols. When confronted by police, the two turned and fired. Police
returned the fire, killing both men."
Next is a video of Angelo Castro.
"We have no positive I.D. on the two shooters. Fortunately, the suite the
two were attempting to break into was unoccupied at the time. We have
no idea at this time what the motive for their actions might have been."
"Jesus," Jimmy says from his bed, "They were trying to kill Nick and
Jimmy. Maybe we could call the station and get the news tip of the week
reward."
"No positive I.D.," I say. "Does that mean they didn't have I.D.s? Or
they're not sure if they're who the I.D.s say they are?"
Before Jimmy can answer, my cell phone rings. It's the love of my life.
"You guys must be busy," Dawn says. "Cassandra and I figure you've
been running from nightclub to racetrack and back again. Do you need us
to send money?"
"We wish," I say. "We've been focused on this deal for that house that
Muriel wants."
"Babylon? You've been up there? What's it like?"
"The place is beautiful, but there's a strange group hanging out up there.
We're still trying to figure out who the players are. The old lady, Carole,
seems okay, like she's trying to give Muriel a deal on the place, but
something ain't right. Some guy with big bucks, David Rockwell,

offered twice the amount Carole will sell to Muriel. She turned him down. This Rockwell guy is married to Mary Ashford Stevens, the writer."

"I know her stuff," Dawn says. "She must have two dozen books out, and they're all the same. Blonde gold-digger gets millionaire stud."

"Yeah," I say. "I think that's Mary Ashford Stevens's life story. Tony Stomps says she was married to Aaron Ross, the Hollywood producer. When she divorced him, he lost almost all that he had."

"Tony Stomps? Is he involved in this? Nick, are you guys in trouble?"

"No, not so you'd notice," I say. "Tony's coming up with Bruno tomorrow so they can evaluate the structural integrity of Babylon."

"Bruno? The only thing Bruno knows about structural integrity is where to place the bomb."

I look over at Jimmy, who's been listening to the conversation. He rolls his eyes.

"It ain't that bad, Babe," I say. "This Babylon thing is hard to figure out. Jimmy thinks that if we get new eyes to look at the project, we might get a clearer picture of it."

Jimmy flips me the bird and drinks from his can of beer.

"Yeah, it would be nice to get some answers," Dawn says. "Like, why is it called Babylon? That's an ancient city in Iraq. It was destroyed centuries ago."

"Good question. We walked down into the canyon on the lower part of the property. There's a large marker there that says BABY LON, all in capital letters. Did someone make a mistake in casting the concrete marker? Who is LON, I wonder? Did someone have a baby named Lon, or is it all a mistake of some sort?"

"What is it on? Some sort of a gravestone, maybe?"

"No, it's on a large concrete cylinder, the size of a big culvert. The kind you see at Boulder City by the dam. They told us it was part of a drainage system that never got built."

"So, if it never got built, why did they put a concrete plaque on it?"

"Don't know."

"Look, I'm going to look something up. Call you back in a few minutes?"

"Yeah, is Molly okay?"

"She's fine. She's in bed. She wonders what you two are up to."

"Yeah, I know. I miss her."

"I know. I'll call back soon."

Dawn rings off.

I look at Jimmy. He looks tired. It's been a hell of a day, a hell of a dangerous day thanks to the white vans and Babylon or Baby Lon.

"I been thinking about that Babylon/ BABY LON thing, too," Jimmy says. "Those white van guys, did they think we were carrying out something from that concrete cylinder with the label on it? What the hell did they think we had? Plutonium?"

We both stare at the black bags.

Jimmy grabs the Geiger counter and turns it on.

We both watch the dial and wait for the clicking sound as we get closer to the bags.

Nothing.

I open the first bag. It's a tripod for the telescope. It comes out easy and assembles almost by itself.

"It is what it is," Jimmy says.

The second bag opens. Inside are tubes and lenses that make up a telescope. An instruction booklet falls out of a smaller box. Apparently, some software attachment on a small motor allows the user to stay focused on a particular constellation while the world spins.

The Geiger counter stays silent.

"Nothing to worry about here," Jimmy says.

"No, whatever they were looking for is still up there at Babylon," I say.

"The kid in the elevator. Remember what she said?"

"Yeah, the mirror made it look like water."

"So, when's the last time it rained in Fairfax?"

"It hasn't rained in California in months."

"So, the water under the grating in the concrete cylinder is a mirror. Guess what might be hiding under it."

I'm about to answer when my cell phone rings.

"I had to check on that Baby Lon thing," Dawn says. "Don't know if it helps, but Lon is an old German name meaning 'Ready for battle.' Any of that ring a bell?"

"It just might," I say. "Jimmy and I are kicking it around, now."

"I'll let you go, then. Stay safe, both of you."

I turn toward the telescope and notice another small box still in the black bag, which has tipped on its side. It's heavy for its size. As I slip it out of the bag, it opens and what's inside falls to the carpet.

It's a piece of metal, gold in color.

Stamped in it are the words:

DEUTSCHE REICHSBANK

1 KILO

FEINGOLD

999.9

Above the words is the Nazi Eagle perched on a swastika.

A small piece of notepaper drops out of the small box in my hand.

"Help get me out of this mess I've inherited from Lacey. If you're reading this note, you've made it safely out of here. There's more, but no time now. Carole."

Chapter Thirty-two

Jimmy:

We stare down at the Nazi gold bar on the carpet.
"Is this for real?" Nick asks. "A kilo? What's that weigh, about two pounds and something?"
"Yeah." I do a quick calculation based on hearsay about the price of gold in pawn shops I've browsed in recently. "Could be worth 35- 40 thousand dollars."
Nick picks up the bar and turns it toward me.
"How many Jewish dental crowns are in this thing?"
I look at Carole's note that fell out of the box that the gold bar was in.
"It sounds like there may be a lot more of this and maybe a lot more trouble."
"Yeah, like we haven't had enough already," Nick says. "Who the hell are these guys? It's obvious that they had no qualms about trying to kill us."
I look around the room. The telescope and its black carrying cases sit in a corner. In the opposite corner is the two-wheeled hand truck with all the nuclear safety equipment.
"You thinking what I'm thinking?" Nick asks.
"Yeah, we better get to the van and find out if we missed something."
Several cop cars and unmarked cruisers are still at the Fairmont, where the shooting of Zombie Guy and the Fat Fuck went down earlier in the evening. It's now probably one of the safest places in town with all the heat hanging around.
A block and a half down California Street, where we stashed the white van in a no parking zone, it's a bit more on the dicey side. A drunk sits on the sidewalk against a brownstone building. He sips from a cheap port bottle and yells everyone his version of the news story that unfolded on the hotel's eighth floor.
"Couple of drug dealers shot two cops, and now the joint is surrounded. Candy-assed San Francisco Police are too chicken to go after them. They're waiting for the Marines to show up."

He takes another pull from his bottle.

"Semper fi, that's what I say. I was in fuckin' Nam, amigos."

Three car lengths past the derelict's version of News at Eleven is the white van, right where we parked it. Nick writes down the tag numbers and the vehicle identification number.

The cargo area is clean, just as we left it. A look toward the front reveals two jackets, each shoved under a seat. Beneath the jacket under the seat on the left is a sawed-off twelve-gauge shotgun and a box of shells.

"You don't suppose this was meant for us, do you?" Nick asks.

"Only a couple of the shells," I say.

We wipe everything clean on the van, grab the jackets, the shotgun, and the shells, and start to head for our hotel.

Just then, a car pulls up behind the van, flooding the rear doors with its halogen headlights.

"Hey," someone yells, "Your friends, the two guys from the ballpark, they around here? They're supposed to tip me a hundred for finding you guys. I been cruising the area waiting for them."

It's the cab driver who tipped off Zombie Guy and the Fat Fuck to our whereabouts.

"Yeah, they were out looking for you," Nick says. "They're right down the street. Wait here, and we'll go get them. I think they each had a hundred for you."

Back at the Mark Hopkins, there are choices to be made. Should we call the cops on the cabbie, claiming that he and the drunk were seen trying to break into a white van? Or should we let it go at that and see what we can find about who owns the van and where our newly deceased attackers are connected?

"We get the cops involved, and they're only going to fuck things up," Nick says. "Some Junior G Man will get the cabbie talking about where he picked us up, how we got off the ferry at the ballpark, and how he dropped us off for the Fairmont and room 801. Once they get that far, it's a quick step to the van on California Street, and maybe if they're good, a half step more to the white van with two bodies inside, sitting in a canyon in Fairfax."

"We can trace the VIN on the van easy enough," I say.

"Let's look through their jackets. Maybe they left their IDs in them."

Nick grabs one and tosses the other to me.

The wallet is easy to find and easy to dig through. There's seven hundred dollars in c-notes and a driver's license issued in Nevada, nothing else.

"Want me to go first?" Nick asks.

"Yeah, what is this? Liar's Poker?"

"I got eight hundred and twenty bucks and a Nevada license made out to

Gerald R. Ford," Nick says. "Thing is, Zombie Guy's picture is on it."
"That's it?"
"That's it. Nada mas. What are you holding?"
"You got me beat on the money," I say, "But maybe I can do you better on the Nevada Driver's License. How does Gideon C. Bible grab you?"
"Is the Fat Fuck's kisser on it?"
"Yup."
"You win."
Checking the VIN is our next task. Our two contacts for that are both in Vegas. Roland Rivers is a politically connected guy who runs an office out of the county jail just off the strip. The other is Detective Jake Glover, a happy-hour-connected cop from South Las Vegas.
"So, who do you like for the VIN check?" I ask.
"We could call Roland," Nick says. "Trouble with that is he owes us a few favors, and if we call him now, he's probably in his Jacuzzi with some babe, so he'll get to it tomorrow."
"True," I say.
"Glover's probably half loaded at the Happy Wanderer Bar and Grill. You know he could use the money. Offer him two hundred?"
I nod.
Nick punches in a number on his burner phone and puts it on speaker. Loud music from Journey and people laughing are the first things we hear.
"Yeah, Glover here. What the hell do you want?"
"I got a VIN number that needs tracing and two hundred bucks for the man who does it."
"Just a goddamn minute... Hey, barkeep, turn down that jukebox. I can't even hear myself think ...Yeah, it's too goddamn loud. How in the hell can a cop make an extra buck with all of that going on?"
Nick rolls his eyes.
I'm about to lose it to laughter.
"Okay, Nick," Glover says. "Give me the number. I'll have it for you in an hour."
"We need to do something else," Nick says when he gets off the phone with Glover. "We can't have that cab driver hanging around by the van. If the cops get interested in it, we could be back in the picture."
"So, we should do like we said we would," I say. "We'll have our friends, Gerald R. Ford and Gideon C. Bible each drop a hundred on him."
Midnight San Francisco has quieted down.
No more flashing blue lights. The cops have left the Fairmont.
Smoke from distant fires clings to everything.

We make our way down California Street toward the white van. Except something is wrong.

The van is gone.

The cab is still where we left it. It sits idling. The driver sits behind the wheel, except something is definitely wrong. Part of his head is missing, resulting from three bullet holes in the windshield.

We turn to where the drunk was sitting.

He's still there, bottle in hand.

He's propped against the brownstone wall.

He's sitting in a puddle of piss.

A bullet hole is in the center of his forehead.

He's done yelling the news to passersby.

Chapter Thirty-three

Nick:

We make our way back to the Mark Hopkins after finding the drunk and the cabbie, both dead of gunshot wounds. One is sprawled on the sidewalk in a puddle of piss. The other sits in his taxi's front seat, one slot removed from where the white van was parked. Our best guess is that whoever shot both of them took the van and high-tailed it out of the area.

"I don't see how they can get a fix on us," Jimmy says. "Even if they trace our rental Jeep, they won't have the Mark Hopkins for our address. They'll have Milwaukee Avenue in Chicago."

"Yeah, lucky us," I say. "We get invited to a private showing for a real estate transaction and end up as targets in a rolling shooting gallery. We don't even know who's trying to get us."

My burner phone rings. It's Jake Glover, the best police detective money can buy. I put him on speaker.

"These goddamn cell phones you guys give me ain't worth a shit," he says. "I couldn't work your VIN at the lounge. Too loud there. Couldn't hear shit, so I had to go back to my office."

"Yeah? You find out anything?"

"Give you the headline, for starters, or you want the whole sob story?"

"Both," Jimmy yells at the phone.

"Donnie Mascarella, the amphetamine king of Sin City and several nearby states," Glover says. "That's his white van you guys are

interested in. He runs an outfit called LA-SF-VEGAS Freedom
Leasing—that's what the van is registered to. It's supposed to be a good
deal for people dying to get out of San Francisco and LA. They rent one
of Donnie's vans or trucks to move their furniture to Vegas. He gives
them a cheap rate. They grab it quick. The thing is, they don't know
they're also hauling a couple hundred pounds of amphetamine."

"So, he's getting the dope from the gangs in SF and LA?" Jimmy asks.

"Not the way the DEA guys have it scoped," Glover says. "They figure
it's coming in from what used to be called Burma. Myanmar. It's a hell
of a lot cheaper there. The theory is that Donnie buys used cars from
Americans living there. Gives them a decent buck, then ships the car
with a load of dope hidden in it to one of the port cities, LA or San
Fran."

"So, what happens then to the car?" Jimmy asks.

"He gets some dirtbag with a driver's license to pick up the car and drive
it to a chop shop. Funny thing, one of Donnie's moving vehicles is sitting
there waiting, ready to take on cargo headed for our fair city."

"How long has he been doing this?" I ask.

"Maybe a couple years."

"So, why don't they bust him?" Jimmy asks.

"Good question. The best I can figure is there's something a lot bigger
involved. That Myanmar crew is pretty dirty. Christ, their government
might be worse than ours."

"So, Donnie's crew is running around carte blanche?" Jimmy asks

"Nah, not that free. The little guys get busted enough to keep Donnie
worried, but the bigger guys? Pretty much hands-off. 'Let's give them
enough rope,' the feds say, but I don't know what for. You know
Donnie's connected, don't you? He's the nephew of Little Philly
Petrillo."

We thank Glover for the info and ring-off. Minutes go by as we stare at
each other while we think.

We're tired after a long day of trying to figure things out while dodging
bullets.

Jimmy finally speaks.

"Donnie's boys aren't walking around with Geiger counters to check out
the radium dials on the watches they steal."

"No, it's a lot bigger than that."

"What did your wife say about Baby Lon? Lon means ready for battle?"

"Yeah, in German."

"We could use a pipeline into what the feds know about this. Don't we
have a congressman who owes us?"

"Ernesto Rivera has the district covering the Pilsen neighborhood in

Chicago. He and Jacky are tight. I think our people got him elected."
"Well?" Jimmy asks.
"Maybe too direct," I say. "We go to him, and he'll talk to Jacky. Then you'll get Jacky butting in like he knows everything. That means a confrontation between Jacky and Muriel. They'll fight over the house in Fairfax, what's going on with Carole, and poor Cousin Teddy. We don't need that."
Jimmy scratches his head and sips from his can of beer.
"Indirectly could work even better," he says.
"You're not referring to the congressman's son who has connections in Vegas law enforcement and politics, are you?"
"One in the same," Jimmy says.
"We'll call Roland Rivers at his office at the jail in the morning," I say. "For now, I suggest sleep."

Jimmy:

Coffee, sourdough, juice, and eggs are eaten. It's time to call Roland. He's happy to hear from us and is interested in what we're doing in California. He claims to be up on all the reports from law enforcement agencies.
"Let's see," he says. "Reports of arson and a gang leader shot by police in Barstow, forest fires all over the state, three guys arrested for streaking in the Mission District, two gunmen shot by police at the Fairmont. Any of that have to do with you?"
"We didn't start the forest fires," Nick says.
"I'll bet. What can I do for you guys?"
It's nice to have a friend with a sympathetic ear to lend. He listens to our lengthy tale of journeying from Barstow to Fairfax. He's familiar with many of the players in our story, having met some of them socially and some semi-professionally, like Teddy Bender, who once begged a jail cell from Roland for an overnighter when he was out of money and had a loan shark chasing him.
On a professional basis, he's had Donnie Mascarella in a cell overnight while police were getting mixed signals from prosecutors.
"Donnie's one nasty son of a bitch," Roland says. "He's got a connection with some of the military over in Myanmar. There's a good probability that they've been dealing with North Korea. You could call it a half-assed attempt to build a nuke, but that's what they were saying about North Korea twenty years ago. The Burmese aren't worried about their nice-guy image. Hell, during the Second World War, they sided with the Japanese."

"So, if Donnie's boys happened to find plutonium up in Fairfax?" Nick asks.

"Hard to say," Roland says. "It could be enough to do something big with, or it might be an addition to whatever Myanmar's acquired so far. My pop is on the congressional non-proliferation panel. From what he tells me, everything in Myanmar is in the early stages, so whatever Donnie and the boys come up with makes them heroes in the eyes of the hard-liners there."

"My question is, how did any plutonium get to Fairfax in the first place?" Nick asks.

"You could go way back into the forties and find reports of the books not balancing at Los Alamos," Roland says. "Some of that was physicists doing a piss-poor job as accountants, and some might have been thefts by Russian agents. Then there's the strong possibility, knowing the Benders, that it's all bullshit. There never was any plutonium at Fairfax."

"So, Donnie and the boys might be willing to kill over nothing?" Nick asks.

"Yeah, they've done it before," Roland says. "You need to keep your eyes on what's real. That guy David Rockwell and his old lady, Mary Ashford Stevens, aren't exactly Mickey and Minnie Mouse. They're trying to get that actor, Tucson Phoenix, to run for president. He's a real right-wing gun nut in favor of using nukes on Muslim countries."

"That doesn't surprise me," Nick says. "They seem like the types that would kill you for a nickel and charge you for the bullet."

"Rockwell tells people at cocktail parties that he comes by it all honestly," Roland says. "He claims to be the third or fourth cousin of George Lincoln Rockwell, the American Nazi that got gunned down by one of his own followers back in the sixties."

"People actually own up to things like that?" I ask.

"Yeah, Rockwell figures his chosen audience likes that kind of bravado. He says, 'I'm a little bit nicer than old George Lincoln and a whole lot smarter.'"

"I had him and his old lady figured for some kind of phonies," Nick says.

"Yeah," Roland says. "They're 24-karat charmers."

Chapter Thirty-four

Nick:

"Where the hell is all this going?" Jimmy drinks the last of his orange juice and burps. "You got Donnie Mascarella running what's left of the Philly Petrillo gang. Those guys really are trying to kill us. My bet is they're after weapons-grade uranium, plutonium, whatever you want to call it, for their slimy friends in Myanmar. Do they figure on moving in and searching the joint once Carole leaves Babylon and Rockwell's boys are no longer running security there?"

I'm holding the Nazi gold bar in my hands. It casts a warm glow, a reflection of the lights in our suite. Outside our window, at the Mark Hopkins, it looks like another dreary, smoke-filled day in San Francisco. California continues to burn.

"How do you figure this fits in?" I hold up the gold bar. "Did the Russians really send two hundred kilos of gold from Berlin to the Bay Area? If the gold is here, what's it doing stashed away in Fairfax?"

"If it's really all here. Maybe what you're holding is part of a down payment for what Donnie's boys are after," Jimmy says. "Big Philly was probably behind that Illinois National Guard rip-off back in the forties. Was he putting the word out that he also had access to stuff from Los Alamos, and he'd take gold in exchange for atomic materials? Or is this all bullshit like Roland says it could be?"

"Yeah, who can you trust?"

"Big Philly was a bullshitter," Jimmy says. "He claimed that he was in on the White Sox World Series fix in 1919 like he cashed in big. The trouble with that line was Big Philly was about five years old at the time."

I pour more coffee into our cups and stare at the mirror, trying to think. I look tired. If I were home, Dawn would tell me to go and take a nap. I've had it up to here with the Benders and this deadly puzzle they've involved us in. Maybe none of this is the truth. Maybe it's all based on out-of-control bullshit stories.

But then I look at the gold bar with the Nazi emblem on it. What did Carole Bender's scribbled note say?

"Help get me out of this mess I've inherited from Lacey. If you're reading this note, you've made it safely out of here. There's more, but no time now. Carole."

More of what? I wonder. More gold? More mess? Who did she think would be trying to stop us? Rockwell? The white van guys? The FBI? The Russians?

"Okay," Jimmy says. "We know that Big Philly hung out at Babylon a lot. Let's say he picked up on a few secrets like two hundred kilos of gold for anyone who could deliver the goods the Russians were looking for."

"Yeah," I say. "Now we're at the first fork in the road. Does he let on that his crew is the one that took down the Illinois National Guard Armory? Does he say that he can deliver atomic goods for the right price? Does he talk about a Los Alamos robbery of nuke stuff to get the attention of the Russians?"

"Maybe," Jimmy says. "Second fork in the road. If Big Philly doesn't have the nuke goods, he's only in it for the chance to rob someone of the gold. But maybe he's got a pipeline into Los Alamos. It's what? Nineteen Forty-eight? The Russians are interested in anything nuclear they can steal from the USA. There's also someone else in the game that we haven't mentioned. In '48, Mao is on his way to taking over China. He doesn't trust the Russians or the USA. You don't think he's without a spy or two in San Francisco, do you? There's a big Chinese population in the Bay Area."

"Wait," I say. "Remember, Donnie's boys are running around with Geiger counters. That means they're expecting to find nuke materials up at Babylon. If Big Philly scored at Los Alamos, that score is still sitting there. Those boys didn't bring nuke safety equipment so they could handle gold bars."

"True."

"But maybe it's only a story manufactured by Big Philly," I say. "He passes it down to Little Philly, who adds his own brand of bullshit to the story. By the time Donnie gets the story, it's back to all the nuke stuff being real and hidden at Babylon."

"This stuff is hard to figure," Jimmy says. "There's someone we're leaving out who's important in this thought process. Lacey Bender."

"She's long gone, I'm afraid. I don't think we can get her to talk unless we have a séance at a Jewish cemetery in Chicago."

"Yeah, even then, she'd probably take the fifth," Jimmy says. "Think about it, though. Lacey was a total opportunist. She made her first fortune as a bookie. Bookies make their dough by balancing the odds and taking the vig. If they get a five percent cut out of the action consistently, they're happy. They never use their own dough. It's always someone else paying the freight. Plus, they're usually ready with a high-interest loan."

"You just described banking."

"Same difference. It's like escrow, charging money to hold someone's deposit until the deal goes down. Maybe Lacey was doing the same, brokering the deal for a cut of the action."

I think about Lacey profiting from the pro-Nazi American Bund meetings in the thirties and later from the pro-Russian communist gatherings in the late thirties and early forties.

"If there was a buck out there to be made," Jimmy says, "She was there, and she was ready."

Jimmy:

Hashing things out with Nick makes us both smarter. We decide that the ingredients for mass destruction weapons are hidden at Babylon. Or only exist in a bullshit story by Lacey Bender and/or Big Philly Petrillo to get gold from the Russians. We also decide that Big Philly's nephew, Donnie Mascarella, believes the makings for mass destruction weapons are there. He wants to deliver them to his pals in Myanmar. He's also willing to kill people just to find out.

Then we have Rockwell and his old lady Mary Ashford Stevens. Have they heard the stories about Nazi gold and nuke materials at Babylon? "Damn right they have," Nick says. "Those types are always in it for themselves. Rockwell would love to have anything with a swastika on it, and dear old Mary Ashford doesn't care what's on it as long as it's gold."

"So," I say, "They play up to Carole like they're friends—friends with money to buy Babylon. Rockwell thinks he's playing it sharp by offering five point five million for Babylon when the appraised value is six mil."

"Sure," Nick says. "Rockwell figures if the gold is there, he gets over eight million in return. If the nuke materials are also there, he's got bargaining chips with right-wingers all over the world. He gets a bit of a shock when we show up on Muriel's behalf and get a deal on the place. Both he and Mary Ashford beg off when they hear the magical phrase 'Chicago money' coming from Carole's lips."

"Chicago money?" I ask. "Is Chicago money more powerful than Nazi gold?"

"It must be," Nick says. "We haven't handed over a dime of it, and already people are trying to kill us."

"Rockwell figures that Carole is moving to Hawaii and that it will take a few weeks for Jacky and Muriel to move in," I say. "He'll show everyone what a sport he is by keeping his security boys on duty in the interim. That's when he'll take the place apart, looking for the goodies."

"When Donnie's boys see Carole moving out, they'll want to move in, too," Nick says. "That could turn Babylon into a war zone. Think of it. Gold bars, weapons of mass destruction, armed and dangerous thugs with itchy trigger fingers. It sounds like American foreign policy."

"Yeah, there has to be a way to keep them from destroying Babylon," I say. "How can we get them off the reservation?"

I look at Nick.

He has that grin that says an outrageous plan could work.

Chapter Thirty-five

Nick:

My carefully laid plan, outrageous though it may be, runs into the Bender curse.

We're almost done explaining Babylon with its touch of Nazi gold and chance of nuclear fission to our newly arrived LA associates, Tony and Bruno when my cell phone rings.

It's Muriel.

I put her on speaker and give everyone in the room the be quiet sign.

She sounds like she's somewhere between hysteria and waiting for the Wellbutrin to kick in.

"It's horrible," she says. "Some shvartzer motorcycle gang has kidnapped Teddy."

In the background, we hear Eddie Scarponi.

"Hey, it ain't that bad. He got away, didn't he? He's still alive."

My guess is that Eddie's driving Muriel to another shrink appointment. She's too nervous to drive and loves bending Eddie's ear about her nerve-wracking lifestyle. Her being married to a multi-millionaire who gives her everything she wants is tough on her. It's tough on Eddie, too. He has to listen to the drama while he works his way past the demolition derby drivers in the Windy City.

"Yes, luckily, he got away from those…Well, I'm not going to say it," Muriel says.

"She's talkin' about the --."

"And I don't want you saying it either, Eddie," Muriel says. "We're better than that. We won't stoop to their level. You know how they can get."

"I was going to say, 'soul brothers motorcycle club.' Ain't that what they call themselves?"

"Yes," Muriel says. "Something like that."

"So, Teddy got away from his kidnappers?" I ask.

Jimmy, Tony, and Bruno sit on the long sofa, shaking their heads. At one time or another, each has heard a version of this routine before. Troubles with Teddy and hysterics from Muriel get dropped like wet garbage into unsuspecting laps.

"They almost killed him," Muriel says. "I thought you had him safely out of danger and on his way to something good. The doctor says they

loaded his system with drugs and alcohol and…."
Now, uncontrolled sobs are coming out of Muriel.
"Oh, my god, oh my god," she says between gasps."
"Hand me the phone," Eddie says. "You need to settle down. I'll handle it."
I can picture him reaching into the back seat of the Lincoln from the driver's seat as he navigates his way across the Michigan Avenue Bridge. A minute goes by that features sobbing and snorting from Muriel. Eddie finally gets on the phone.
"The meat wagon picked up Teddy off a sidewalk in San Rafael. They hauled him over to Marin General. The Doc says he was really out of it. Too much booze and some kind of drugs the Titsoons fed him before they took his dough and kicked him out of the car. No broken bones, but he's scraped up pretty bad from what they say. Cops took a basic report, like what happened is no big deal to them. The hospital says they'll release him to you or Jimmy."
I watch as Jimmy whacks himself on the forehead.
"Please, give me the phone back," Muriel says.
"Hold on, Nick. The lady wants to talk."
"I was trying to call Carole Bender at Babylon when I got the call about Teddy," Muriel says. "I wanted to see how the house deal was going."
Jimmy whacks himself on the forehead again.
"Oh yeah?" I say.
I always come up with something witty like that when Teddy and Muriel are forcing me to have an interesting day.
"Some guy named Julius answered the phone," Muriel says. "He said Carole couldn't come to the phone. She was taking her nap. I told him to wake her up, and he refused. Who is this thug, anyway? Just then, the call-waiting thing on my iPhone kicked in with the call about Teddy."
"Muriel, you need to settle down and let us professionals take care of Teddy and Babylon. We're going to see Carole later today. We have an appointment. You know she's up in years and needs some rest."
Muriel blows her nose and sniffs.
I don't like what I'm hearing about Julius. It sounds like he's trying to control Carole, but I'm not about to share my thoughts on that with Muriel.
"I'm sure that Julius is handling the situation," I say. "We've met him. We know him. Don't worry."
"Okay, Nick. Do what you can for poor Teddy. I trust you guys."
"Good. Give the phone back to Eddie. I want to ask him about something."
"Talk to me, Nick," Eddie says. "I'm listening."

I'm happy to hear the "I'm listening." It means he's not on speaker on his end. If he was on speaker, he'd say, "We're listening."

"How much of this shit does Jacky know about?" I ask.

"Not a word," Eddie says.

"My guess is that if she told him about Teddy and his shit, it would start World War Three."

"You got that right."

"So, you're on the way to her shrink?"

"Yeah, gonna have to ring off. Going into the parking structure now. Take it easy, Nick."

Easy for him to say, I think. He'll wait in the lobby-level coffee shop, shooting the breeze with people about the Cubs and the Bears while Muriel gets her head shrunk by Dr. Feelgood at three hundred per hour.

Jimmy:

Nick gets off the phone with Muriel, and I'm already in my flight mood. I want to run. I want to take everything I love and run off with it. I have a list. Sell our house. Cash in all the money certificates and stocks and run off. Grab my lovely wife. Talk Nick and Dawn into coming with and bringing their little princess Molly. Toss Zorro and his squeaky rabbit toy into the back seat and run. Run. Run. Run.

But then I realize for the umpteenth time that there's no place to go.

It's all been done.

It's all been done in.

Paradise is lost.

California's burning.

Florida is under water at high tide.

Bullets take their toll in all our major cities, and all we're offered are prayers and lame excuses while we wait for the final heatwave.

"This may not be too bad," Tony Stomps says. "There's a way we can put Teddy on ice that Muriel will approve of."

I realize then that I haven't been listening to the end of Nick's report to Bruno and Tony on the Babylon situation. He's gotten our LA boys up to date and involved in planning.

"You guys don't remember Doc Webster, do you?"

Everyone looks at Tony, waiting for him to continue.

"Yeah. He used to be a Michigan Boulevard doctor back in Chicago. He got wind of how drugs were an integral part of the music and entertainment industry in the Bay Area. A little bit of research and checking the facts on his calculator told him that drug recovery could make a sizable buck, maybe even better than pushing heroin and LSD.

Plus, it was all legal."

"So, what's that to us?" Nick asks.

Tony stands up from the sofa and tosses his hands into the air like his fifteen-to-one shot has just won the Kentucky Derby.

"He's right here in Marin. He's got the Fairweather Bridge Clinic. Better yet, he owes us."

"Are we supposed to sit around here all day admiring your shit-eating grin? Or are you going to tell how he owes us?" Nick asks.

"Chico Bolero," Tony says. "Mister Obnoxious Heavy-weight Champ thought he could run out on a hefty bill from Fairweather Bridge. He ran up over two million straightening out his wife and two of his girlfriends at Doc Webster's place. Then he thought he could skip paying."

"What happened then?" Nick asks.

Tony looks toward the couch.

"Tell him, Bruno."

"Chico had some car trouble," Bruno says. "He parked his Rolls Royce in front of his Brentwood estate. As he got to the front door of his home, something maybe over-heated or maybe short-circuited. Capisce? His fancy car exploded. Inside the front door of the house, Chico found a bill from Doc Webster saying his account was in arrears and now he owed three million."

"He paid the next day," Tony says. "He had the junkyard haul off what was left of the Rolls. No cops, no problem."

"And we never got a taste of that?" I ask.

"Jacky wanted it to be a favor," Tony says. "You know how he says, 'Favors are sometimes better than cash.' He may be right in this case."

Chapter Thirty-six

Nick:

Two hours ago, I wanted to kill Teddy Bender. His loose cannon act meant another major blockade in getting things settled at Babylon. The drugged-out drunk that we left sound asleep on a bench in Fairfax the afternoon before turns up as a street crime victim in Greenbrae. Do I believe poor Teddy? He claims that a bunch of black guys grabbed him, drugged him, and tossed him out of a car after taking all his money.

"There are a few discrepancies with Theodore's story," Doc Webster says. "The police say that a rental Cadillac in Theodore's name was found in a ditch against a tree near where they found him bleeding on the sidewalk."

Doc Webster, the second part of the Teddy/ Webster equation, is ready to do anything he can to smooth things for Teddy and our crew. You could say that he's the positive end of the equation. For the three-million-dollar favor our boys did when they collected his bill from Heavyweight blowhard Chico Bolero, he should be positive.

"Hey, I talked with the coppers about Theodore, and they won't pursue anything," Doc says. "As far as the hospital, well… I'm something of a legend around here. We have a copacetic relationship between Fairweather Bridge and the health care people in Marin. Our annual rock show extravaganza raises funds for many programs around the Bay Area."

Jimmy and I are sitting in Doc's office at Fairweather. Teddy has been sedated and admitted into Fairweather for an inpatient stay of sixty to ninety days. The place is a paradise among the hills with formal gardens, swimming pools, exercise rooms, and gourmet food.

"I'm delighted you guys called me in your hour of need," Doc says. "I'm so grateful to Jacky and your guys for helping me with that Chico asshole. It's time I gave something back."

Doc presses a button on the intercom on his desk.

"Maria, please bring us some refreshments. Uh, coffees all around and some sparkling water? Okay for you guys?"

We both nod.

Doc is one of those guys that has found new life by moving west. There's still a bit of Chicago in his speech, but the three-piece suit favored by high-priced Michigan Boulevard doctors has been replaced by a silk shirt, designer jeans, and high-end moccasins. An elaborate leather lace holds a turquoise Kokopelli pendant that rides a foot below his neck.

"Excuse my curiosity," Jimmy says. "That wouldn't be a fertility god hanging from your neck, would it?"

Doc laughs.

"It is, as a matter of fact. I guess it's been doing as advertised. I'm lucky to be married to a beautiful woman, and we have five kids together. Maybe you remember Angel Mascara, the punk rocker sensation? Kill Me with Your Bleeding Love? Heroin Heartbeat Shutdown? Dance Me Through Your Deadhead Dreams?"

"Wow, you're married to her?" Jimmy asks. "I thought she was dead of an overdose."

"Publicity," Doc says. "Angel grew up a Mormon, but when the punk craze hit, she saw a good thing and grabbed it. She was in the Tabernacle Choir when the group Blending Your Blood came to Salt Lake. Their featured singer did O.D. there. What do you know? Angel filled in and the rest, as they say, is history."

"So, she helps you here at the clinic?" I ask.

"That's putting it mildly. She has a lot of connections with music people. Some need our help, and others have friends who have been helped here. We do a major concert every year with help from some of the popular groups. All the proceeds go to charities around the Bay Area. We have a concert coming up in about four weeks. If you're here, then send me a guest list, and you'll have deluxe seating on me."

I look at Jimmy. I know what he thinks before he says it.

"We're a bit leery of concerts," he says. "We were supposed to be guests at the Highway 91 concert in Vegas. Damn near went, taking our wives and Nick's little daughter. My wife's bronchitis made us think twice, and we all stayed home watching Harry Potter when the massacre went down."

"Jesus, you were lucky," Doc says. "That was awful."

"Yeah," Jimmy says. "I still have nightmares about it."

Our coffee and sparkling water arrive, delivered by Maria on a teak tray with anchors carved into the wood.

"Well, there must be some other way I can help you guys," Doc says.

"You know I used to play golf with Jacky back in Chicago when I could get him away from all the business pressures. Geez, it would be fun to hang out with him again."

"You might get your wish," Jimmy says. "Nick and I are out here trying to close a deal on a house in Fairfax for Jacky and Muriel."

"You're not referring to Babylon, are you?" Doc asks.

Jimmy:

I'm starting to think that maybe there is a God who likes to put you through hell before he takes off his mask and smiles at you. Doc Webster knows something about Babylon.

"Look," he says. "I want to help you guys, but my hands are tied if I adhere to the patient confidentiality code. On the other hand, if we decide that we're talkin' Chicago here and no one later has any comebacks hitting them in the ass, I can talk. Okay?"

"All we need is info that will help," Nick says. "We don't publish reports on what we do, and if you want, we'll forget we even met you."

We start with Carole Bender.

"I see her as an outpatient these days," Doc says. "We've had her here several times as an inpatient for several weeks at a time. Try as we may, we haven't gotten to the core of her anxiety. Something happened back when she was a young girl. Something very threatening keeps giving her nightmares. She sometimes acts out violently, throwing objects around and even firing a rifle into the canyon at perceived intruders. Police have been involved, but nothing has ever been found down there. No intruders. I've asked her what she sees when she fires the rifle. What is she looking at?"

"And what does she say?" Nick asks.

"Ghosts, maybe. Something that won't stay dead."

"She wants to quitclaim the property to Jacky and Muriel," I say. "She tells us she's had enough of Babylon. She wants to spend the years she has left in Paris. I think she's pretty secretive about that. We heard her give two of her friends a different story about moving to Hawaii."

"Oh?"

"Yeah, Mary Ashford Stevens and her husband, David Rockwell. They were up there. We had a drink with them. Rockwell's security company is there around the clock. He says it's to keep Carole safe."

Doc is silent for a minute. He puts the fingertips of both hands together and stares at us.

"What impression did you have of them?" He asks.

"I thought she was a real bitch," Nick says. "Rockwell seemed wound pretty tight. There's a lot of that whacko right-wing shit around lately. They wanted to buy the place from Carole, but she says she's not interested. She wants Jacky and Muriel to have it. They offered her twice what Muriel and Jacky will get it for."

"We've had Mary Ashford Stevens up here after every one of her divorces. Once, it was part of a court decree when she attempted to shoot her third husband. Anybody else would have done time in the slammer, but Mary Ashford got hold of an expensive lawyer who knew where enough of the bodies were buried on the judge's side. I could give you the fancy textbook name for it, but basically, Mary Ashford Stevens cares only for Mary Ashford Stevens. I wouldn't be surprised if she's killed people in her past."

"What about Rockwell?" I ask. "Anything on him?"

"He does her bidding. She likes rich men that she can push around. She makes them try to be as macho as possible. The tougher, the better. That's what eventually gets them into trouble. About the time they fall on their asses, she takes them to divorce court and threatens to go public with a major sob story about their illegal activities."

"In Rockwell's case, it might be stories about his neo-fascist antics," Nick says. "Something like that gets out, and his business interests could go down the drain."

"Yeah," Doc says. "I've heard about his American Nazi pedigree. Mary

117

Ashford may be pushing him to go ballistic on that. Like I say, she uses sex to push her husbands. It gets bizarre. They either break their butts to please Mary, or they can go sleep with the dog."

"Any of them refuse?" I ask. "Tell her to go away?"

"Her first husband was Roger Crowder, the financier," Doc says. "She wanted him to channel ten million dollars to her account in Panama. She had something going down there, she said. That's how she put it. Something going down there. He refused at first. It was illegal, but then he gave in."

"Why?" Nick asks.

"Her cousin showed up with a gun. Crowder could either do it, or they'd kill him."

"Her cousin?" I ask.

"Yeah," Doc says. "You know she's connected, don't you? She used to be Mary Ann Petrillo."

Chapter Thirty-seven

Nick:

Sharing coffees and fizz waters with Doc Webster proves to be a great source of information. He's just told Jimmy and me that Mary Ashford Stevens is a vicious money-grubber who would kill to get her way. She's also a Petrillo family member, the wonderful killers from the white vans run by Mary's cousin Donnie Mascarella.

"Figures," Jimmy says. "Remember how Rockwell's security guards weren't worried about the phony surveyors from the white vans? Rockwell probably told them to ignore them as threats."

"And he did that why?" I ask. "Was it because Rockwell is in on the deal with cousin Donnie and the boys, wanting to dig up nuke materials to ship them off to Myanmar? Or is Rockwell just taking orders from Mary Ashford Stevens?"

I look at Doc Webster. His head swivels back and forth from me to Jimmy and back.

"Nuke materials? Myanmar?" Doc stares at us over the top of his aviator sunglasses.

"Yeah," Jimmy says. "Toss in the possibility of eight million bucks in Nazi gold bars and people trying to kill us at the Fairmont. Soon you'll start getting the whole megillah."

"Jesus, I heard about the shooting at the Fairmont," Doc says. "They were after you guys? Don't they know any better than to fuck with our crew?"

I like it when I hear the words "fuck with our crew." Doc has just reaffirmed his allegiance to our team. If he takes it any further, he'll be receiving a burner cell phone every month from Pulaski Road in Chicago.

We fill him in on how helping Muriel buy a house has led to life-threatening situations involving neo-Nazis and foreign governments with connections to North Korea.

"So, what about Rockwell?" Jimmy asks.

"If I had to bet, Rockwell is just doing Mary Ashford's bidding," Doc says. "Remember, she's always in control. I don't know this Donnie guy, but unless he's some kind of a god, Mary's pulling his chain, too. If that wasn't the case, Mary would be long gone. It's her way or the highway."

"So, the most logical conclusion is that Mary's running the show and Donnie and Rockwell are either lackeys or dupes," Jimmy says.

"Rockwell may not even know about Donnie being a close relative of Mary's."

We sip our coffees in silence for a minute. Somewhere off in another part of Fairweather Bridge, a harpsichord plays "Here Comes the Sun."

"It's good to analyze the parties involved," Doc says. "Mary's not going to take a back seat to anyone. Rockwell will go along as long as he thinks he's a macho stud for Mary. I don't know this Donnie Mascarella, but he better have more than one deal up his sleeve. If the nuke stuff is all he's got, Mary will take him out as soon as she can."

"Even if he's a relative?" I ask.

"You could ask Mary's mother," Doc says. "She's living in some mosquito-infested trailer park near Lake Okeechobee. Mary has nothing to do with her. She told Mom that she'd have some drugged-up Cuban come up from Miami and slit her throat if she kept bothering her."

I look at Jimmy, wondering if he's thinking what I'm thinking. Has best-selling chick-lit novelist Mary Ashford Stevens already taken Carole Bender out of the play? Are Rockwell's boys taking Babylon apart, looking for treasures?

"Muriel tried to talk to Carole on the phone," Jimmy says. "The security guy in charge, Julius, refused. He said she was taking a nap."

"That's not like Carole," Doc says. "She hardly ever naps. She always takes calls. She's hungry for connection. When salespeople cold call her, she gets into conversations with them. I think she's even had some in for drinks."

"I don't like this," Jimmy says. "This could get ugly and rough."

"Maria," Doc says into his intercom. "Get Carole Bender on the phone for me. I don't have her number handy."

Doc looks at Jimmy and me and winks.

"We'll see what this Julius asshole is up to."

"It's ringing," Maria's voice comes over the intercom.

"Babylon, may I help you?" The voice sounds like Julius.

"This is Doctor Webster. I'd like to talk with Carole Bender, please."

"She's indisposed right now. Can't come to the phone. Can I take a message?"

"Yes, is this Julius?"

"Uh, uh yeah."

"Julius, you say Carole Bender is indisposed and can't come to the phone right now. Correct?"

"Uh, yeah. Maybe later if you call back."

"Julius, do you know what a 5150 order is?"

"No. What is it?"

"It's an order to bring someone into an institution for treatment for a mental disorder. I have such an order ready to be executed on Carole Bender. I'll be arriving shortly with the police to execute that order. You say Carole is safe."

"Uh, yeah, she is."

"Good. By the way, this phone conversation is being recorded. It will be part of the legal proceedings should anything of a negative nature come up regarding Carole Bender's treatment."

"Uh, yeah. Okay."

Click.

Jimmy:

We head out for Babylon, cutting our way through the smoke that has drifted into Marin County from someplace where forests, houses, and people have burned to death. Doc Webster is in the lead in his Mercedes, followed by the Fairweather Bridge ambulance, then us.

"We'll pick up a police escort in Fairfax and possibly another from the county sheriff's office," Doc says. "They like what we do at Fairweather. We even have a program for officers under stress to spend a long weekend chilling out. No charge, of course. We believe in networking."

If networking gives you a police escort as opposed to a ride in a police van, I'm a believer, too. I'm thinking ahead to what we'll find at Babylon, knowing that if anything wrong has happened to Carole, there'll be hell to pay. Muriel will have a meltdown. Jacky will accuse us of getting in over our heads and not asking him for help.

On the other hand, if Carole is okay, Muriel is still capable of having a meltdown. As far as us asking Jacky for help, he'll want to know why we can't handle a simple house sale when he's already okayed the three-million-dollar sale price.

Nick is on the speakerphone with Bruno and Tony. They've been scouting the road to Babylon. We want to know what happened to the white van that veered off the road, taking two guys who tried to kill us to the canyon floor. Was it still down there? Were their bodies rotting in the heat?

"Interesting stuff," Tony says. "We stopped in a driveway across from where the van went down into the canyon. At least the nearest we could figure from the busted glass on the road and the busted-up bushes and trees. We couldn't see any van at the bottom, so we went back to where we parked."

"That's when we ran into Mr. Shaughnessy," Bruno says. "He lives in the house where we parked. He didn't see the van go down into the canyon, but he saw them bring it back up with a big wrecker from some outfit called LA-SF-VEGAS Freedom Leasing."

"That's the company run by Donnie Mascarella," Nick says. "Did they haul up any bodies?"

"No, not that he could see, but here's the good part," Tony says. "Shaughnessy says he went across the street to watch the van get hauled up onto the flatbed. He says some Asian guy was out there yelling at one of the guys in charge."

"What was his problem?" Nick asks.

"Shaughnessy couldn't figure that out," Tony says. "But the guy was swearing in Burmese. 'Lee gon, lee gon.' Shaughnessy used to work at the embassy in Rangoon. He says it's a small world. You step outside your house in Fairfax, and some guy you vaguely remember from Myanmar is yelling 'dick head, dick head' in a language you haven't heard spoken in years."

"Shaughnessy knew him from before?" I ask.

"Not by name, but he recognized him as one of those connected guys that had a free pass from some of the more questionable types in the government."

"Did Shaughnessy talk to the guy?" I ask.

"No. Never got the chance. The 'dick head, dick head' guy saw Shaughnessy standing on the side of the road and immediately shut up. He jumped into a silver BMW and took off toward downtown Fairfax. It sounds to me like Donnie's playmates from Myanmar are on the scene. At least one of them is."

"Yeah," Nick says. "It sounds like the Myanmar group might have its doubts about the way Donnie's boys are handling things. It could get dangerous."

"Yeah," Tony says. "Not only for Donnie's crew, but maybe for us, too."

Chapter Thirty-eight

Nick:

Our caravan drives through Greenbrae on its way to Fairfax and our planned rescue of Carole Bender from Babylon and David Rockwell's henchmen if Carole needs rescuing. The jury is still out on that. Nevertheless, we come armed with enough shrink forms to choke the proverbial horse. It's all bluster and bullshit, but it comes delivered by Doc Webster. He certainly should be able to out bullshit the likes of Julius, the security guard, and David Rockwell, Nazi wannabe if he's even present.

Finding out from Bruno and Tony that the Burmese have landed amongst us, or at least one of them has, puts a new spin on things. It draws commentary from one of my favorite critics.

"This goddamn shit is for the birds," Jimmy says. "Every time we get involved in Muriel's bullshit, it gets worse. We're supposed to be up here on a business trip, buying billiard tables for the casino, checking out the talent for the lounge at Dominos. Instead, we're dodging bullets over a fucking house closing. How the hell does this happen?"

Traffic slows as we enter San Anselmo. A line of cars with turn signals on is attempting to move into our lane. Somewhere up ahead is an accident or construction.

"The trouble with this deal is that Jacky and Muriel don't talk to each other," Jimmy says. "If they did, we'd never be involved in Babylon. She'd say she'd want to buy it, and he'd say, 'No, we're going to Rio or Paris instead.' and that would be it. She'd have her luxury, and we'd avoid all this bullshit."

"You're sure of that?" I ask.

"No. That's the trouble. Both of them think that we can't wait to get involved in some crazy bullshit. Like we're dying to get out on the road and get away from running the Dominos. We're executives, you know. We have respected positions in Vegas. Chamber of Commerce meetings. Mayor's luncheons. Non-profit fundraisers."

"I know exactly how you feel about those things," I say.

Jimmy grumbles a low, slow growl.

"It seems to me that...."

"...Save it, Nick. I know what you're going to say. I hate going to those things. I usually send our in-house lawyer Marlene or try to weasel Dawn and Cassandra into going."

I'm about to answer Jimmy when my burner phone rings. It's Jacky in his run-away-locomotive mode.

"Here's what's happening. Both you guys listening, right? I talked it over with Muriel and called Gene Cornell into the picture. We've okayed the deal on the house, this Babylon joint. It's still standing, right? Well, even if it isn't, Gene says the lot alone is worth six million, so we ain't dumb taking it for three, right? Now, I've wired the three mil to Carole's account at Wells Fargo in San Rafael and put two other wires in the bunch – one for two hundred thousand for Murray Bender and another for the same amount for Teddy Bender. Keep 'em happy, right? So, we're spending three point four on our end. Carole can vacate right away, and you guys will stay at least long enough to secure the place with new locks and security fencing all around it. Where are you guys now?"

I look at Jimmy. He shrugs.

"We're on our way there," I say. "An old friend of yours is driving up with us in another vehicle. Doc Webster has treated Carole as a patient for a few years. We're having him check on her. He's also treating Teddy."

"Yeah, that's all good," Jacky bulldozes on. "Muriel told me Teddy got jacked up by some street shvuggies. Listen, you need any help with heavy lifting, call Tony and Bruno. Have them fly up."

"Yeah, good idea," Jimmy says. "We had a little run-in with the leftovers from the Petrillo gang. They're interested in Babylon, too."

"Who's running that crew? Donnie Mascarella?"

"Yeah," Jimmy says. "Word is he's running dope from Myanmar."

"And what's he giving them in exchange?"

Jimmy:

How do you answer Jacky's question, "What's Donnie Mascarella giving the crew from Myanmar?"

Do we go full disclosure and drop nuke materials and Nazi gold bars into Jacky's lap? Do we describe, shot for shot, how we took down white van number one and then snookered white van number two's boys into a fatal shootout with the SF cops? Should we have already reported that to the boss? Even though we have little evidence to support our suspicions that someone soon will try trading plutonium for Nazi plunder in Jacky's new house? In this place where Frankie Rat Pack supposedly screwed Marilyn Monroe clones?

I look at Nick.

He shrugs.

I shrug back.

If traffic noises from a half-mile backup can be described as silence, we have silence, a silence that seems to stretch on for minutes.

Of course, it's only been seconds, and then we realize that we could have dumped all the suspected grief into Jacky's lap, and it wouldn't have registered a bit. He's been busy having another conversation on his end. With Muriel?

Eddie Scarponi?

No. he's been talking with Gene Cornell, aka Yevgeny Kornikova, a world-class hustler who walked out of Russia under Putin's nose with most of the proceeds from the Moscow Circus International. The fact that Gene's married to Putin's second cousin Anastasia gives him a certain amount of immunity from harm.

The fact that Gene is vice-chair of Congressman Ernesto Rivera's re-election campaign elevates him from someone who absconded with funds to someone who can be a valuable conduit between influential people. It's no accident that Gene books most of the significant talent into the main theatre at the Galloping Dominos Casino. It's also probably no accident that Anastasia's Conversational Russian courses at Northwestern University are favorites of State Department personnel.

"Yeah, back to you guys." Jacky is back on the phone and ready to bulldoze some more. "This Donnie Mascarella character, he's running what's left of the Petrillo bunch. Big Philly's dead, Little Philly's in jail, and Donnie's trying to carry on the family tradition, which in my estimation is to fill the world with bullshit."

I look at Nick. He rolls his eyes as Jacky continues.

"Big Philly tried to take the Dominicans, Trujillo and company, for a ride back in the fifties. Supposedly, he had weapons stolen from the Illinois National Guard Armory. He'd sell them to the Trujillos for a bundle, half down, half later. They were dumb enough to fall for it. Big Philly never delivered. He told them the boat that left New Orleans got hijacked by Castro's boys. They say that's why Big Philly mysteriously disappeared in the late fifties. Later on, Little Philly tried the same bullshit line on the Contras in Nicaragua and a couple African nations. No takers. Word had gotten around."

"Yeah, we heard some of that," Nick says. "Donnie might be trying the same sort of deal with the people from Myanmar, Jacky. You just never know. He could be…."

"Yeah, he could be carrying on the family tradition," Jacky says. "Only this time, what's he going to tell them? He's got a nuke for sale? Listen, boys. This is a simple deal. Forget Donnie. Just take care of the house. Take care of Carole. All the money has been transferred; the papers have been taken care of. Relax and enjoy yourselves in the Bay Area. Gotta run. Take care."

Traffic starts to move. A police cruiser has pulled in front of Doc Webster's car and leads the way with its blue light flashing. The ambulance from Fairweather Bridge Clinic follows Doc. A package delivery truck and a beer truck have pulled into our lane behind the ambulance before we can react. We're staring at a light beer logo.

"Nothing like a police escort," Nick says. "You don't suppose we should be concerned about the white van following us, do you?"

I see two Asian faces through the front window of the van. Are they two guys on their way to lay carpets, or are they sent by the Burmese guy who yells "Dick head, dick head"?

"Are we being paranoid? Or just careful?" Nick asks.

"I vote for careful," I say.

Nick turns and pulls his Glock, resting the barrel on the top of his seat, pointing at the van.

"I vote for careful, too," he says.

Chapter Thirty-nine

Nick:

We drive along with the top down, windows up, and air conditioner on full --- the preferred California cruising style of Jimmy Cox. He slows the Caddy down to a crawl. We're sitting behind the beer truck that's wormed its way into our police escort convoy.

"I could go after a beer," he says, "But not like this."

The white van stays on our tail. I've got a decent view of it through the passenger side mirror. The two Asian guys in the front seat talk back and forth with each other. Are they arguing about what to do about us? Or are they just a couple guys who could care less about Nick and Jimmy?

I hold the Glock just below the top of my seat, pointed in their direction, waiting for any sort of dangerous move. There's more talking back and forth. The guy in the passenger seat reaches back behind his chair and retrieves something. He holds it like a pistol.

I get ready.

Then I notice. It's a cordless power tool.

He shows it to the driver: the driver nods and laughs.

Who's the joke on? I wonder, is it on us?

The passenger seat guy puts the power drill back behind his seat. He laughs.

Traffic is heavy. The sky looks and smells like what used to pass for air near the steel mills in East Chicago. When did California Dreamin' leave the state, I wonder?

"Those guys behind us up to some shit?" Jimmy asks.

"Guy had a power drill, showing it to his buddy. I damn near shot him. Thought he had a piece."

Now the guy has something else in his hands from behind the seat. I make out a cylindrical shape. Two of them. He's got one in each hand, and he's laughing like he just put one over on someone, us, maybe?

I'm tense. I'm ready.

He hands one to his buddy and puts his feet up on the dashboard.

Beer bottles. They both take a swig and laugh some more.

"What now?" Jimmy asks. "They trying to kill us?"

"If they drink enough beer, they might slam into us," I say. "No worry at this speed."

We move ahead.

The white van follows.

We slow down and stop just past an intersection.

The white van turns left toward a sign that says, "Downtown San Anselmo." I look back and see the back doors on the van are tied with a rope to keep something from sliding out.

Carpenters? Carpet installers?

My burner phone rings.

It's Tony Stomps.

"We drove up to Babylon. Drove past it to take a look. Two security guys with dogs, the kind you hate. Didn't see much else, so we drove back down toward town to look for food and a place for Bruno to take a dump. Where are you guys?"

"Stuck in traffic in San Anselmo," I say. "We're supposed to have a cop car leading the way, but we've been separated. I think we're about eight cars back from Doc Webster. Somehow we're gridlocked."

Horns honk up ahead of us. Somewhere off in the distance, a siren wails. Maybe another of Doc's friends coming with a squad car to deliver us to Babylon? I look around for any signs of a cop car or a white van. Nothing.

"So, we go into this sandwich and beer joint in Fairfax," Tony says. "Who do we see? Some guy who looks like a Little Philly Petrillo knock-off. He's sitting there arguing with an Asian guy who's saying, 'Donnie, we straighten this shit out real soon. No dick head, dick head stuff. Old lady no sell house? So what? We go in and take it.' Donnie asks, 'What about the old lady? What do we do with her?' The Asian guy just sits there and laughs."

"That must be the guy that Shaughnessy saw. Didn't he say that the guy kept yelling 'dick head' at the guys pulling the white van out of the canyon?"

"Yeah, it gets better," Tony says. "Donnie tells this guy that Rockwell's boys will help with the heavy lifting and digging. They've scoped out some possible sites where stuff might be buried. Dick head guy says, 'Good. Need good help. Offer big reward. Gold sometime turn into lead.' Then he laughs like hell."

"What happened then?"

"They finished their beers and took off. This Asian guy had a couple of his paisano lackeys with him. They were camped out in a booth nearby. When the 'Dick Head' guy stood up to leave, they jumped up like their assholes were on fire. Far as I know, Donnie only had some fat-ass torpedo waiting for him outside in a black Buick."

"Yeah, he might be a little light on personnel these days," Jimmy says. "I always thought that driving those vans was dangerous."

I'm about to say something to Tony when I see people getting out of their cars and looking at something ahead of us. I hear another siren getting closer to us.

Someone's running toward us from up ahead.

I aim the Glock. I'm ready.

"Tony, I can't talk. Call you back," I manage.

The running figure is in my sights. He's carrying something. Why is he running toward us? Everyone else is heading the other way toward the sirens. Is this guy from the white van crew? I refuse to die from instant lead poisoning in San Anselmo.

"Wait, don't fire," Jimmy yells. "It's Doc Webster."

Jimmy:

Doc's in a panic. We get him into the back seat fast. He tries to tell us what went down, and it sounds like, "Habba habba shot. Umma, two guys. Umma silencers. The cop. A white van cut off. Got ambulance driver. Silencers. Two Asian."

That's enough for me. It's no time to sit and talk. We do that, and someone else will be saying, "Habba habba" about us. I have just enough room to clear the truck ahead of us. It's time to get out of Dodge.

The beautiful rose bushes planted in the San Anselmo Garden Club's median strip are no match for the Caddy. We drive through the plants and bounce over the curb into the southbound lane.

It's empty of traffic except for the two guys from the white van. They're running toward us. Both have a pistol with a suppressor on the barrel—one of the guys fires at us on the run.

"Thub, thub," the gun sounds. The Caddy's rear passenger side window shatters.

Nick points his gun as the two guys stop to aim. The Glock barks four times, and the two Asian guys fall to the pavement. Blood flows from their heads and chests.

"I knew they were shits," Nick says. "I came so close to wasting them a few minutes back, but who could say for sure?"

"You couldn't know for sure," I say. "They looked like carpenters on their way to a remodel job."

I think about how the white van turned off at the sign that said, "Downtown San Anselmo." That's how they got ahead of the traffic mess-up. Somewhere there's a side street that will get us ahead of all this.

Traffic is light, and we cruise along through a pleasant-looking town. One block over on the highway, it's all tied up. We've just been shot at by two thugs and came close to buying the farm. I should be thinking about the next danger waiting for us, but I'm not.

The downtown is full of unique shops and restaurants, and I'm thinking how nice it would be to stroll along with Cassandra. She loves places like this. And then I wonder. What the hell am I doing this for? I should just walk away from it. I don't need people shooting at me. I don't need Muriel and her crackpot family.

A sidewalk café has people enjoying sandwiches and drinks. That should be us, I think. I picture us sitting with our crew, the one that matters most to us --- Nick, Dawn, Molly, and our dog Zorro.

"Why can't we have this kind of life?" I ask.

"Maybe later," Nick says. "Turn right. Then make a quick left back onto the main road we just left. We'll be out of the woods and on the way to Babylon."

It snaps me back to the present. I know how he means it, but we're not out of the woods. If anything, we're going in deeper. Others are counting on us --- Carole, Tony, Bruno.

I look in the rearview mirror.

No white van. I take a deep breath and let it out.

I look again.
Something else is missing.
"Where the hell is Doc?"
Nick turns and looks into the back seat.
"He's down on the floor," Nick says. "There's blood coming from his head."

Chapter Forty

Nick:

This ain't right, I'm telling myself as I stare down at Doc Webster, laid-out face down on the backseat floor of the Caddy. His head is bloody. Pieces of glass from the shattered passenger side window are scattered like rough-cut jewels. Some sparkle like diamonds. Others have the look of rubies from the blood and the red leather upholstery.

"This is all we fuckin' need," Jimmy says.

He swings the Caddy into a shopping mall parking lot and heads for the shade of a tree, away from the cluster of parked cars.

Crazy thoughts race through my head. Losing Doc means a lot of negatives dumped on Nick and Jimmy. For starters, we both like Doc. He's one of the good guys. He's on our side.

He's also a three-million-dollar favor owed to Jacky that we've just started to collect on. Jesus, no Doc means no treatment for Teddy Bender. Who the hell wants that clown out on the street? What about springing Carole Bender from Babylon with Doc's ambulance, police escort, and bullshit 5150 order?

"See anyone following us?" Jimmy asks.

I look up from Doc's bloody head and scan the area we've just left. I don't see anything, but I start to feel it. Behind us, there's a mess. From what Doc tried to tell us, as he jumped into the car, the two Asian guys shot a cop and the Fairview Bridge ambulance driver. Now, the two shooters are lying dead on the street in San Anselmo.

Now I wonder. Were there just the two guys that tried to kill us? Or are there more of them? Had someone else in their group cut off the traffic flow? Or is gridlock now a common feature of Californication?

"I don't see anyone trailing us," I say. "But how do we know? These guys aren't wearing uniforms with matching hats."

The Glock is wet in my sweaty hand. I check the magazine and reload.

"CTSD," Jimmy says. "That's us, and it ain't funny anymore."

He's right. Continuous Traumatic Stress Disorder was funny the first time he joked about us having it. We laughed like hell.

Now, I'm feeling like hell.

Jimmy eases into a secluded parking spot under a tree and brings the Caddy to a halt. What next? Crazy thoughts are galloping through my brain. Do we clean up what's left of Doc and prop him up in the back seat? Pretend he's okay as we serve the papers to Julius up at Babylon for Carole's commitment into Fairweather Bridge? Or do we say to hell with it? We can't be driving around with a stiff in the back of the car? We'll put him on a park bench somewhere for a while? That could work. Then I think that won't work. Jacky would be pissed.

I can hear him yelling, "You guys fuck up a simple house closing, get a friend of ours killed, and dump his body on a park bench across from a taco joint? What about his wife? Are we going to feature Angel Mascara, an aging Punk rocker, in our show lounge at Dominos for the next twenty years? What about his kids? Don't you guys ever think?"

"We gotta think," Jimmy says. "Those two Asian guys were driving one of Donnie's white van specials. Think about it. Tony says Donnie was at a meeting with Dick Head Man, who had two of his boys with him. Donnie's only backup was some fat torpedo who sat in a black Buick, keeping the a/c cold. It sounds to me like Mister Dick Head is calling the shots. I think Donnie's short-handed. We knocked off four of his crew. He may not have much left."

Two cop cars and an ambulance roar past the shopping mall with their sirens on, headed for the mess in San Anselmo.

"So," Jimmy says. "When Donnie says that Rockwell's boys will do the digging at Babylon, Mister Dick Head tells Donnie that Rockwell's boys might end up as landfill. He adds that he doesn't need a deed to Babylon. Dick Head's just going to go up there and take what he wants."

"You know what that means?" I ask.

"Yeah, it means that once Dick Head is in, he doesn't need Donnie anymore."

I'm about to say something to Jimmy when a loud bass track followed by over-driven guitar fills the car. The unmistakable voice of Angel Mascara growls out, "Kill me with your loving tonight, bleed for my forgiveness tomorrow." Her platinum hit is coming out of Doc's iPhone as a ring tone.

"Jesus," Jimmy says. "What next? Haven't we had enough?"

"You want to answer it and tell her what's happened?" I look down at Doc. Where the hell is his phone? Do I have to jump into the back seat and roll what's left of him for the damn iPhone? Should we let it go to voice mail?

"Excuse me," a voice says. "I really should take this call. She's probably worried."

Doc's hand retrieves his phone from his designer jeans' back pocket and brings it to his mouth.

"Yeah, Babe. Yeah, there was trouble, but I'm okay. I'm with Nick and Jimmy. Everything's fine."

Jimmy:

Doc puts his phone on speaker, so Angel can hear what everyone has to say. Mostly it's reassurance that whatever she's hearing about shootings in San Anselmo on the news, it hasn't involved us in any negative way.

"Oh, a few scratches." Doc winks and rolls his eyes. "Nothing to worry about."

I'm hoping he's right as I look at his blood-streaked face. Was it the glass fragments from the window that made him bleed? I don't think he took a bullet. He was smart. When the shooting started, he went low and didn't come up until he knew it was safe.

Angel doesn't convince easily.

"Those Bender people were always involved with a bad crowd," she says. "Hoodlums running around shooting each other. It's just terrible some of the stories you hear about what went on at that house. I'm so glad that someone respectable is taking it over."

Nick tries to jump in to get her off the track.

"Angel, we heard your platinum hit just now on Doc's iPhone when you called. We were wondering if you would consider performing at the Galloping Dominos in Vegas. We could put together a Punk revival festival, maybe get a few groups from the Punk movement to do a weekend series?"

Doc gives Nick a thumbs up and manages a smile.

"That's a wonderful idea," Angel says. "I think the world needs all the Punk it can get these days. We could include some grunge acts, too. My agent Joey Polito will handle the contract side. I know a few of the groups are still hanging out in the Bay Area. The Dormant Flowers and the Arsenic Impersonators would be great as part of the show. I'd have to find a lead guitarist. Owen Crawford overdosed a few years back, but there are guys around who could do it. Some of them have been through rehab at Fairweather Bridge. It sounds exciting. We should talk."

"I'm sure you'll find a lot of fans in Vegas," Nick says.

"I'm sure," Angel says. "Hey, we could probably get Tonic Colonic."

"That would be great," I say, wondering if Tonic Colonic is a person, a

131

group, or a medical procedure.

"It'll be great," Nick says.

Angel is finally satisfied and rings off.

Doc does an assessment of his condition in the Caddy's rearview mirror and gives Nick a list of items he needs from the shopping mall's drugstore.

"Bring us back some cold beers, too," I yell as Nick takes off.

A minute later, my burner phone rings. It's Bruno.

"The radio says there was some shooting in San Anselmo. You guys still among the living?"

"Yeah, they got Doc's ambulance driver and his cop friend, but Nick got them, two Asian guys in a white van."

"We got a line on who they are," Bruno says. "When we left the restaurant where Donnie had his meeting, we headed back toward Babylon to check out the scene. On the way, we saw Shaughnessy in his yard, so we stopped. Tony asks him if the guy he saw yelling 'Dick head" at the tow truck drivers had any tattoos. Shaughnessy says he didn't get close enough to see. Tony tells him we saw an Asian guy with a tattoo on his arm --- a knife stabbing the sun. Shaughnessy says, 'That sounds like Maung.'"

"Yeah? So, what's that mean?"

"He asks if the guy had anyone with him. I say he's got two guys that have the same tattoo. 'That is Maung,' Shaughnessy says. "He's a big shot in the secret police in Myanmar and a real bad actor, runs drugs and whore houses for Western tourists. Does it all with his four brothers and keeps all the money in the family."

"We got news for Maung," I say. "He's only got two brothers. Nick did some family planning for him."

"I get it," Bruno says. "Where you guys now?"

"We're on our way to Fairfax. Doc got thirsty, so we sent Nick to bring back some cold beers. How about we meet in that downtown parking lot across from the restaurants?"

"Sounds good."

Bruno rings off as Nick approaches with patchwork for Doc and refreshments for all.

Soon, it looks like only a tiny alley cat attacked Doc's face. A bandage here and there, some tape and gauze, covered by sunglasses and a cheap Giants cap, and Doc looks like a ringside bettor at a Filipino cockfight.

"Don't worry." Doc slurps his beer and raises the can. "I'm ready to go. I'm in touch with my inner child."

"That's great," Nick says. "What does your inner child have to say?"

"He says, 'This is a great crew we have here.'"

"It is a great crew," I say as I pull out onto the road toward Babylon. I might have gone too far when I said Nick and I had Continuous Traumatic Stress Disorder.

Maybe my beautiful wife knows us better than we know ourselves. "If they ever want to kill you and Nick," Cassandra says, "They won't need bullets. They'll just make you sit behind a desk every day."

Chapter Forty-one

Nick:

As we drive toward Fairfax, I start to worry. We're on our way to take possession of Babylon. Jimmy says that we have every right to walk in and toss everybody out as Jacky and Muriel's legal representatives. He doesn't mention the part about how we might have to shoot our way in. We're also on a mission to rescue Carole Bender, Muriel's aunt. Recent phone calls to Babylon asking for Aunt Carole get answered by Julius, one of David Rockwell's security thugs. Julius says Carole can't come to the phone. She's napping. Doc Webster says that Carole hardly ever sleeps. She loves to answer the phone and loves long conversations, even with strangers.

We know Rockwell is a wealthy Nazi wannabe under the control of his wife, the best-selling-author-and-gold-digger Mary Ashford Stevens. Mary Ashford is also a cousin of Donnie Mascarella, who runs what's left of the Big Philly Petrillo gang. As far as we can tell, Donnie's gang consists of Donnie and the fat-ass driver of his black Buick. The rest of Donnie's crew is on ice. Two went over the side of the canyon in a white van. Two more were killed by the SFPD when they tried to break into a room at the Fairmont to kill Jimmy and me.

We've had problems with white vans. We know at least two of them are registered to Donnie's moving company.

Two guys in a third white van just tried to kill us in San Anselmo. This crew came from a sleazeball named Maung. His two Burmese brothers died in the attempt.

Maung is a business partner of Donnie's. Together they bring dope in from Myanmar and get it delivered to Vegas and points east.

So, why are all these characters involved in a simple house closing? What's in it for them?

Rockwell believes that there are eight million bucks in Nazi gold bars hidden on the property. The gold was supposedly hustled out of Berlin in 1945 by the Russians as Hitler's Third Reich fell apart. Why is the gold at Babylon? Could it be that the Russians wanted to use it for payment to Big Philly Petrillo for nuclear materials and information stolen from Los Alamos Lab in the late forties?

On the other hand, Maung wants to get his hands on that nuclear stuff that Big Philly may have hidden at Babylon. Some of the politicians in Myanmar are jealous of North Korea. They'd like to see their country join the H-Bomb set.

I can hear you asking, "You got any proof that any of this is going down, Nick? Or are you just breaking our balls with bullshit?"

I could tell how Donnie's boys had tools and protective gear for handling nuke materials, but you could say, "That's Donnie's way of working a con on Maung."

No argument, there. The Petrillo gang has always been long on bullshit when hustling a buck. It's been said that back in the fifties, they pulled off a scam on the Dominican Republic, "selling" them weapons supposedly stolen from the Illinois National Guard Armory.

We do have proof of the Nazi gold bars. Well, at least we have one gold bar that Carole smuggled out to us in a telescope case. Jimmy's got it in his laptop case. We haven't had it analyzed, but it might be the real thing.

So, at least eight people are dead over what may or may not be hidden in Babylon. My gut feeling is that someone in this mix stands to benefit from this deal either way. Nukes or no nukes. Nazi gold or no gold.

We have proof of something else: this group of cutthroats is ready to kill us.

The Caddy moves toward Downtown Fairfax. Doc sips his beer in the back seat.

"You're quiet," Jimmy says to me. "You figure it all out?"

"Yeah, something that Doc told us rings true," I say.

Before I can say anything else, Doc's iPhone blasts out music. This time the ring tone is Carlos Santana's "Maria, Maria."

"Hey, Maria," Doc says. He sips more beer and holds the phone up so we can see the photo of Maria, his assistant from Fairweather Bridge.

"Angel told me about you being okay. I hope that's true," Maria says.

"Jesus, they've got Wally in intensive care with a gunshot to the leg and one to the shoulder. The ambulance has been impounded by the cops. Speaking of cops, your friend Wes took one in the gut, and another grazed his head. He's in ICU, too."

"That's actually good news," Doc says. "I thought they were both dead."

"No, my friend Suzi at Marin General says they're both probably going to make it. So, where are you? What are you doing?"

Doc winks at me.

"I'm with Nick and Jimmy. We're headed to Babylon to take care of things."

"Then you're really okay?"

"Yeah, never felt better. I love the action." Doc sips from his beer.

"We're all worried about you."

"I know. I'll try hard to stay safe. Hey, we have to run. We're meeting the rest of our crew in Fairfax."

"We're rooting for you, Doc. Stay safe." Maria clicks off.

I get stuck on something Maria says. The ambulance driver and the cop were wounded, not killed. Then I think how the two shooters ran toward us and only managed to shoot out the rear passenger window on the Caddy. Before the shooting, they were drinking beers and joking. Were they trying to screw up the courage? Maybe Maung's brothers were more about bullshit than really being tough guys. Having a tattoo on your arm of a knife stabbing the sun might scare people in Myanmar. It didn't do much for them here.

Jimmy:

We look closely at the scene as we roll into Fairfax. We need to connect with Tony and Bruno. They're supposed to meet us in the downtown parking lot, across from the bars and restaurants. Happy hour is in full swing. The aromas of pizza and beer fill the air. The sound of Credence Clearwater Revival's "Bad Moon Rising" spills out from one of the bars. Fairfax really does live in the sixties.

We want to avoid Maung and his two brothers. The same goes for Donnie Mascarella and his fat-ass driver and the dynamic duo of David Rockwell and his keeper Mary Ashford Stevens. I'm hoping that all of them have taken off to haunt another venue.

I know better, of course. It doesn't take a genius to figure out sharks in the water that smell blood. They're either at Babylon or lurking somewhere nearby. I look around for a white van and then think how crazy that is. They could be driving anything. Hell, they could be taking aim at us as we sit here.

Losing our police escort puts a different light on things. The plan was to follow Doc's cop friend, Wes, up the canyon. A little flashing lights and siren action would have put some fear into whoever is standing guard at Babylon.

"Maybe we'll have to improvise," Nick says.

Then I notice something.

Across the street, a Fairfax cop carries a cup of coffee toward his squad car. He's a young guy, maybe in his mid-twenties. A heavily bearded bum staggers up to the cop and shakes a paper cup at him, panhandling. The cop laughs at something the beggar says, then he drops some coins into the bum's cup.

"You see that?" Nick asks.

"Yeah, I think we just got our police escort back," I say. "Wait here." Officer Jeffrey Lawrence listens politely when I tell him about my predicament.

"Aunt Carole, she's up in years," I say. "I can't get her to answer the phone. She's on some kind of medication. This has happened before, but I'm worried. I get lost trying to find her place."

"Where does she live?" Officer Lawrence asks.

I give him the street address. He writes it down in a notebook.

"Is that up the canyon?" He asks.

"It is. Some people know the place better as Babylon."

"Hey, I've heard about it. Nice looking place. Didn't movie stars used to hang out there?"

"That's the place," I say. "Could you show me the way to get there?"

"I know where it is," Officer Lawrence says. "Can't say that I've ever been inside. Why don't you follow me up there, and we'll check on your aunt?"

Bruno and Tony spot us from across the parking lot and call on the burner phone.

"Looks like we have a police escort," Nick says. "Stay behind us."

"Hey," Tony says. "This is one for the books. We're trailing a cop."

"Get in line," Nick says. "We're going to visit dear old Aunt Carole."

Darkness approaches as we bump along the canyon road.

"Goddamn it," Doc says from the backseat. "This is the life. You guys really know how to live."

Beside me, Nick checks the magazines in our Glocks and nods.

"We're good to go."

Ahead, Officer Lawrence switches on his roof rack lights, blasting blue flashes at roadside trees as we climb toward Babylon.

Chapter Forty-two

Nick:

Officer Lawrence leads our caravan up Canyon Ridge Road toward Babylon, flashing the blue lights atop his squad car. We have a police escort.

"Why such a gung-ho leader?" I ask Jimmy. "You bless him with a c note?"

"No, I think he wants to see where a bunch of drunk movie stars got laid."

We pass by the gap in the roadside brush where White Van Number One took its dive to the canyon floor. I wonder if the bodies of Donnie Mascarella's two thugs are still down there stinking up the neighborhood. Or were they tucked inside of the wrecked white van and taken to the auto-crushing machine? With a class act like Donnie's, you could bet either way on their final resting place.

As we get closer to Babylon, I'm hoping that Carole Bender is safe. All we need for Muriel to go into mental meltdown is to tell her that Aunt Carole has fallen prey to the sort of sleaze buckets the Benders are famous for hanging with.

I expect to see the two attack dogs, Heinrich and Himmler, hanging out in front of Babylon. A couple of handlers will probably be holding the dogs in check, and maybe a couple uniforms in vehicles from Rockwell's security outfit will be on the parking pad. I'm expecting confrontation even though we have a cop leading the way.

Do I feel like a louse, lying to our cop about our mission to Babylon? I mean, we are worried about dear old Aunt Carole. We told Officer Lawrence we were. Okay, it was weapons of mass medication on the old girl that we said we were worried about. Actually, Jimmy said it. He left out the parts about Nazi gold, nukes, and narcotics. It was a sin of omission anyone might make.

Okay, I do feel like a louse, but I'm hoping we can fake it until we make it. With any luck, we can cop our way in, present Doc's legal papers, and somehow get the advantage on whoever's there to give us shit. I could cross my fingers, but it makes it harder to handle a Glock.

"Jesus," Doc says from the back seat. "Shouldn't I have a piece? Shouldn't I be carrying? Shouldn't I go in heavy?"

He sounds like he's channeling Uncle Junior on "The Sopranos."

"Doc, take it easy," Jimmy says. "We know you're a tough guy. Keep an eye on Nick. Make sure he doesn't fly off the handle. Capisce?"

Doc loves the capisce bit. He takes another drink from his beer.

"Yeah, capisce. We'll keep Nick on the straight and narrow." He shoves a foot-long pretzel stick in his mouth. He's the Marin County version of Al Capone.

Canyon Ridge Road is anything but straight. It's dark, narrow, and filled with curves. Behind us, I can see the headlights of the rented Escalade carrying Tony and Bruno. Another set of headlights is behind them, close on their tail.

"You got any idea of who's joining our parade?" Jimmy asks.

"I've been watching the headlights."

"There are other people who live up this road," Jimmy says.

"Yeah, maybe just someone trying to get home," I say.

"Yeah, maybe not. Maung's still got two brothers left."

"I hope they shoot as bad as the first two."

We push on, bouncing behind Officer Lawrence.

The headlights behind Tony and Bruno disappear. Did they turn off into a driveway? Did they just turn off their lights?

My burner phone rings.

"That was a FedEx driver making a delivery," Tony says. "He got so close. Bruno was getting ready to duck."

"Antsy?"

"Yeah, this gig sucks. If I didn't like you guys, I'd be back in LA."

Officer Lawrence leads us around the next bend in Canyon Ridge Road, and we come upon Babylon.

It's everything we didn't figure on: no attack dogs, no handlers, no security personnel or vehicles. The parking pad is lighted and deserted.

Officer Lawrence pulls the squad car onto the pad.

We pull in beside him.

Tony parks the Escalade across the road on the shoulder next to a vertical cliff wall.

Officer Lawrence speaks into his microphone.

"I'm code six at 88 Canyon Ridge Road."

"Ten-four, Lawrence," the radio says.

"That means I'm out of the vehicle, investigating," Lawrence says.

"Nick, Jimmy," a voice yells from the open deck above the parking pad. "Is that you boys? I see you brought some friends."

"Yes, we were worried about you," Jimmy says. "Thought maybe you took too much medicine. The officer was kind enough to help us get up here."

"What a wonderful man. Please bring him in."

"Aunt Carole?" Lawrence asks.

"The one and only," Carole says. "You should come up and meet her."

Jimmy:

The double wooden doors to Babylon open. Gary, the security guard who took us on a tour of Babylon's property, motions us to come in.

"She's upstairs and ready for guests," he says.

Nick leads officer Lawrence up the stairs, followed by Doc, Tony, and

Bruno.

I hang back.

"What gives?" I ask.

"She told us this morning that if anyone called, we should say she's taking a nap," Gary says. "She told me that she didn't want to talk to anyone. She was waiting for a deal on the house to close. As soon as she got confirmation out of Chicago, things would change, big time."

I look around at the parking pad.

"You're the only one here?"

"Yeah, Carole listened in on the phone call from Doctor Webster. She knew you guys were on the way. Julius got freaked out when he heard everything was being recorded. The first thing he did was call David Rockwell."

"What happened then?"

Gary rolls his eyes.

"Rockwell told him not to piss in his pants over it. 'They say they're on the way,' he told Julius. 'That doesn't mean they're actually going to show up. Things can change.'"

How cozy, I think. Rockwell gets word to Maung so his boys can kill us before we get to Babylon. Did he go past Donnie and his fat-assed driver, figuring they didn't count? Or did he honor another thief by letting Donnie think that he was in charge of taking us out?

Then I realize I have it wrong.

Rockwell runs to mama with his problems.

I remember what Doc said. Mary Ashford Stevens is always in charge. If anyone gave the go-ahead for the hit on us, it was best-selling Mary.

"So, why is the place so empty?" I ask. "Nighttime means dogs and extra guys up here from Rockwell's security service."

"A little while after Doc Webster's call, Carole came out of her suite holding a batch of papers that were emailed to her. The deal had gone through on the house, and the new owners wanted everyone out. She turned to Julius and said, 'You got two minutes to get all your security shit out of Babylon. The cops are on their way, and so are the boys from Chicago. You don't want to meet either group.'"

"Did Julius call Rockwell then to ask for his advice?"

"No, what Carole said was enough for Julius. He got the two handlers to shove the dogs into the truck, and he took off in the security patrol car."

"But you stuck around?"

"Yeah, she asked me to. I would have offered anyway. She doesn't like to be alone. She has a way about her that draws you in. I tell her she's just a crazy old lady who knows how to play the piano and drink at the same time. She tells me, 'If you're so smart, Fatso, fix us another drink.'"

Carole's voice drifts down the staircase from the large gathering area. "I'm so glad, Officer Lawrence, that you could help my nephews and friends find their way to Babylon. Yes. That's the largest Steinway they make. It took a small crane to get it into the house…You play?… Only a little?… Blues? I love the blues…Sit down, and at least get the feel of the keys."

Tentative notes from the piano are followed by more robust notes and chords. A melody starts to flow, and Carole begins to sing.

"Baby, won't you please come home, 'cause your mama's all alone…."

Chapter Forty-three

Nick:

Officer Lawrence turns out to be more than just a police escort. As he insists Carole should call him, Jeff is not only a blues piano player, but he also knows a lot about Fairfax.

"I grew up here," he says, as he riffs Carole into another song, "After You've Gone."

She sings the first verse and starts to laugh.

"Jeff, that Steinway sounds great the way you play it. Tell us more about you."

"My parents own the Pizza 4 Da People restaurant downtown," Jeff says. "I grew up here and went through all the tie-dye stuff and the alternative lifestyle fads. Getting a look at the inside of Babylon is a treat for me. For years I've heard about how Hitch and other great film people hung out here. It must have been great fun, Aunt Carole."

"Some of it was." Carole smiles. "You should just call me Carole. That Aunt stuff sounds like I'm some stuffy old prude out of Agatha Christie." Jeff smiles. "Carole it is. I love your singing."

Carole smiles and pats Jeff's arm.

"Let me give you a tour of the place. We have oil portraits of some of our movie friends. You might find them interesting."

"Great, lead on," Jeff says.

They head down the hallway toward the elaborate suites.

"We need to get organized," Tony says, hustling Doc off to the kitchen. "Give me a hand. We're going to need some coffee and food. We may have to tough it out for a while. I see a large espresso machine, and I'm betting there's plenty of groceries."

I walk to the railing on the Canyon Ridge Road side of Babylon. The road is dark and empty of traffic. Jimmy comes over and stands next to me.

"Expecting company?"

"Yeah, and it ain't Larry the Cable Guy."

The smell of garlic bread and coffee begins to cover the stench wafting in from fires across the Bay.

Soon, Carole and Jeff are back. They stand at the railing, looking into the dark canyon side of Babylon.

"How far down does the property extend?" Jeff asks.

"I can show you." Carole grabs a flashlight and aims it at the southeast property marker.

"I see it," Jeff says. "Past that marker is no man's land. Goes down about another five hundred feet. Ever been down there?"

Carole shakes her head.

"Lots of stories about it," Jeff says. "Old bootleggers used to hide there from the feds back in the twenties. Some say a few are buried down there."

"Really?" Carole stares into the dark. "Do you think it's true?"

"I didn't see any headstones, but if you wanted to get rid of someone, you'd probably use an unmarked grave."

"I know how steep it is on our property. Does it go that way through all the overgrowth down to the bottom? Could there be empty champagne bottles from some of my party guests down there?"

Jeff nods and smiles.

"There's a lot of old junk that's rolled down the slopes. I ride my Yamaha dirt bike down there with some friends. We ride through this large concrete drainpipe that leads down there. A few months back, I found an old bootlegger's still. My dad loves it. It's on display at the restaurant. He collects antiques."

Carole puts her hand on Jeff's shoulder.

"Ever see any ghosts down there?"

"I don't think so." Jeff laughs. "Seen some old hippies who looked like ghosts. They were taking care of their pot plants. It's all the property of some drainage district. It has a long name with preservation or conservation in it. There's a lot of dried brush down there this time of year. We need rain. There's nothing down there now to drain."

"I may have seen ghosts," Carole says. "Moving around in the dark. A couple of times, I got spooked and took a shot at something down there. I never hit anything except a possum. Made me feel like hell when I found out what I had done."

Carole reaches for a switch box and turns on the lights. The entire back of the lot is lit. Nothing is moving.

"Your lights only cover up to the property marker," Jeff says.

"Yeah, I didn't think I could light up someone else's property. I didn't want to get sued by the guy who owns the property behind me."

Jeff laughs.

"Carole, some guy growing pot down there isn't going to sue you. You shouldn't be shooting at things, though. Just call Fairfax PD. We're a great bunch. We make house calls."

"I'll be sure to let my niece and her husband know that. I'm transferring the property over to them. They own the Galloping Dominos Casino in Las Vegas. My nephews and their friends here help to run the place."

"You're not sticking around?" Jeff asks.

"I'm going to live in Paris for a while. I have a house lined up near Notre Dame."

"Wow, I've always wanted to go there."

"Give me your business card, and I'll send you a special invitation once I'm settled," Carole says.

"Great. We could do the Louvre and some of those old Hemingway haunts."

"Yes, we could. We should."

Jeff hands Carole his card.

The radio clipped to Jeff's shirt barks, "Lawrence, are you ten-seven or ten-eight?"

"I'm ten-eight."

"Check out a ten-ninety-one b at 668 Roscoe."

"Ten-four," Jeff says. "I've got to run, Carole. Wonderful meeting you."

"Something dangerous?" Carole hugs Jeff.

"A barking dog. Could be the crime wave of the day."

Jeff gives Carole a hug and heads to his patrol car.

"If I were forty years younger," Carole says as Jeff pulls away. "He'd never get out of my bedroom."

Jimmy:

It's time to get it together. Bruno goes downstairs to guard the front of Babylon with Gary. I do a quick Google search for outfits that put up security fencing in an emergency and call one of them. Can they come out tonight and surround Babylon with razor wire and chain link fencing? Not tonight, but morning, about ten? Fine, I say.

I could have called a few other outfits, but the answer would be the same. No one's going to come out in the dark and work on rugged land that slopes at a forty-five-degree angle. We've done the easy part. We've covered our asses with Jacky, who told us to take possession of Babylon and order security fencing. By rights, we can install the fence and take off tomorrow afternoon.

Except we know that what works on paper in Chicago can get us killed in Fairfax. We've had an ongoing firefight since leaving Babylon yesterday.

Now, it's talk turkey with Carole time.

We crowd around a large coffee table in the gathering area. Tony and Doc bring in some snacks and drinks. Carole leans back in her chair and wraps a serape around her shoulders.

"Tell me straight what you guys know," she says.

Nick looks at me. I nod.

"We got your note and the golden paperweight that came with it," Nick says. "Before we go into that, you should know that two thugs in one of those white vans tried to run us off Canyon Ridge Road as we left here with your gift bags. They took a full magazine and dropped like dead weights into the canyon."

"Dead?"

"Yeah, they might be fertilizing pot plants where Officer Jeff rides his bike."

"I was wondering," Carole says. "Both the vans left and never came back."

"Yeah," Nick says. "Van number two tried to get us at the ferry terminal, but they missed the boat. They tried to get us at the ballpark later. We gave one of their flunkies some phony info about staying at the Fairmont. That's where the SFPD took them out when they tried to break into a room that they thought we were staying in."

"They're both dead?" Carole asks.

"Yeah, but that wasn't the end of the blood-letting. Someone from their outfit came back to collect their van. In the process, they shot an old drunk sitting next to the van and the cab driver who tipped off the two shooters about where we were staying."

"So, six people are dead?"

"No, it gets worse. We're playing high-stakes poker here," Nick says. "Two more guys tried to take out Doc, his ambulance driver, and an off-duty cop friend of his in San Anselmo."

Carole gasps.

"They shot you, Doc?"

"They tried. I just got cuts from flying glass," Doc says. "The ambulance driver and the cop are in the ICU at Marin General. They say they have a fifty-fifty chance to make it."

Tony reaches over to the coffee table in front of Carole and pours her a shot of Jack Daniels. "This will help," he says.

"The two shooters? What happened to them?" Carole slugs the whiskey in one gulp and holds the glass out for more."

"Nick took them out," I say. "We left them dead on the street in San Anselmo."

"Oh, my god." Carole sips more whiskey. "How did it ever get this bad?"

"That's what we want to know," Nick says. "This was supposed to be a simple house closing. Eight people are dead, two are hanging onto life, and Jimmy just ordered razor wire to secure this place."

"Oh, my god. This is bad."

"I left out the part about your nephew Teddy. He was found beaten and bloody in Greenbrae. He showed up with his friends from a black motorcycle gang. Their specialty was pushing meth out of a run-down donut shop in Barstow. Teddy's been placed in a ninety-day program at Fairweather Bridge Clinic. His friends are in the slammer on drug charges."

"Why? What did they come here for?"

"It wasn't for the fresh air and sunshine. Somehow, they got the notion that something valuable was here. They weren't alone. Your friend Mary Ashford Stevens and husband number eight are
also sniffing around, then there's Donnie Mascarella and his boys from Burma. They're after it, too."

"Who, what is it they're after?"

"That's what we want to know. It's time you came clean. I'm tired of ducking bullets over your bullshit."

Chapter Forty-four

Nick:

Okay, I know my yelling, "I'm tired of ducking bullets over your bullshit." at Carole has an effect.

For a minute, the room is dead quiet. The house is dead quiet. Even outside on Canyon Ridge Road, it's dead quiet. I start to wonder if all of Fairfax has heard my yell and gone silent. Maybe everyone is tired of ducking bullets over someone else's bullshit.

Then Carole squeaks something in almost a whisper.

"Okay."

She looks at Doc, sitting next to her. He offers his hand. She grabs it.

"The reason we never got to my breakthrough in therapy is because of me." she coughs and clears her throat. "I couldn't tell the truth. It was safer to deal in lies. That's how I was raised by Lacey."
She looks around the table and continues.
"Hell, if I said anything truthful to someone we didn't trust, we could all end up in the slammer or dead. You can talk about all the wonderful entertainers who hung out here but don't forget the creeps and the killers. They were more than happy to deal with us, too."
She grabs a cigarette and lights it.
"It's a bitch, Doc." She clears her throat and swallows. "We could have had a breakthrough years ago. I know you wouldn't have revealed anything about some of the shit I was living through, but I was trained to be a liar. I learned how to move the conversation away from anything dangerous to something that sounded serious but never got close to threatening us with the truth."
"I know how you feel," Jimmy says. "I've had some hard truths in my life that I didn't want to accept. I only hurt myself with denial. This situation is different. People have tried to kill us and some of our friends because of what they think is here in Babylon. They think we know what it is and where it is. The problem is we don't know. We're in a dangerous position."
Carole raises her empty glass at Tony.
"I know. I worry about leaving a terrible situation for Muriel and Jacky to deal with. I don't want that."
Tony pours whiskey into her glass.
"Mind if I just let go?" Carole asks.
"Go ahead," Jimmy says. "You're among friends."
"I was just a kid," Carole says. "I had just turned eight. It was back in 1948. Some fascinating people were hanging out up here, too. One of them was a nice guy named Mickey Saturday. He really had it bad for Lacey. I think she fell for him, too. I don't know how long they knew each other, but I always got the drift that there was a history there."
"What did this guy do?" Jimmy asks. "Was he connected?"
"In a way, but I found that out later. There was another guy who spent a lot of time up here, Philly Petrillo. They didn't call him Big Philly then. It was just Philly. Anyway, he and Mickey Saturday had been working some sort of deal. I'd hear bits of their conversation. Philly would say things like 'cross my palm with the gold, and your old uncle Joe will get a big bang out of it.' I figured it had something to do with gambling. Vegas was just getting started."
Jimmy looks around the table and says to the group, "Let her talk. We can ask questions later. Go ahead, Carole."

145

"I always liked Saturday. He was like an uncle to me, bringing me comic books and stuff. One night, I woke up and thought I heard him in the house. He was talking with Lacey and Philly. It was right here where the railing overlooks the canyon. Philly was saying that Saturday had come up short on the gold, and he had to leave. Saturday said he still had some money. Lacey butts in and says that the FBI could show up at any minute. They couldn't have that. I'm listening in from around that corner over there. I'm about to come in to say hello when I hear a gunshot. I peek around the door jamb and see Saturday go over the railing. I screamed."

"What happened then?" Jimmy asks.

"Philly goes ape shit over me seeing what happened. 'This goddamn kid is a pain in the ass,' he yells. 'Maybe I should do her, too.' Lacey has to calm him down. 'Don't worry about the kid,' she says. 'Carole knows how to behave. She's a Bender.' Then she tells Philly that he shouldn't have shot Saturday. There had to have been a better way. 'Yeah, I should have shot him twice,' Philly says. That's when she tells Philly, 'Don't push it, or I'll bring half of Chicago down on you.' She says he has his own work cut out for him. He'd better hurry up and get rid of Saturday, or all their asses will be in a jam."

"So, did Philly get rid of Saturday?" Jimmy asks.

"I didn't see what happened after that. Lacey took me to my room. I was in hysterics. She wasn't much better. She was shaking all over, telling me that everything was going to be alright. She held me in my bed until I fell asleep. In the morning, Philly was gone, Saturday was gone. I looked at the place where Saturday went over the railing. I didn't know what I would see. Blood? A dead body? There was nothing. It could have all been a nightmare, but I knew it was real."

Carole stops and sips her drink. Around the table, everyone is silent. Doc breaks the silence. "You're safe, Carole. We can protect you."

I look at Carole, and I start putting pieces together. This guy Saturday is the Russian who disappeared in 1948. There was something wrong with the deal he had going with Big Philly. Was Saturday trying to pass off fake gold bars to Philly in exchange for nuke stuff? Or was the promise of nuke stuff just some Big Philly bullshit story designed to steal gold from the Russians?

I look up and see Jimmy standing behind Carole. He's holding the gold bar that she gave us. I watch as he turns and heads toward the kitchen and the digital scale he pointed out to me when we had our tour.

"Saturday getting shot was traumatic to me," Carole says. "I couldn't believe it happened. I was used to crazy stuff going on in Babylon, high stakes poker, whores working on johns out in the open. This wasn't a fun time for high rollers. This was murder. It stopped me in my tracks. I still have nightmares about that."

Jimmy is back from the kitchen with one word.

"Lead."

"Oh, yeah, the gold bar is phony. Instead of a kilo, it's a little over a pound," Carole says. "Philly killed Saturday because it wasn't gold. Even though the FBI was closing in, Philly still thought he could take delivery of real Nazi gold. He'd get Saturday safely out of the picture, and no one would be the wiser. When it turned out there wasn't any gold, that was the end of Saturday, and it left Philly with a body to dispose of. Great way to raise an eight-year-old kid, eh?"

"So, there wasn't any gold," Jimmy says. "Does that mean there weren't any nuke materials?"

"I never saw any, but that doesn't mean there wasn't any. They weren't going to let a kid in on what they were doing. Hell, whatever it is, could still be down there somewhere in the canyon. I'm willing to bet that Saturday is down there in an unmarked grave."

"And Big Philly?" Jimmy asks.

"He'd show up every once in a while," Carole says. "He was always trying to make a big deal happen. His trouble was he screwed too many people along the way. Lots of enemies. So many, he couldn't keep track. We had a big party for my eighteenth birthday, and he showed up. That was the last time I saw him. Hell, I don't think anyone saw him after that."

I look at Jimmy. He nods.

"According to his Persons of Interest File," I say, "Big Philly walked in here and never walked out."

Carole sips more whiskey.

"Yeah, I figured it out later. Lacey had given me a '57 T-Bird for my birthday. As the party started to wind down around two in the morning, she said, 'You should take your Bird out for a spin. Take Marco with you.' Marco was this handsome guy from the Dominican Republic. He was there with his uncle, a distillery owner. We took off for the nearest motel. When we got back around dawn, most of the cars were gone, but Philly's Caddy was still here. I figured he stayed over. Marco got into his Corvette and took off. I never saw him again."

"And you never saw Philly again?" Jimmy asks.

"I woke up in the middle of the afternoon. A tow truck was hoisting Philly's Caddy and pulling away. He was nowhere around. It was no secret he had screwed the Dominicans bad. I figured they finally got him. Is he down there with Saturday? I couldn't swear to it, but sometimes I think I see one of them trying to climb up from the canyon."

"And that's when you take shots at them?" Jimmy asks.

"Yeah, stupid, I know. How do you kill someone who's already dead?"

"But they're not real," Doc says. "They're leftover bad experiences that you haven't gotten rid of."

"Maybe so," Carole says. "They won't go away, so I'm going away instead."

Chapter Forty-five

Jimmy:

Carole Bender gives us some answers about Babylon, but a lot of what she's telling us leads to more questions. I sit watching as Doc Webster holds Carole's hand and tries to soothe her. Tony is quick to pour Jack Daniels into her glass, and Nick sits there making subtle motions for me to do something.

I turn toward Carole and try my damnedest to be the Mister Rogers version of Mister District Attorney.

"Lacey Bender lost her husband Oscar in the early thirties when he died. Yet, you say that in 1948, you were eight years old. I don't recall anything about Lacey remarrying. Can you help me out here?"

Carole smiles.

"Lacey wasn't what you'd call a nun. She was good-looking and loved men. One of the men she loved was my dad, a stunt pilot and racecar driver named Dieter von Ritter. Some of the old-timers told me the two of them got into a lot of heavy breathing back in the late thirties. The story goes that when it started to look like war was coming between the United States and Germany, Dieter was called back to Berlin. I've tried searching for information on him, looking through old Luftwaffe information, but I got nowhere. For all I know, he could have been a spy. I've heard he worked with the German Consulate. Either way, he's one of the millions lost forever in the war."

"Wasn't he in a bad spot if the Nazis found out he had been romantically involved with a Jew and had a half-Jewish daughter?" Nick asks.

"Maybe so, but Lacey wasn't going to tell them," Carole says. "I was an infant when he left. That was November of 1941…But from all Lacey told me, Dieter was an excellent pilot. He took her stunt flying several times. The Luftwaffe probably would have welcomed him."

I place the phony gold bar on the table in front of her.

"Tell us about this. It didn't just show up, did it?"

Carole shakes her head.

"The night I saw Mickey Saturday get shot, the gold bar was sitting in a puddle of booze next to the drink glasses on a small table. It was near that railing overlooking the canyon.
That was the first time I saw it.
I looked for it the next morning. It was gone. Everything was cleaned up. Even the table and chairs were gone."
"So, somehow, you found the gold bar again," Nick says.
"Seventy years later, it literally dropped back into my life," Carole says.
"I was packing up some personal belongings a couple days before you guys showed up. A small, ornate mirror I wanted to take with me was hanging in my room. A couple of screws fastened it to the wooden panel. When I took out the second screw, the gold bar fell out of the wall. I was shocked.
It took me back to that terrible night. I got scared. I started to wonder about the so-called ghosts and the possibility of buried bodies and weapons somewhere on the property. Maybe the gold was phony, but were the weapons fake, too?"
Carole sticks her empty glass toward Tony.
Her hand shakes.
He pours more whiskey.
She sips.
"I immediately did what Jimmy just did. I weighed out the gold bar, and it came up short. It was a phony."
"So, why did you smuggle it out to us?" Nick asks.
"I knew I couldn't deal with it alone. I needed your help. You guys are part of our family, part of our crew. I started to see things in a different light. Was all this security from David Rockwell there to keep me prisoner or to keep me safe? I didn't like the vibes I was getting."
"I thought you were tight with Rockwell and his wife?" I ask. "Care to explain?"
"Mary Ashford Stevens and I go back a long way. I take her for the bitch she is. She's in it for Mary Ashford, no one else. You know, she's part of the Petrillo crew. She got back in touch with me a couple years ago. I had her over for one of my parties. That's where she met Rockwell. He was here as a tag-along with that actor, Tucson Phoenix, the gun nut. I think they both came wanting to pick up whores. Tucson got one of the $500 bimbos. Rockwell got Mary Ashford. He's been paying for her ever since."
"You got that right." Tony laughs. "I saw how she took Aaron Ross to the cleaners in LA."
"One of her many victims of love."
Carole nods and laughs.

"She got back in touch with you?" Nick asks. "Any particular reason?"

"Jesus, you guys are good." Carole sips more whiskey. "She's got a heavy white powder habit. Could I help her out? After all, I was connected... Shit. So was she, but she didn't trust any of the Petrillos. I set her up with B.J. Forman. He's been the main connection for a lot of music groups in the Bay Area. I get a ten percent taste from what Mary buys... about a thousand a month."

"She's doing a thousand dollars of coke every month?" Nick asks.

"No, that's what I get. She's moving ten grand. I don't think she's making coke-flavored smoothies with it, though. Both Mary and David use gift packs of blow to grease a lot of wheels. She supplies some major book critics, and he's got his right-wing buddies who love to snort."

I look at Doc. He nods and silently mouths that he knows B.J. Forman. I figure he's been a featured player at Doc's revolving door clinic.

"What can you tell us about that concrete cylinder down on the back slope?" Nick asks. "What's inside the Babylon or Baby Lon container?"

"I don't know much about it," Carole says. "I've been down there a few times, but it's been years. Maybe it's part of that drainage district thing that Officer Lawrence was talking about. I saw a rattler down there once. That was enough for me. I had no reason to go prying into an old concrete drain. It's been there as long as I've been here."

I look at Nick. I can tell we agree that she's not going to help us on this one.

"It's getting late," Carole says. "And I've got to tell you I'm not feeling so hot. I'm an old lady who could use some of Doc's clinic treatment. Doc looks like he could use some of it, too."

Doc stands up and walks over toward the railing facing Canyon Ridge Road. He holds his cell phone up to me. I nod. Best to get Carole safe, I figure.

"I'll be happy to come back tomorrow and collect my things," she says. "I've made some arrangements for someone to move my stuff. After all, the place is no longer mine. It's in your hands, boys."

It doesn't take long for an ambulance and two Marin County Sheriff's cars to arrive. Doc has used his influence. Carole and Doc get into the back of the ambulance. Gary decides he's had enough of Babylon. He hitches a ride to Greenbrae with one of the cops.

We watch from the railing as the vehicles disappear down Canyon Ridge Road into the darkness. Bruno crosses the road and moves the rented Cadillac to the parking pad in front of Babylon. He leans against the large planter near the double doors to Babylon and lights a cigarette. There's silence.

I look at my aging El Dorado sitting near Bruno. The rear windows are shattered, and a bullet hole is in the passenger side door. It looks like a dying dinosaur. I wonder if we're all dying dinosaurs who haven't read the memo yet.

The smoke from thousands of burning trees and buildings somewhere to the east settles into the canyon. A slight breeze kicks up. Will it bring more stench, or will it finally clear the air?

For several minutes no one speaks. Then Tony breaks the silence.

"One thing's for sure," he says. "We're in control of Babylon and all its mysteries."

"Yeah, for as long as we can hold it," Nick says.

He points to distant headlights making their way up through the heavy smog on Canyon Ridge Road.

"I wouldn't count on them being the cavalry," he says.

Chapter Forty-six

Nick:

I watch with the rest of our crew as the distant headlights make their way up Canyon Ridge Road. They stop for a few minutes at places then move on. Why the delays? Is this Major Maung and his brothers coming to Babylon to find the nuke materials we may not have? Is the Donnie Mascarella gang part of this onslaught? I know what you're going to say, "Some gang, fat Donnie and his lazy-assed driver." The rest of his tough guys can't make it due to a sudden onset of fatal lead poisoning.

I notice a third set of headlights. Could this be David Rockwell and Mary Ashford Stevens? Are they coming for the Nazi gold bars that we don't have?

It can't be people looking for a house-party-in-progress.

I think about the three cars and our cast of characters. They're all part of some conspiracy that doesn't make sense.

Donnie and Maung want nuke materials so the major can be a hero back in Myanmar. Donnie gets rewarded with tons of illicit drugs from the boys in Rangoon. If they find gold bars, so much the better.

Rockwell and Mary Ashford Stevens are after the gold bars. He loves the Nazi inscriptions on them. She loves what they're made of. Should they run into nuke materials, Rockwell can peddle them to some fascist.

My guess is that Rockwell's had his security team search the house while they were protecting Carole. Being on-site 24/7 gave the security guys plenty of opportunity to case the joint. They couldn't go down to the concrete structure and tear that open without raising a response. Hell, Carole would have shot them.

So, Rockwell would tell Donnie and Maung that what they were looking for wasn't in the house in the ideal world. He'd point at the small Baby Lon bunker on the back slope. Maung would find the nuke stuff. Donnie would get tons of drugs, and Rockwell would walk with eight million in Nazi gold. Everyone would get their fair share of the deal.

Except, this isn't high school economics. Everyone wants more than their share Maung wants it all. Donnie would probably share the gold with Maung to keep the drug flow going. Rockwell wants the gold bars and whatever he can claim of the nuke stuff.

And then there's Mary Ashford Stevens. How did Carole put it? "I take her for the bitch she is. She's in it for Mary Ashford, no one else."

Tony breaks the silence.

"I think they're looking for a way to walk down into the canyon so they can come up behind the house," Tony says. "We noticed a couple spots where the road widens out, and there's parking if you do it right."

"Hard to see Rockwell or Mary fighting their way through brush and rattlers," Jimmy says.

"Rockwell's got some stooges working for him," I say. "Julius is a real shit bird, and Kenny, the dog handler, looks like he'd do anything for Rockwell."

"That leaves Donnie and his driver," Tony says. "They might get down into the canyon. The big question is, can they get up from there?"

I walk over to the fireplace. The famous double-barreled 12-gauge shotgun we saw in the celebrity photos is still there. Above it hangs a 9mm Mauser, a relic from WW II, but kept in good shape. Next to the fireplace is a small table with a drawer in it. Inside are two boxes of ammo. These will do.

A fourth set of headlights joins the others at the wide spot just around the curve from Babylon. Jimmy looks at me with that what-do-you-guess-is-happening-look.

"Okay," I say. "Like playing hunches, here's my bet. Maung and his brothers are the lead car. Donnie and his fat driver are in car number two. I put Rockwell and Mary Ashford in car number three. That gives them a chance to keep an eye on the Donnie and Maung teams. Car number four has Rockwell's flunkies. I'll say bitchy twit Julius and maybe Kenny the dog handler."

Jimmy looks around the room, then looks down the road where the vehicles have just put out their lights.

"We should at least have a double sawbuck on this."

He hands Tony a twenty and looks at me.

"You're in," I say, handing over two tens. "Now, what's your bet?"

"I like Maung first. In second, I put Mary and spouse. That means Donnie and his driver are third. Fourth is the dregs of Julius, the dog handlers, or whatever they can throw together."

"You guys are both wrong," Tony says. He takes a twenty out of his pocket and puts it with the other bills under a beer bottle. "Bitchy Mary and Mr. Nazi are head of the parade followed by Maung, then Donnie's black Buick. Whatever else is behind is fourth. Mary's always in charge."

Jimmy:

The road is dark. All the lights of Babylon have been turned off. Bruno sits behind the large planter with the double-barreled 12-gauge shotgun. Tony is one floor up near the roadside railing. He holds the 9 mm. Mauser. Nick and I sneak past bushes toward the vehicles that have stopped just around the bend from Babylon.

You could say that we're nuts for doing this on a wager of sixty bucks, and you'd be right. But the bet is just Nick's way of getting us up off our assets and taking the game to the enemy. We figure we can get close enough in this smog-darkened night to find out what we're up against.

As we draw closer, we can hear an argument in progress.

"Now you tell us. Why you no bring attack dogs?" Maung asks.

"Too noisy. They bark," someone says.

"I don't want to hear from you," Maung says. "You nothing. You just shut up, dickhead."

"Jesus, man."

"That's enough, Kenny," Rockwell says. "Major Maung deserves your respect."

"I was respecting him," Kenny says. "Does he want the goddamn dog to tell the whole fucking world that we're ready to take a fuckin' bullet?"

"You shut up," Maung says. "Maybe you the one take the bullet, dickhead."

"Okay, enough," Rockwell says. "I know that Donnie's boys plotted the trail down to the canyon when they were posing as surveyors."

"Damn right. They did a good job. I pay well, and I get results," Donnie says. "It's a straight shot, marked with a yellow cord tied to bushes. They even ran the cord just short of the property line for Babylon. From there, it's only maybe twenty feet to the concrete bunker."

"Then you lead the way, Donnie," Maung says. "Take driver with. Two brothers next. Rockwell, take Kenny dickhead next. I follow."

"What about me?" Mary Ashford Stevens asks.

"Hah." Maung says. "No place for woman. You wait here. You can move cars. Better you go home. Everyone hear enough shit from you. Men got work to do."

"Shit?" Mary Ashford starts to say. "What do you…?"

"Mary, please," Rockwell says. "Come on. We're this close to getting it."

"Yeah, close, alright," Mary says. "Go ahead, go play with the boys."

I peek around the bush I'm hiding behind. Rockwell and Kenny shoulder their rifles and follow the others down the trail. Maung turns toward Mary Ashford Stevens. He rubs his holstered sidearm, then his crotch, and spits.

"Asshole," she says as Maung leaves the road and heads down the steep trail.

For a minute, the only sounds are from the men edging their way down the slope. Then a car starts. Mary's had enough, I think. She's leaving. Then another motor starts. Soon, all four vehicles are running.

"What the hell?" Nick whispers.

The white van is first.

It moves to the head of the trail.

Mary gets out.

The van creeps forward to the edge of the path and plunges downward. Thuds and screams are followed by another vehicle moving to the trailhead. It's Donnie's Buick. Mary gets out, and a second vehicle heads to the bottom of the canyon. More thuds this time but just a few groans. The dog handler's pickup is the third entrant in the race to the bottom: more thuds, no screams, no wails.

Smoke comes up the trail.

A small fire has started in one of the wrecked vehicles.

Mary Ashford Stevens lights a cigarette.

She gets into her Mercedes and drives away.

Chapter Forty-seven

Nick:

Firefighters are at the inferno in five minutes.

High-pressure hoses shoot water at the wrecked vehicles. They're heaped on a flat area halfway down the steep slope.

"Did you see the cars drive off the road?" Fire Captain Dave Collins asks.

"No," Jimmy says. "We heard a crash. It sounded like Demolition Derby. That's when we called 9-1-1. Then we came out to investigate. You guys were pulling up when we got here. What do you figure? Some drunk fall asleep at the wheel?"

A firefighter climbs up to the roadside from the crash site. "We've got three vehicles, burnt to a crisp," he says. "Looks like seven fatalities, Dave."

Captain Collins nods and looks at us.

"Your house nearby?"

"Yeah," Jimmy says. "We're over there at the house called Babylon. We're worried about the fire spreading."

"I've got retardant on the way and another pumper. We should have it under control in a little while. We were lucky that the vehicles landed on that old concrete slab. Looks like someone had the idea to build a house here, back in the day. If the burning cars had gone down to the canyon floor, we would have had a big problem. A lot of dry brush down there. Lots of homes might have been destroyed."

"Any way we can help?" Jimmy asks.

"You can check around your property for sparks that might have jumped and started some brush on fire."

"Sure, anything else we can do?" I ask.

"No, I'll be down to see how it's going. I don't expect it to be any worse than it is now. We're lucky there's not much wind tonight."

Shortly after midnight, Collins pulls his car in front of Babylon. Jimmy and I walk over.

"Fire is out. You can relax. I'm keeping one unit up here to monitor the situation. There were seven fatalities. I'm wondering if you might have known any of them."

"We weren't expecting anyone," Jimmy says.

Collins reaches into his shirt pocket and reads from a paper.

"David Rockwell? Donald Mascarella? A Myanmar national, Major Maung?"

"No, they don't ring a bell," Jimmy says. "You say there were seven fatalities?"

"Yes, we haven't identified the others. They were burned pretty bad."

"That's awful," I say.

Captain Collins says goodnight and drives off.

We drag ourselves into Babylon and upstairs to where Tony is leaning on the railing. He takes a swig from a can of beer and belches. The front of his Oakland Raiders jersey says he's been eating something with a lot of mustard on it.

"Pretzels," Tony offers the bag to us. "Great for dipping."

"Too tired to crunch," Jimmy says.

"You guys get some rest," Tony says. "Bruno and I will take the first watch. Get you up about six?"

We nod and head off to one of Babylon's luxury suites. My head hits the pillow, and I'm out.

The next thing I'm aware of is the smell of fresh-brewed coffee. The dream image of my beautiful wife, Dawn, saying, "Nick honey, coffee is ready." morphs into the reality of Tony Stomps standing over my bed.

"It's six am." He says. "Nothing going on. No fires. A cop is taking pictures of the fire scene. I walked down there. He says they got the remains of everybody out around three, three-thirty. He asked me if I knew anything about a militia group in the neighborhood. 'No, why?' I ask."

"What did he say to that?"

"He tells me they found seven guns down there with the bodies. 'Unusual,' he says. Anyhow, they got a big wrecker on the way to clear up what's left. Bruno crapped out about an hour ago. He's on that couch in the game room."

"You made coffee?"

"Yeah, right here. Hey, I'm going to rack out down the hall. Call me if you need me."

I look at the tray with two cups of steaming java on it. When I look up, Tony is gone.

"Must be time to snap out of it," Jimmy says. He swings to a sitting position on the edge of his bed and grabs a cup.

The morning is quiet in Babylon. The kitchen has a good selection of food, the washer/dryer works with ease, and the showers are wonderful. A look outside reveals blue skies. Maybe all the fires are under control. By eight-thirty, we're ready to take on the world. Or at least prepared to take on the guys who are coming to put fencing around the place.

My cell phone rings. It's Doc.

"I hear that you had some trouble after we left," He says. "If it's as safe as I think it might be, maybe we can come up. Carole's got some guys helping her move. She wants to collect her things and catch an Air France flight later today."

"It looks good," I say. "We're waiting for some workers, too. Come on up. We'll tell you all about it."

Jimmy:

About nine-thirty, a parade of trucks comes around the bend. Two of them have small cranes on the back. I'm thinking these fence guys don't fool around. It turns out that only half of the trucks are here to install the fence. The other two are here to help Carole move, "just some personal things."

I tell Bruno and Tony our latest game plan for Carole's move from Babylon.

"I want you guys to keep watch on everything she's packing. I don't want anything we're searching for to slip through our fingers. Take Doc aside when he gets here and tell him to be on the lookout, too."

Doc's BMW trails the trucks up to Babylon. Nick and I greet Carole, Doc, and Angel Mascara. We settle down with coffee at a table overlooking the canyon side of Babylon.

"I just had to meet everyone and to make sure that Carole got packed and made her flight to her new life," Angel says.

She's wearing a purple and pink Blending Your Blood t-shirt. It's a walking reminder to us about our promise to hold a Punk fest at the Galloping Dominos.

I look at Nick. He's about to tell the story about last night's fiery crash. I can tell he's wondering how much he should say with Angel present.

"I guess by now that you know that David Rockwell was one of the fatalities last night," he says.

"Hah," Angel says. "I'll bet that bitch Mary Ashford Stevens got him. They're saying on the radio that she gets his ninety-million-dollar fortune. I bet she's laughing all the way to the bank."

"I wouldn't say that for public consumption," Nick says.

"Take it easy, Hon." Doc gives Angel a hug. "No need to get excited."

"Yeah, yeah, I know. Capisce and all that crap," Angel says. "I heard the same 'so-called' accident got the jerks that tried to kill you guys and Doc. At least that bitch Mary is good for something, not that I'm saying, mind you."

"We understand, dear." Carole pats Angel's arm. "Things can get complicated."

"Well, anyway, it looks like we're out of the woods," I say.

"That's fine, Jimmy." Angel puts down her coffee cup and stands up. "Look, Carole's got a plane to catch, and I'm here to make sure she makes it on time, so we're going to get to work. I think those guys from that emergency fence outfit want to talk to you."

It's hard to argue with Angel. There is a lot of work to be done, and everyone is anxious to get to it. As far as what Angel knows about the

157

"accident" that took the lives of people who were out to get us, I leave it at that. Everyone has a right to their theory.

Marvin, the guy from the fence company, is standing off to the side. He also has a theory. His is about securing Babylon from intruders.

"We run a chalk line about a foot in from your property line, Mister Babylon. Follow me?"

I nod. It would be easier to follow Marvin if he didn't have a lit black cigar clenched in his teeth.

"So, once we establish our lines, we're going to have to pound some pipe into the ground." He shifts the cigar to the other side of his mouth. "Your property is steep in the back, Mister Babylon, so maybe we'll drill pipe in as we go along. Follow me?"

I nod again.

Marvin puffs a toxic cloud and chews on the cigar.

"The holes will be good for the temporary fence, you know. Barbed wire and razor wire will secure it until we come back with the best plan, Mister uh…."

"Cox, just call me Jimmy."

"Yeah, that's right, Mister Jimmy. I figure a place this nice should have electronically keyed gates. Yeah, and video cams and motion sensors. You don't want any piece of trash waltzing in here to attack you or your wife. You married, Mister Babylon?"

He puffs and chews again.

"Yeah, I'm married to Julia Roberts. She's not here right now, or I'd have her autograph your cigar."

"No problem, Mister Roberts. I'm going to have my crew start laying down the chalk lines. We'll be making some noise."

I'm about to say something to Marvin when my burner phone sounds Jacky's ring tone.

"Sorry, got to take this," I say.

"No problem, Mister Babylon," Marvin says. "We're gonna get to work."

I motion to Nick to follow me to the suite we slept in overnight.

The door closes behind us. I hit answer, then speaker.

"I'm getting the impression that you boys have been extra busy," Jacky says.

"Yeah," Nick says. "These house closings can be murder."

"Jimmy, are you writing Nick's punch lines for him?"

"No. He's way too clever. Doesn't need me. What's up?"

"I just got off the phone with our dear friend, Congressman Rivera," Jacky says. "He wanted to know if we knew anything about the sudden demise of a Major Maung and his brothers. Ernesto's subcommittee has had its eyes on Maung. He also says that fat Donnie Mascarella and the rest of his crew are permanently MIA."

"Yeah, we kind of heard that, too," Nick says.

"Heartbreaking, isn't it?" Jacky says. "I've been in tears all morning. I'm so choked up I may have to miss the first inning of the Cubs game. Tell me what you guys know and try to leave out most of the bullshit."

Chapter Forty-eight

Nick:

"Let me get this straight," Jacky says. "You're saying Mary Ashford Stevens, the queen of millionaire romances, killed seven men? She dropped a van, a Buick, and a pickup truck on them as they made their way down some rocky slope?"

"Yeah," Jimmy says. "We saw it all go down. She took some heat from Major Maung. He told her a woman didn't belong there. Then he rubbed his crotch and spit at her. When she didn't get any support from her hubby, David Rockwell, that was all it took."

"One red-hot mama," Jacky says.

"Yeah, the word is that red-hot mama inherits Rockwell's ninety million bucks," Jimmy says. "Who says crime doesn't pay?"

"Those seven guys were going to make their way down the slope. Then they could come up to Babylon from the steep side of the property," I say. "We figure Rockwell's boys searched the house while they were serving as security for Carole."

"Yeah, that's cute. The security guys get paid for casing the joint." Jacky says. "So, they figure whatever's valuable is hiding somewhere outside the house."

"Most likely in a concrete bunker that looks like a big drainpipe," Jimmy says. "We're ready to check it out as soon as we get everyone cleared out of here. Carole's got some movers here to take her stuff from the house. They should all be gone by this afternoon."

"Yeah, and we got Marvin, the fence guy putting up barbed wire and razor wire to secure the perimeter," I say.

"So, give me your seat-of-the-pants," Jacky says. "Your hunches. You think there's anything in that bunker?"

I look at Jimmy. He gives me his noncommittal shrug, the I-don't-know-shit-from-Shinola look. It means I'm nominated to take the first guess.

"Our seven fatalities all had a reason for going down into the canyon," I

159

say. "Maung had to believe that there was something that would help Myanmar's Nuke program. Donnie Mascarella had to think so, too. Otherwise, what was the motive, so he could get Maung and his brothers down there and do away with them? Why would he do that? Maung was his drug connection."

"Yeah," Jacky says. "What about Rockwell? What's he doing there? Is he after the Nuke stuff? Does he think there's Nazi gold down there?"

"From what we know of Rockwell, there isn't any love there for Asian people like Maung," Jimmy says. "You know, the master race and all that crap. He'd be the type to kill everyone and take everything."

"So, we're left with that bunker either being full of nuke stuff and/ or Nazi gold, or it's got neither," Jacky says. "Here's how we have to play it, boys. I don't want any free-lancing on this. If there's nuke stuff, we can put it back in safe hands by way of our congressman Ernesto Rivera. It can all go away under the radar."

"That's good," Jimmy says.

"The Nazi gold, if there is any, that's another matter," Jacky says. "If it was any other kind of gold, I'd say we go for it, but I don't want us profiting on this. It's got to go back in some way to help make up for the terrible things that happened to people, some of our relatives. Capisce?"

"I couldn't agree more," Jimmy says.

"I'm with you all the way," I say.

"Okay, do your best. Get Carole moved out and get the fence put up. Keep me in the loop. Now, I'm heading to Wrigley to enjoy the Cubbies."

Jacky clicks off.

Back in the gathering area, things are happening. Carole sits at her piano, playing "Don't Get Around Much Anymore."

"One last tune," she says. "A tribute to a great man."

"Duke Ellington," Doc says.

"I'll never tell," Carole says. She sings a few more bars of the song and stops. She pulls the wooden cover over the keys.

Men from the moving company wheel boxes into a corner near the railing.

"It's all going in a container to Paris," Carole says. "I'd love it, Nick, if you and Jimmy could bring your families over for a visit once I'm settled. You boys have had a rough time in all this crazy stuff."

"Hey, we're going to show up," Jimmy says. "Cassandra knows some great shops there."

"Doc and I are planning on coming," Angel says. "Can't wait to tour the Louvre with you, Carole."

I'm about to say something when Marvin cuts in.

"I need you guys to look at something," he says to Jimmy. "Can you come down into the back area for a look-see, Mister Babylon?"

Jimmy:

We follow Marvin's cigar stench down onto the back slope of Babylon. We were here a few days back with Gary, the security guard. Then, it was quiet, hot, and new to us. Today it's noisy, hot, and tiresome. I have to say I'm getting damn tired of Babylon and the Benders.

Marvin's crew is hacking at brush and pounding steel into the ground. They're supposed to be following the property line. It's one of those futile exercises in legalese. We can't violate the properties next to us by putting our fence right on the property line. The fact that both neighboring parcels are unbuildable adds to the farce.

"One of my boys strayed off the blue line we had," Marvin says. "He thought this was where the property line made a ninety-degree turn. Anyhow, he pounded a pipe support into the ground, and he hit something you need to look at."

A shirtless kid in his late teens is standing next to a hole in the ground. A small mound of dirt beside it holds a shovel. Nick and I stare down into the two-foot-deep hole. We've both seen the shape of this container before. It's a dirt-encrusted version of what we took out of the white van parked near the Fairmont. It's a canister designed for handling nuke materials.

"Didn't know what it was," the kid says. "Figured I better ask before I moved it or covered it up."

A long serial number is stenciled in fading black paint across the lid. Two rusting fasteners secure the cover from opposite sides of the canister.

"Any idea what it is?" The kid grabs the shovel. "I can dig it out if you want. I could open it."

"No, no," Nick says. "We can't bother that. It's part of a monitoring system. They told us to be aware of it when we got hold of the place."

"Yeah," I say. "Delicate sensors. You know the earthquake monitoring. Cover it up. Anyone asks, we'll tell them you never touched it. Jesus, they'd come after all of us looking to collect a big fine."

"Cover it back up, Tyler." Marvin puffs out a cloud of tar from his cigar. "We don't want any trouble from some earthquake experts, do we, Mister Babylon?"

"No, we sure don't," I say. "Hey, there's cold beers and sodas up in the kitchen for you guys. Help yourself."

"You heard him. Break time." Marvin leads his gang of four toward the house.

Nick motions for me to follow him to where the Babylon bunker sits. It hasn't changed since we were here last. I decide the little girl in the elevator at the Mark Hopkins had it right. The "water" under the grating is a mirror. A phony cover means there's something underneath worth hiding.

We head to the tool room under the house to see what we have to work with. The few basic tools there will help some, but we need more.

"We need Tony and Bruno to pick up some equipment for us," Nick says. "We need to rent a GPR, ground-penetrating radar unit. We're also going to need a torch to cut through the metal grill covering the bunker. We'll make a list. There's a good chance that everything we've been looking for and maybe more is in our back yard."

"You think there's more than what might be in that canister and in the bunker?" I ask.

"Take a look around," Nick says. "It's a pretty big yard."

He's right, I decide. If that kid Tyler could find the canister by accident, no telling what a little searching might turn up.

"You're right," I say. "It is a big yard."

"Soon as we get everyone out of here," Nick says, "We're gonna find out what the Benders have been burying."

Chapter Forty-nine

Nick:

Jimmy and I stand in the dusty tool room across from the servant's quarters on the lower level at Babylon. Clancy Booker's description of the place comes to mind.

"It was clean and comfortable but not like the luxury suites upstairs," he said. "The tool room was okay, too. It didn't have a lawnmower because Babylon didn't have a lawn. So, no one could yell, 'Niggah, get out there and cut the grass.' I used to worry about the rattlers down on the back slope. Hell, they were no match for some of the snakes one floor up."

We make a list of tools we need to ferret out what's buried in Babylon's backyard. A quick search of the internet shows a couple builders' supply stores in San Rafael. Two phone calls later, we have a plan. Bruno and Tony will go to pick up all our new toys. Jimmy and I will stay to keep an eye on Marvin's crew. We're hoping that they don't accident their way into plutonium or gold while putting up our fence.

Bruno comes bouncing down the stairs to where we're standing. "Carole's movers are ready to go," he says. "All her stuff is packed. We looked at everything she's taking with. No nukes, no gold, a lot of old lady sweaters and dresses. She's getting ready to leave for the airport with Doc and Angel. Come upstairs and say goodbye."

The parking pad in front of Babylon is a confusing mess of trucks and cars. Marvin's fence materials are blocking the front of the mover's truck. Doc is able to lead Carole and Angel through the maze toward his car. It's parked off to the side of Canyon Ridge Drive.

"I'm so grateful to have met you and Jimmy," Carole says. "You boys have been lifesavers. Give me a big hug."

We each get a big hug from Carole, and both of us have to swear that we'll visit her in Paris. Angel grabs Carole by the arm and leads her toward the waiting car.

"We got a lot of traffic ahead of us," Angel says. "I don't mean to be rude. Sometimes Doc drives like he's in an over-loaded manure truck with faulty brakes. It's time to move ass."

For once, I'm glad that Angel is rude. We need to get people out of here so we can explore what's buried in the backyard.

She opens the back door for Carole, eases her in, and slams the door. Seconds later, Angel's in the front passenger seat telling Doc to "let's go. Get the lead out of your ass."

Doc steers his BMW down Canyon Ridge Drive. Carole and Angel wave. A toot on the horn, and they're gone.

"Someone's got to move all this crap, or I can't get out of here." It's the driver of the flat-bed container truck holding Carole's Paris-bound goods. He's right. Bruno runs to tell Marvin to get his act together. Things need to move.

After what seems like an eternity, Marvin's crew hauls their fence materials off to the side, and the truck can move. The truck driver hands a clipboard to the guy sitting next to him in the front seat.

"Get him to sign us out of here," the driver says. "They took off without verifying we were done."

Another screw-up, courtesy of Marvin, I'm thinking. Carole's rushing off to the airport. Meanwhile, her goods are still here without a sign-out for the movers. I sign the top copy of a multi-copy form next to the space that has the time and date.

"That work for you guys?" I ask.

"Yeah," the driver yells. "Give him the bottom copy, the pink one, and let's get going."

I grab the pink copy and stuff it in my pocket. The flat-bed truck moves down the road, followed by another with a crane on the back.

"I thought that one was Marvin's," Jimmy says.

"Live and learn," I say. "His truck has the smaller crane."

"How fascinating," Jimmy says. "Let's get Bruno and Tony to town before those tool places close."

In minutes, Jimmy and I are watching Marvin's crew from the canyon-side railing. We sip our beers as we view the show. Progress is going along well. Pipe gets pounded into the ground. Wire gets strung, and before long, wire fencing is protecting the back slope of Babylon.

Soon, the action moves to the front of the house. Fence gets attached to supports in moveable concrete bases. In minutes there's a gate connected to the entrance to the parking pad. We're surrounded by steel wire on pipe.

"It's all we can do for you today," Marvin says. He hands us a large chain with a padlock on it for the gate. Three keys come with the envelope he gives me. "It's a copy of the billing to your Chicago company and a basic sketch of what I have in mind for permanent security. We can talk about it tomorrow or the next day. I'll have a couple estimates you can run through your people."

He lights another cigar and adds, "You know, there's a lot of possibilities for this place. I could see extending a large concrete patio over the canyon side. It could have a medium size infinity pool coming off the second-floor overlook. That downslope area isn't worth anything unless you take advantage of the space."

"Sounds good," Jimmy says. "Beats the hell out of dealing with rattlesnakes."

"Yeah, I'll work on a few sketches on that," Marvin says. "No charge."

We watch as Marvin's trucks head down Canyon Ridge Drive.

I look at Jimmy.

"Welcome to Babylon. Enjoy your stay."

"Yeah," he says. "Here's a shovel and a Geiger counter. Get to work."

Jimmy:

Bruno and Tony get back from town as the sun is going down. We could stumble our way on the back slope with the yard lights on, but we take a vote. Unanimously, we decide that morning would be better. We need to rest, eat, and check out Babylon on the inside.

"I'll tell you one thing," Tony says as he finishes his fourth slice of pizza, "This ain't no shit house. The place is beautiful. Quality fixtures, good construction, and comfortable beds. If everything is secure, I'm going to get some shut-eye."

Nick and Bruno follow suit, heading for their beds. One more beer, I tell myself, and I'll go, too. I check the outside lights on both the front and the backyard. The gate is locked tight with the heavy-duty padlock provided by Marvin. It's all been taken care of, but something keeps nagging me. I feel like I'm missing something.

My cell phone rings.

"You guys must be super busy," Cassandra says. "We've been missing you two. Want to tell Cassie about it?"

I know she's sitting by herself when she refers to herself as Cassie. It's our special name for her when the two of us are being close.

"I miss you," I say. "I can't wait to get home. This Babylon thing has been unsettling, to say the least. Every time I turn around, I'm looking at someone else's version of the truth."

She listens as I outline our activities since arriving in the Bay Area several days ago. She loves hearing about characters like Angel Mascara, Charlie Lynch, and Porkchop. I can feel her broad smile as I list some of their quirks and characteristics.

I can also feel her wince as I recite the death toll since we arrived for what was billed as a simple house closing.

"My god, fifteen dead?"

"Yeah, but all we did was four in self-defense. It was a woman who drew the most blood. She killed seven. I'll tell you who she is when I get back home."

"You're such a tease," Cassie says.

We talk for a while about what's going on in Vegas. She tells me about the shrimp scampi she made for Dawn and Molly earlier in the evening. They watched some old Road Runner cartoons before Molly got tired, and Dawn took her home. Zorro went with them across the golf course. He's staying over on his guest doggy cushion in Molly's room.

I love every word she's saying, and I want to be there. I'm tired of Babylon, tired of the Benders and the bullshitters. Maybe, you're just plain tired, Cassie says.

"Get some rest, Babe. Let it all go for a while. You'll think better. I want you back here safe. And take care of Nick while you're at it. We all love his reckless act, too."

I decide she's right and head for bed. The beer and the pizza have made me tired. The thoughts about that kid Tyler finding the nuke canister can wait till tomorrow if that's what it is. He looks like someone I know, but I can't place who. Besides, what difference could it make? He's just some kid. To hell with him. Listen to Cassie. Let it all go for a while.

Then there's that damn song that keeps running through my head. It's the song Carole was singing before she closed her piano. Don't Get Around

Much Anymore. Crazy old broad fucked up the lyrics. The line goes something about missing a Saturday dance, not Mister Saturday's dance. To hell with it. Cassie's right. Let it go. Tomorrow it will all come clear.

Chapter Fifty

Nick:

We manage a decent breakfast from the dwindling supply of groceries Carole left us. Sourdough bread with melted provolone tops the menu. Two strawberry cheesecakes thawed in the microwave are next. The coffee is top of the line, and there's even orange juice. Who can complain about that?

On the early morning news, the over-dressed creep says another jillion acres of forest fires are filling California's air with smoke. One whiff of the air in Fairfax supports his conclusion. When an ad for hemorrhoid ointment comes on, I turn off the TV—no need to remind Jimmy of his problem.

Tony and Bruno go down to their rental car to get the weapons of choice for attacking the backyard slope. The plan is to get rid of all the brush and weeds so we can see what we're dealing with. The ground-penetrating radar unit is supposed to help with that once we get the area cleared.

I look across the table at Jimmy. He's got one of those thousand-mile stares. He's sipping coffee like he's hoping inspiration grows with each drop of caffeine.

"You going to talk with anyone today, or are you trying to be the Vegas version of the Buddha?" I ask.

"We need to find out what's in that Baby Lon bunker," he says, putting down his cup. "That's got to be first. We figure that out, and we'll be on the right track."

"What about the canister that kid Tyler found?"

"Lots of unsettling thoughts," Jimmy says. "Goddamn, kid's ten feet inside the property line. What's he doing there? What, he just walks over and decides to poke into the dirt with a steel pipe? I'll tell you something. That kid is too smart to be stupid. One look at him, and you know he's bright. He didn't do that to be dumb. The first time he pokes into the soil off the fence line, he hits a canister designed to hold nuke materials? Give me a break. What are the odds on that?"

"But you want to leave that one alone for now?"

"Yeah, if it's loaded with nuke crap, it might be above our pay grade. It's possible, if we find out what's in the bunker, we'll have a better idea of where we stand. Maybe there's nuke stuff, maybe there's gold, or hell, a couple dead bodies in there."

I get up and grab the coffee pot to refill our cups.

"So, if you get the bunker open and discover a bunch of nuke canisters sitting there...."

"I'll shut the cover and call Jacky. Let him and Congressman Rivera call in the troops," Jimmy says. "But, maybe there's something valuable. I'm not saying it's Nazi gold, but you can't tell me that with all the shady deals that went on at Babylon over the years...."

"That there isn't a leftover trinket or two?" I ask.

"I ain't saying for sure." Jimmy sips more coffee. "I'll tell you this, though. I got one of those feelings like I had with the last presidential election. All the books went heavy for 'Mrs. Know-it-all.' There was no way the fat bozo was going to take it. I went off the books and nailed down a grand at fifteen to one with Cesar Bourne at Rock-A-Baby Casino. I ain't happy about the election, but the fifteen big ones were a hell of a consolation prize."

I stir some sugar into my cup as I think about what he's saying. We aren't going to get rich if we find nuke materials. But who's to say that there isn't some leftover treasure hiding in the bunker?

"So, the kid pokes the pipe and hits the canister. Maybe there are canisters all over the back slope. We could all go out there and hit a nuke canister," I say.

"Yeah," Jimmy says. "That would be way above our pay grade. At that point, we'd be wise to run like hell."

Bruno and Tony come upstairs to where we're sitting next to the canyon side railing.

"We got all the stuff at the top of the backyard slope." Bruno pours a cup of coffee and grabs a piece of cheesecake. "Any ideas?"

"Jimmy says we need to cut a path to that bunker out there," I say. "Make some room around it so we can work on getting into it. He thinks that Al Capone's loot might be buried in it. He's playing a hunch."

"Let's hope he's right," Tony says. "We could all use a taste. I'm ready to start looking for loose change under cushions."

"Not to worry," Jimmy says. "Jacky's got us covered. He knows this has turned into a bunch of crap. I know he'll be generous."

"What about that canister that the kid poked?" Bruno asks. "You know, the kid brother of that cop that was up here with Carole giving him the deluxe tour."

"Jesus." Jimmy slams down his cup. "That's who he looks like. Why didn't you say he was Officer Lawrence's brother?"

"Hell. I thought you knew," Bruno says. "He came right out and said he was when we took a break for beers. He usually works at their pizza joint. He said this was better pay getting a day's work with Marvin. Couple hundred bucks, I think he said."

"Shit." Jimmy shakes his head and stares at Bruno.

"Hey, he didn't just tell me," Bruno says. "Carole and Doc were standing there, too. In fact, Carole gave him a hug and said she was glad it worked out for him."

Jimmy:

"What sense does any of this make?" Nick asks.

"Wait," I say. You have to hand it to Carole. She wants us to find the nuke container, but not by admitting she knows anything about it. So, she finds out that Jeff Lawrence has a kid brother who could use a few bucks. A phone call to the kid and one to Marvin results in a day job for Tyler."

"How fucking heartwarming," Tony says. "So, how does the kid know where to push the pipe into the ground?"

"You remember the pile of dirt with the shovel in it next to the hole the canister is buried in," I say. "There was something else on that pile, an old wooden handle corkscrew."

"I remember that," Nick says. "A corkscrew sitting there marking the spot wouldn't raise any suspicions. We told the kid to shovel it all back into the hole."

"Yeah, the kid did what Carole told him to do." I look out at the back slope. The half-filled hole looks just like it did when we announced it was beer break time. Carole knew that we weren't going to open the canister while everyone was hanging around. She knew we'd wait till we got everyone safely out of Babylon before we went looking for nukes.

"So, you think that Carole wanted to tip us off about where Big Philly Petrillo hid the nuke stuff?" Nick asks.

"Yeah, maybe so," I say. "If that's the whole extent of what's here, we got it made. We open the Baby Lon bunker and see what's worthwhile. Maybe we're okay by handing over to the Feds what's in the container the kid found."

"My kind of plan," Tony says. "Let's do it."

We're about to go down to whack through the brush when my burner phone rings.

It's Jacky.

"You guys got the place all to yourself, right? Good. I want you to find what's there and don't try any heroics like you're all of a sudden, scientists. Things are happening. I talked with Marvin. He's okay. I like his security plans for Babylon, so he'll be starting with the permanent fence and all that in a couple days."

"We got all the tools," Nick says. "In fact, we were just getting ready to find out what's hidden on the back slope."

"That's good, really good." Jacky clears his throat. "I got a little pressure on this end. My lovely bride wants to know when we can get out there to enjoy the place."

More bullshit from Muriel, I'm thinking. All we need is for her to show up.

"Good question," I say. "As far as I can tell, Carole's housekeeper has quit. The food supply is getting a little sparse around the edges. The place could use some real help. It's beautiful here, but it needs a lot of cleaning and upkeep."

There's a pause on Jacky's end, and I think maybe we've gotten a reprieve from a Muriel visit. Then Jacky clears his throat.

"Okay. So, here's the deal. I'm sending out Eddie Scarponi and his wife Marie to organize the place. She's a go-getter, runs that Franklin Park Italian Festival every year. The Papaleo brothers will come for heavy lifting. They'll be there the day after tomorrow, late. Eddie will call you when they get in."

"You want us to pick them up?" Nick asks.

"No, let them rent cars. I just don't want them getting lost."

"That's just great," Tony says after Jacky hangs up. "That goddamn Marie is worse than Muriel. She thinks she's the D.A. She wants to know everything about everyone. If we want to discover anything, we'd better do it now. And those Papaleos, didn't they do time for running some real estate scam?"

"Yeah, disappearing rent-to-own floating condos in Florida," Nick says. "Let's get to work."

Chapter Fifty-one

Nick:

The bush hacking tools take a little getting used to. This top-of-the-line equipment has complicated instructions in six different languages. But nowhere do they say anything about standing on a 45-degree slope while trying to avoid chopping off your leg.

"The slow approach is the best," Jimmy says. "Look, we been at this for only a couple of hours, and we got the top part of the lot cleared."

"Yeah, and no one's lost a hand or a foot," Tony says. He's got a "Babylon" towel wrapped around his forehead to catch the sweat.

The top part Jimmy is referring to is about a ten-foot swath next to the house. At this rate, I think we won't get to the bunker till late afternoon.

Bruno's weed eater coughs a few times and stops.

"Would you believe we're out of gas?" He asks.

"So, fill it up," Jimmy says.

"Uh, for that, we need to go to town," Bruno says. "We should have bought that five-gallon can and filled it up."

"We only got the two-gallon can," Tony says. "There's about a quarter gallon left in it. The way the guy at the rental place talked about the tools, I thought the two gallons would be enough."

Things start to complicate. We're not only running out of gas; we're running out of decent food and close to being out of beer.

Tony and Bruno head for town while Jimmy and I use up the rest of the gas. We manage another five-foot sweep across the lot. We're getting closer to the bunker. All the busted-up brush and weeds are off to one side in a big pile. The ground we've cleared is loose gravel mixed with a scattering of dirt.

"Find any gold yet?" Jimmy wipes the sweat off his face with a hanky.

"No, I'm only doing this for the exercise," I say. "Find any rattlers?"

"It's all bullshit," Jimmy says. "The goddamn Benders lied about everything else. Let's say there's no gold, no rattlers, no nukes. All there is, are the four of us out here sweating our asses off because somebody laid a good bullshit story off on us."

Out of gas but not out of beer, we head into the house to our favored spot by the rail overlooking the canyon side. We're halfway through the first beer when Jimmy stands up and looks around. "Right where we're sitting, that's where that guy Saturday bought the farm. The way Carole tells it, Big Philly shot him, and he went right over that rail to the slope below. Jesus, a hell of a thing for an eight-year-old kid to see."

Of course, I have to look over the rail to see where Saturday might have landed seventy years ago.

"There's a problem with that story if this is where it happened." I point down toward the backyard slope. Below floor level is a six-foot wooden extension hanging out at a slight angle. It's an overhang protecting the downstairs area by the toolshed and the servant's room. The edge of the overhang has an eight-inch redwood beam that prevents stuff from going over the side. A fork, a shot glass, and a crushed cigarette pack are part of the current exhibit next to the board.

"Jesus." Jimmy stares at what I'm looking at. "That would make it hard for a body to hit that and roll off onto the slope."

"So, an eight-year-old sees things differently," I say. "Or they built the extension onto the house later. I know the electricity has been updated. Hell, in the twenties when this place went up, you had two-prong plugs and not much need for 220-volt outlets."

"Maybe so," Jimmy says. "The plumbing has been brought up to date, too."

We sit in silence, drinking our beers, happy for the break. Quiet feels good. We get over this next hump, the bunker, and whatever else is in the backyard, and I'm ready to pack it in. Hand the joint over to Marie and Eddie Scarponi and head for home. They can fool around getting things ship-shape for Muriel and Jacky. I can do without all that.

"Just suppose." Jimmy leans forward and puts his elbows on the table. "What if Carole did lie about Saturday getting shot and falling over the railing? It's far-fetched, I know, but why would she do that? Years of therapy with Doc, telling him that story over and over again? This make any sense?"

"No, of course not," I say. "Besides, what's in it for us if we find out that dear old Aunt Carole lied about it? Isn't lying what the Benders do?"

"I'll be damn glad to get out of here." Jimmy sips his beer and leans back.

He smiles, shakes his head, and lets out a deep breath. It doesn't fool me.

Inside, I know he's grinding.

Jimmy:

Tony and Bruno come back with food, beer, and gas, ten gallons of it. I'm tempted to ask Bruno if it's enough to burn down Babylon, but I decide we'd better see what we can find on the back slope first.

The work moves along. We're getting good at working the tools. By late afternoon we've cleared the entire back slope. We're ready to take on the bunker.

There's something different about the bunker. It's like one of those large cast-concrete sewer pipes that you see where highways are being built. With all the weeds and brush removed you see that it's surrounded by a patio made from multi-colored brick. It looks like a place where people might have sat and enjoyed the view of the canyon.

"Just say the word, and I'll burn our way through the top grating," Bruno says, holding a propane torch. "It's probably rusted in place."

I tell him to wait. The rust on the grating doesn't seem to be rust. It looks like someone has painted it to look like rust. Off to one side of the grating, I notice a padlock under a bunch of dead leaves.

"Who wants to try picking a lock?" I ask.

"Let me get some of that spray oil from the tool shed," Bruno says. "It'll make it go easier. I'm usually pretty good with those weatherproof locks."

In minutes he's back with the oil. He also has a large ring with a half dozen keys on it.

"Hey, they were hanging on the wall. I figure what the hell."

The fourth key opens the padlock. Bruno swings the grating open on its hinges and lets it fall toward the house. The metal mirror that gave the appearance of water is next to come off. Beneath it is a varnished plywood cover with fold-out handles attached to each end. Tony grabs the handle opposite Bruno, and they lift.

We stand staring down into a dark hole. Nick turns on a flashlight. There's a metal ladder bolted to the side of the bunker opposite the hinges. It's hard to see much from up top, but it looks like the ladder goes down about ten feet to a concrete floor. Nick is about to go down the ladder when Tony stops him.

"Let's get one of the Geiger counters first. It doesn't hurt to play it safe." Tony comes back from our collection of nuke-handling merchandise with a Geiger counter and a six-pack of beer.

"Better not try to do this when we're thirsty," he says.

We lower the wand down into the hole and get no signal telling us it's hot. Whatever's down there, it isn't plutonium.

"I'm going down there," I say. "I've got my Glock in case there's a snake."

"Get Jimmy," Tony says. "He thinks he's fucking Bruce Willis. Just remember those bullets ricochet."

"He's not going to shoot anyone," Nick says. "He just uses the handgrip of the gun to hit things."

I get to the concrete floor and reach up for the flashlight. I turn around. It's larger down here than I thought. Ten feet in diameter? I'm guessing. I focus the flashlight on wooden crates off to one side. Ammunition crates? Stenciled lettering on one container reads "Illinois Nat'l Guard." I open the busted wooden top on the crate. Inside are parts of what looks like Army-issued .45 caliber sidearms. Another case next to the sidearms has a half-dozen Army-issued field glasses. I flashback on the field glasses Carole had when we first visited Babylon.

"Any snakes down there?" Nick asks.

"Come and see."

Everyone gets the tour, and we do an inventory of what Babylon has been hiding. Tony says he can probably put together eight .45 caliber pistols from the parts left in the crate. Fourteen pairs of field glasses are off in another box on the other side of the bunker. A large container of bayonets has crayon markings on it that say "Cuba." Another crate of canteens is marked "Dominican Rep."

Bruno finds a belt of .50 caliber machine gun bullets behind another crate marked "Miami."

"All those stories that Big Philly Petrillo ran stolen guns to Latin America. Looks like they weren't bullshit," Nick says. "This must be the leftovers."

"Yeah," Tony says. "What does that say about him stealing from Los Alamos? Think there's any leftover plutonium here?"

Chapter Fifty-two

Nick:

We unload everything out of the bunker and take it upstairs as the sun starts to set. The plywood cover gets topped by the metallic mirror surface. The grating gets locked in place, and the key goes back to the tool room. As far as anyone else is concerned, we opened the bunker and found it empty. Our best guess is that the bunker served as a cistern to catch water off the roof of Babylon at one time back in the day.

Somehow, everything we've taken out of the bunker needs to disappear. We need to get rid of the crates that have anything to do with the Illinois National Guard. The circular fireplace in the middle of the second floor gathering area will do the trick. Even though it's eighty-five degrees outside, we opt for a fire. More smoke added to what's drifting in from wildfires to the east won't get noticed.

Stuff we're trying to keep like the sidearms, and the field glasses need to be boxed. The crates of bayonets and canteens need to be repacked to deliver them to whoever will have them. As luck would have it, Carole's movers have left a stack of cardboard boxes ready for taping. They've even left a roll of mover's tape.

We sit like campers around the fire, tossing in parts of crates. It seems like someone should be telling ghost stories. Instead, we drink our beers and eat pizza. We've parceled out all the keepers from the Baby Lon bunker into four stacks of boxes. A fifth pile off to the side holds the bayonets and canteens.

"Hey, I think I got a guy down in LA that will take that stuff," Bruno says. "It ain't going to bring much, but if we lay it on him like a favor, it could do us some good down the line. He runs a shop where preppers and survivalists hang out."

"Yeah, it's Keith Marsh he's talking about," Tony says. "All around good people. We should do that for him."

"Sounds good," I say.

I toss more pieces of Illinois National Guard crates onto the fire.

"Yeah, fine," Jimmy says. "Too bad we don't have marshmallows."

"Believe it or not, there's some out in the kitchen." Bruno gets to his feet. "There's a whole collection of candies and nuts in the cabinet near the sink."

Halfway through the second bag of marshmallows, I get up to go to the can. On the way back, I take the meandering route, checking out Babylon suites to see what's been left behind. Other than towels and bed linens, the luxurious suites are empty and clean. Maybe too clean, I think.

I get to Carole's old abode and look around. It, too, is clean. You can call me nuts, but somehow, I find that troubling. There's something I should see here, but I can't remember what it is. I feel like I'm turning into some old fart who can't remember why he walked into his kitchen.

I stand there, staring at the empty walls. Everything has been taken off the walls and packed away into the moving container. It's all on the way to Paris, even her small ornate mirror. Then I remember what Carole said when we asked her about where she found the phony Nazi gold bar.

"I was packing up some personal belongings a couple days before you guys showed up. A small, ornate mirror I wanted to take with me was hanging in my room. A couple of screws fastened it to the wooden panel. When I took out the second screw, the gold bar fell out of the wall. I was shocked."

I turn on all the lights in Carole's suite. The dimmers are up all the way. I don't see any hole in a wood panel for a gold bar to fall out of. In fact, I don't see any wood panel. I chalk it up to another Bender lie. Hell, I tell myself, there probably wasn't any ornate mirror, either.

Jimmy sticks his head in the doorway.

"Where the hell you been? We thought you got lost."

"I was going around double-checking things."

"Any significant discovery you'd want to share? Find any gold, plutonium, Philly Petrillo?

"It's more Bender bullshit," I say. "Carole told us that the phony gold bar dropped out of a hole in the wall. You see any holes?"

"Of course not," Jimmy says. "You got to quit believing what you hear from the Benders. Tomorrow we check the place for nukes. We'll put our trust in the Geiger counters, not the Benders."

Jimmy:

I sit staring at the Illinois National Guard crates going up in flames. Tony's telling a funny story about how he and Jacky accidentally won a big jackpot in Atlantic City.

Instead of enjoying the evening, I'm grinding about what Nick told me. I'm adding the missing hole in the disappeared wood panel to my list of what bothers me about the Benders:

The phony gold bar didn't drop out of the wall.

The rust on the bunker grating is paint.

A kid hired by Marvin, the fence man, turns out to be Officer Jeff Lawrence's brother. The kid goes right to the place the nuke canister's buried. It turns out Carole got him the job, and no doubt told him where to poke a pipe and hit the canister.

So, how did Carole know which fence company would be building our emergency barricade?

Then there's the story about Mr. Saturday getting shot and tumbling over the railing to the slope below. Nice touch, except Saturday would have had to jump through a ton of redwood lumber to end up on the slope. The wooden overhang is part of the house, and it looks like it's been there ever since Lacey Bender took over the deed.

I feel like I've caught some sort of Bender disease. Every involvement with Muriel, Teddy, and Carole leads to more complications. This was supposed to be a simple trip. Go give Teddy a financial boost. Check out Babylon for a house closing so Muriel and Jacky can enjoy the Bay Area. While you're doing these simple things, have some fun.

Some fun.

We've been lied to, threatened, and shot at. We've also had to clean up Teddy's crap so Muriel wouldn't go off the deep end.

That song about a Barnum and Bailey World keeps running through my head. Phony as can be. Who the hell paints rust on a grating, I wonder? Then I think of something else.

"Turn on the lights for the back slope," I say. "We've got to check something out."

"What? Kind of late, ain't it?" Bruno asks.

"Something's been grinding on me," I say. "I want us to check out that container that kid Tyler poked into. My bullshit detector has been sounding an alarm."

"Mine, too." Nick tosses his empty beer can into the fire. "We're getting someone else's version of what's been happening here."

"The nuke handling materials are down in the tool shed," Tony says. "We've got all the protective clothing and the two Geiger counters."

"Maybe what we really could have used around here was a lie detector," Nick says.

In minutes, we're down on the backyard slope staring at the half-filled hole the container is in. Tony lowers the wand from the Geiger counter into the hole.

No clicks.

Nick lowers the wand from the other Geiger counter.

"Just to be sure," he says.

No clicks.

Bruno scoops some dirt out of the hole. Soon, we're staring at the top of the canister with its two rusting fastener bolts. Except, a closer look tells us the bolts aren't rusting. It's another paint job.

I'm about to reach into the hole with heavy-duty tongs to pull out the canister when Nick yells.

"Wait."

He points to something shiny sticking up from the dirt.

Next to the container, there's a plastic bag with an envelope inside. I grab it with the tongs and bring it out of the hole.

"What do you think it is?" Nick asks.

"Another chapter in the ongoing Bender saga," I say.

Chapter Fifty-three

Nick:

Morning arrives, and I find Jimmy sitting by the table next to the canyon side railing. He's drinking coffee and reading the note from Carole again. We fished it out of the hole sitting next to the nuke container last night and brought it upstairs to read.

"Take another read," Jimmy says. "tell me what you think. Can we trust her?"

"I thought we hashed this out last night. Everyone thought it was legit."

"You know how much I trust the Benders," Jimmy says. "I'm surprised it wasn't written in disappearing ink."

I fill my coffee cup, and I read:

Hey Guys,
I want you to know that there are no nuclear materials at Babylon. Big
Philly used the old container to show people that he could deliver nuke
stuff, but it was all bullshit.
By now, you boys have cleaned out the bunker. Yes, Big Philly did knock
off the Illinois National Guard, way back in another era. Jesus, I feel like
a damn dinosaur. Please take the merchandise and do with it what you
will. Please don't leave anything incriminating for Muriel and Jacky to
deal with.
I know you're wondering about Tyler Lawrence working for Marvin. His
finding Big Philly's old nuke container is my doing. I knew you'd be
searching for nuke stuff and stolen Army weapons. You'd also be looking
for emergency fence companies in Marin County. Fact is, Marvin owns
all the companies that do emergency board-ups and fence work in Marin.
His company has been up to Babylon to work on plumbing and
electricity. He's an old friend.
Tyler has delivered pizza to Babylon, and several times he's hung out for
a while to help eat what he brought. He's a charming young man. I
wanted to tell you where the container was without causing a ruckus. I
figured if Tyler ran into it, you guys would wait until everyone got out of
range. Then you'd check to see if plutonium was in the container. You
can go out and check all you want, but I know for a fact that you won't
find any makings for weapons of mass destruction.
Well, I'm off to what's left of the rest of my life. It's been nice meeting
you guys, and please don't forget about Paris.

Carole

"What do you think? Jimmy asks.
"We should run that ground-penetrating radar unit around on the back
slope this morning. If nothing shows up, I'd say we're done here, except
to turn the place over to Eddie and Marie later today."
We manage to put together a decent breakfast. Soon we're down on the
back slope using the GPR. I wonder if we'll discover if anything unusual
is buried under the dusty gravel. Big surprises appear, but nothing that
would detonate to any degree.
A silver cigarette case with Lucky Strikes tucked inside in their original
packaging is first on the list.
"Jesus, it must be sixty years old," says Bruno, the lucky finder. "If you
lit one of these things and inhaled, you'd drop a load in your pants."
Jimmy finds a gold-plated Dunhill lighter from the same era as the
cigarette case.

"I don't think they belonged to the same guy," he says. "The Benders wouldn't hang with anybody tacky enough to wear silver and gold together."

A small collection of pocket change turns up. Toss in a bottle opener, half a dozen bottle caps, and a rusty pocketknife. That about covers it.

"I'm satisfied," Jimmy says. "If you guys are, too, we can take these tools back and get ready to hand the joint over to Eddie and Marie."

"I'm keeping the phony nuke container," I say. "I'll use it to decorate my office at Dominos."

We return the tools to the rental place in town. Everything gets packed in the boxes left by the movers. The nuke handling equipment, along with the Geiger counters, get FedEx-ed to Vegas.

Tony and Bruno take their share of the weapons and all the canteens and bayonets. The Escalade they rented is packed, ready to make the 400-mile run to LA. By mid-afternoon, everything is packed in our vehicles. When Eddie and Marie show up, we're out of here.

About two in the afternoon, Marvin's crew arrives to do some work on the permanent fencing. I tell him about Eddie and Marie coming in later to take over Babylon.

"Yeah, I heard they were coming," Marvin says. "I spoke with Jacky earlier today. He's going to go ahead with that patio I told you about, the one with the infinity pool."

"Good," Jimmy says. "I'm glad you got it covered."

I can tell by the way Jimmy says this that he's had it. He's tired of all the Bender shit and wants to get on the road. Just then, my burner phone rings. It's Jacky.

I give him the basic report that the joint is clean of weapon materials and ready to hand over to the Scarponis.

"Marvin's going to do some of the work he and I agreed on," Jacky says. "Eddie and Marie will get the heads up on that from me. Give them the keys. I'm hitting each of the four of you with 50 large. You've done a hell of a job. I hope you guys all have a safe trip home."

After a few okays and greats, the call ends. Suddenly, I feel free.

Jimmy:

Marie and Eddie arrive in a rented Caddy just after three. Both are in a good mood and seem happy to be in Fairfax.

"We had a nice flight," Marie says. "I was anxious to get out here and see what we can do before Jacky and Muriel come out. We left the Papaleo brothers in Chicago. We didn't want to bother with their crap."

"Yeah, we thought it was best," Eddie says. "Marie's brother is a retired cop from Petaluma. He and his wife Patty will be showing up tonight to help with the place."

We tour them through Babylon. They're impressed.

"With a kitchen like this, we can do banquets." Marie waves her arms at the restaurant size appliances.

"No wonder a lot of heavy hitters hung out here," Eddie says. "This place is beautiful. Jesus, the oil paintings of those movie stars, the view of the canyon, the Jacuzzis."

We introduce them to Marvin and hand over the keys to Babylon. By five, we've had our farewell drinks with Eddie and Marie. We're in the Caddy and on the way down the winding road leading out.

"You know I don't care if I never see this joint again," I say. "I'm happy to be out of here."

"Oh, but don't you feel that there's a small part of yourself that you've left behind at Babylon?" Nick asks.

I glance over at him in the passenger seat. He's got one of those smirks that looks like it might burst into a belly laugh.

"What the hell do you mean? A small part of me? Yeah, maybe the nightmare I had about Muriel showing up before we could escape. They can have that."

"When we loaded all the stuff into the trunk, did you notice anything missing?" Nick's smirk gets more intense.

"I give up," I say. "I'm on overload. I'm happy everything fits in the trunk, and we're out of there. What am I missing?"

"Just those black trash bags. The ones with the blood-soaked sheets from your bout with hemorrhoids at Murray's. I smuggled them into one of the deluxe suites. I took Eddie aside and told him we had to get a little tough to set things right at Babylon. We tried our best to get rid of all the evidence, but the sheets somehow got left. It would be good if he could help us out, capisce?"

"You're a crazy son of a bitch. You know that, don't you? What did Eddie do, piss in his pants?"

"No, he took it in stride. He just wanted to make sure that we didn't bury anyone on the property. I told him, no, but he could talk with Jeff Lawrence, one of the local cops. He has some theories about who might be buried down in the canyon."

We both laugh and punch each other in the arm.

"Head for the Mark Hopkins," Nick says. "We can use some rest before we head for home. I'm glad this Babylon stuff is all over."

"Let's hope so," I say.

Inside, I still feel that somehow, we've been conned.

Chapter Fifty-four

Nick:

How do we celebrate being finally free of Babylon?

I could tell you how we call our wives and have them fly up to SF from Vegas. Cable car rides, ferries to Sausalito for open-air jazz concerts, and an Alcatraz tour make us happy. Even four-year-old Molly falls in love with The City. She especially loves the cannolis at Stella Bakery and the sea lions at Pier 39.

Or, I could tell you about us meeting up with our wives and Molly in LA and staying at Tony's place in Beverly Hills. Tours of Disneyland, movie studios and the Getty Museum spark everyone's interest.

I could tell you all that, but it would be lies.

Those things we'll save for other times.

Jimmy drives from Babylon back to our suite at the Mark Hopkins. We walk down the hill, have a good dinner at an Italian place in North Beach, and grab a taxi back to the hotel.

"I gotta tell you," Jimmy says. "I'm beat, had enough."

"I hear you, loud and clear."

We decide to rack out early and leave for Vegas at daybreak. We've both had too much of California burning and Bender bullshit.

Jimmy's Caddy, with the two bullet-riddled rear windows, is our way back to Sin City. Jimmy knows a guy there who can handle the repairs.

We're missing our families and friends. Somehow, they make up for the dry, hot desert and the crazies who flock to Vegas searching for something most can't define.

We listen to music on the satellite radio station as we drive. Part of me wonders if Jimmy and I are a couple of those crazies still searching for something we can't define.

Near Bakersfield, the jazz station announcer says, "Here's a classic vocal from Mel Torme." The song "Don't Get Around Much Anymore" plays.

"That's one of those songs Carole was playing," Jimmy says.

We listen as Mel makes his way through the Duke Ellington classic.

"She had different words," Jimmy says when the song ends. "Goofy old broad. Think she was losing it?"

"Hard to tell," I say. "Maybe Paris will be good for her."

"Next up on Jazz Classics," the radio voice says, "Charlie Parker with 'After You've Gone.'"

I try my best to remember what Carole was singing just before the movers packed everything up. Then, I remember Jimmy saying that the canyon side railing was where Saturday took his plunge. Except, when we both looked, there was no way he could have tumbled over the barrier onto the backyard slope.

"She wasn't that goofy," I say to Jimmy. "I think she was cluing us into something that we later discovered on our own."

"Okay, Sherlock, let me in on what we got clued into."

I turn down the radio and do my best to croak out the words I remember Carole singing.

"Mister Saturday danced. Waltzed his way out the door. Hit the highway without me...."

"Ah. so," Jimmy says. "She was letting us know that Saturday doing a header onto the slope was bullshit. He walked. Somehow, he got away."

"There's another line she sang, but I can't remember it. I almost had it. Damn, it's frustrating. That's when Marvin showed up with his cigar."

"The one-man poison gas attack," Jimmy says.

"Yeah," I say. "And right after that, Jacky called."

"I'll be cherishing all those golden memories," Jimmy says.

We pull into a steak and egger for food and a bathroom.

"So, Saturday got away." Jimmy grabs the ketchup as our BLT clubs arrive. "Good for him, whoever he was. He's probably long gone by now or somewhere in his nineties. Just another character the Benders hung with."

"Yeah, makes you wonder about him and Carole's supposed father, Dieter von Ritter," I say. "Saturday's supposedly carrying water for the Russians, while old Dieter is a dyed in the wool Nazi agent."

"And both have disappeared into the Bender mystery file," Jimmy says. "No trace of either. The Germans have no record of Dieter, and if Saturday went back to Moscow, he probably died in a gulag."

I sip some lemonade and bite into a French fry.

"Knowing what I know from both of those countries," Jimmy says. "If I was in either of their shoes, I'd find someplace else to go."

We arrive in Vegas in the late afternoon, happy to be home. Dawn and Cassandra have poolside steaks and salads waiting for us. The entertainment features Molly and Zorro doing backflips into the pool. We hear about what it's like to drive the electric cars Dawn and Cassandra have rented.

About three beers after dinner, we call it a night. There's the real business to catch up with at the Galloping Dominos in the morning.

Jimmy:

131

Things get busy our first day back at Dominos, and they don't look like they're going to let up. Murray and Clancy arrive and walk us through their plans for the upcoming Noir Fest. More crime writers, more old actors, new t-shirts, and hats.

A couple days later, Angel Mascara's agent Joey Polito shows up to help plan the Punk and Grunge Fest. It's surprisingly like the Noir Fest. There are Punk and Grunge writers and old Punk and Grunge groups. Also, there are new t-shirts and hats to go with all the punk-ing and grunge-ing. There's an orthodontist's convention coming in, too. It means that a lot of manufacturers selling their latest equipment will be in the house. I ask Lynn Thomas, the coordinator for the gathering, what to expect this year.

"There will be a lot of media types who cover medical news," she says. "Some of the old-timers will be talking about how it used to be done, and now it's better. New stuff, of course, will be there on display."

"Any hats or t-shirts?" I ask.

"Hey, not only that but hoodies, pens, pencils, and giveaway trips to Hawaii and Baja," she says. "We like to get a little crazy, you know."

One day leads to another, and soon we're into September. A mid-morning coffee break gets interrupted with a phone call from Dawn to Nick.

Moses Truthseeker is at the house with the first of the billiard tables. Can we head over so he can tell us all about it? He's also got my table on his truck and needs advice on where to put it.

Moses' crew has placed Nick's table in the middle of the large rec room that faces the golf course. It sits there looking like a well-cared-for antique.

"Beautiful," Nick says. "What kind of wood is that?"

"There's mahogany, oak, and teak trimming the table," Moses says. "The tile inlays are made from composite materials designed to mimic precious stones."

"And the beautiful legs?" Dawn asks. "Mahogany? Koa?"

Moses grins.

"Not wood, at all," he says. "It's a special composite. Very strong, doesn't get bothered by the change in humidity. Keeps the table level and true. It also allows the thick legs to have hollow places where extra balls, chalk, and cue tips can be stored."

He unlatches something on one of the legs beneath the table. A door swings out, revealing extra balls, racked nine to a shelf.

"Jesus, Jimmy," Nick says. "We've seen these legs before on Carole's piano. Hell, I even signed the slip for the movers for that entire load. That was the rest of her Mr. Saturday Danced song. She's gone to see him once more, only this time she's bearing gifts."

"I saved that slip," Dawn says. "I found it in your pants as I was about to toss them into the washing machine."

In minutes, she's back, slip in hand.

"If that shipment was going to Paris," Dawn says," Its first stop was Vietnam."

Chapter Fifty-five

Nick:

Fucking Saigon. Okay, to be precise, Ho Chi Minh City. That's where the load of Carole's possessions went. The load I signed for as shipper. The load with the Steinway in it. The Steinway with composite legs. With doors hiding racks that can hold billiard balls. Or gold bars with Nazi emblems engraved on them. Or what else, for shit's sake? Plutonium?

How liable am I for signing a shipping ticket?

"I wouldn't sweat it," our good friend Roland Rivers says. "I've run it past my pop, the congressman. He says whatever you sent has already gone into the labyrinth of Viet Nam politics. Plus, the US doesn't mind if our Vietnamese friends hint to China that they have nuke plans."

"So, what? They run around showing off a small ball of plutonium to scare off the Red Chinese Army?" I ask.

"It means they're into the game," Roland says. "If they have weapons-grade plutonium showing up here and there, it's hard for anyone to figure how much they have. If they let a few undercover Chinese agents see what they have, it could be used as a bluff. They show one ace. Nobody knows how many they have in their hand."

Jimmy reaches for our beer mugs and fills them from the pitcher the four of us are sharing. The fourth member of our afternoon burger and beer break is Detective Jake Glover.

"You guys worry too much," Glover says. "Think about it. You had a successful trip. Straightened out the Babylon house thing for Jacky. In the process, Donny Mascarella and his crew bit the dust. Some dickhead and his crew from Burma dropped off the face of the earth. And that goof Rockwell isn't running around imitating Hitler."

He's right, of course. I could add that Teddy Bender is in therapy rather than running a meth lab/whore house. Another bonus, we now have a Punk and Grunge fest headed to the Dominos. It all looks great. It would be even better if we planned any of it.

Jimmy must be reading my mind again.

"Of course, you guys know that Nick and I knew it would all work out," he says. "We're just like that woman from Honolulu that won three hundred thousand on the slots at Dominos last June. They asked her if she was surprised. 'No,' she said. 'I knew I was going to win big. I have my lucky frog purse with me.'"

"Now there's a woman who knows how to live," Glover says. "Tell me, which one of you guys carries the frog purse?"

The letter arrives the next day. It's delivered by Antonio, our US Postal Service letter carrier. He's always ready with a joke about the shortcomings of the Bears and other Chicago stumbling attempts at professional behavior.

"Didn't need to look at the rest of the address," Antonio says. "I saw HMFs-In-Charge, and it had to be you and Jimmy."

He hands over an envelope with colorful stamps stuck above the address:

To: Nick and Jimmy HMFs-In-Charge
The Galloping Dominos Casino
Las Vegas, Nevada, USA

I open it to find fancy perfumed stationery with old-school penmanship.

September 11, 2018

To: Nick and Jimmy HMFs-In-Charge

The Galloping Dominos Casino

Las Vegas, Nevada, USA

Dear Nick and Jimmy,

So, it ain't exactly Paris. Shoot me. Actually, it's a lot more like Paris than you'd think. The sidewalk cafes are bustling with people from all over the world. And there's a Notre Dame Cathedral nearby. Maybe it's not as elegant as what you'd find in France, but it fills the bill. There's good art all over the place, and the Vietnamese coffee with heavy cream is addictive. I'm staying in the Hotel Continental Saigon while my nearby house gets a good going over before I move in. The house is one of those old walled-in places with gardens and citrus trees around it. At one time, it belonged to a hotshot in the American mission during the war. Then it became a school, and now it's mine.

Well, mine and someone else's, I should say. The truth is Mickey Saturday is here, all 96 years of him. I know you caught my version of "Don't Get Around Much Anymore." You probably wondered why an old bag like me couldn't get it straight. Did I forget the words? No. I was just teasing you with some clues. "Mister Saturday danced. Waltzed his way out the door."
Mickey is one of the two treasured mystery men in my life. The other is my daddy, Dieter von Ritter. Both saw things differently than those they were supposed to be working for.

Dieter was a National Socialist, a Nazi. The trouble for Dieter was he was more socialist than he was Nazi. He also had a problem. There was a paper trail about how he shipped his Jewish relatives to New York. When things got tense in 1941, Dieter got recalled to Berlin from the consulate in SF. Damn, Dieter mistook Stockholm for Berlin and ended up in Sweden under the name Nils Anderson. The Svenskas were happy to have him. He had inside info from Hitler's playbook, and he also knew a lot about airplane design. After the war, Dieter helped the Swedes peddle fighter jets to Israel. He was also a help to countries that wanted to get rid of the Brits and the French colonialists. I have a cherished photo of Dieter standing next to Ho Chi Minh.

Saturday, on the other hand, was recalled back to the Soviet Union. That was when the Russians tried to blockade Berlin. He says that sort of

*belligerence was never his style. California weather played against his
return to chilly Moscow. Cuba's weather was beautiful for a while, and
Vietnam's was even better. The fact that he was skilled in running guns
to those places made him an honored part of the crew.*

*With not much chance of Dieter and Saturday returning to Babylon,
Lacey and I sat on what was in the bunker. Big Philly couldn't make the
big deal with anyone for what he took from Los Alamos. The gold bars
that Saturday left behind got stored away, too. We thought that somehow
one of the guys would come back for the goods. We would get letters
from both, but never any solid plans to come back. It was too hot for both
of them in the States. Dieter passed away about a year after Saigon fell
to the liberating armies. He's buried in a hero's cemetery about five
kilometers from my new home.*

*I met with Saturday several times in Mexico. Once, we even took a plane
to Cuba for a couple weeks of sightseeing. We never got to a workable
plan to move what we had stored in Babylon. It was always too hot. The
Feds were looking.*
*Finally, we came up with the Old Lady Retires to Paris plan. Sell
Babylon for three million. Pack the furniture. Kill the bank accounts and
go. Simple, eh?*

*But then all hell broke loose with Donny, Rockwell, and the Burmese.
You guys showing up made it easier in some ways and harder in others. I
have to ask. Do people always find violent ways to die when you two are
on the scene? I thought for sure that somehow you guys and your crew
would foil my plans. The last day, when we were about to pack the*

Steinway, Bruno gave the piano a close inspection. Then he looked at the legs and found the one with the latches. He opened it and found a hidden stash of marijuana and porn magazines. I got the naughty old lady routine from him, and we shared a laugh. He looked at the other legs, but they had no latches. They had been carefully sealed up to appear solid. Then he told the movers that the piano could be crated and shipped along with the oversized piano bench That's another place where he should have looked.

Well, what more can I say? I'm with a person I love. He used to read me the funnies and bring me toys when I was a kid. He's still pretty sharp. He plays chess and Bridge with his friends at one of the cafes. Now I look forward to taking care of him. If you guys are ever in Ho Chi Minh City, look us up. I play the piano at the Hotel Continental during the afternoon, three days a week.

Carol

Jimmy puts down the letter after reading it a second time. A smile spreads across his face.

"I gotta hand it to that old broad," he says. "That took a lot of guts on her part. I wonder if we'll ever hear any more from her?"

I look at Carole's letter sitting next to its colorfully stamped envelope on my desk.

"Maybe we will," I say. "But for now, that's all she wrote."

THE END

ABOUT THE AUTHOR

Veteran print and broadcast writer Ray Pace is a member of the Authors Guild. He lives in Waikoloa Village on the Big Island of Hawaii. He is the founding President of the Hawaii Writers Guild and a member of the Waimea Writers Support Group.

His works of fiction are
Disappearing Act, A Las Vegas Love Story, Sort Of...,
Hemingway in Hawaii,
Bearstone Blackie, Detective, and
Captain Mike's Honolulu Fright Night Tour, a ghost story.

Hemingway, Memories of Les is a memoir dealing with Pace's friendship with Leicester Hemingway, author of My Brother Ernest Hemingway.

Made in the USA
Middletown, DE
08 November 2021

51639289R00109